Nanny For The Firemen

CASSIE COLE
Romance Author

Copyright © 2021 Juicy Gems Publishing

All rights reserved. No part of this publication may be reproduced, distributed, or transmitted in any form without prior consent of the author.

Edited by Robin Morris

Follow me on social media to stay up-to-date on new releases, announcements, and prize giveaways!

www.cassiecoleromance.com

Books by Cassie Cole

Broken In

Drilled

Five Alarm Christmas

All In

Triple Team

Shared by her Bodyguards

Saved by the SEALs

The Proposition

Full Contact

Sealed With A Kiss

Smolder

The Naughty List

Christmas Package

Trained At The Gym

Undercover Action

The Study Group

Tiger Queen

Triple Play

Nanny With Benefits

Extra Credit

Hail Mary

Snowbound

Frostbitten

Unwrapped

Naughty Resolution

Her Lucky Charm

Nanny for the Billionaire

Shared by the Cowboys

Nanny for the SEALs

Nanny for the Firemen

Nanny for the Santas (Dec 2021)

Books Written As
K.T. Quinn

Only You

Make You Mine

Yours Forever

First Down (Nov 2021)

1

Clara

I hated—and I mean *hated*—working at my mom's restaurant.

"Clara!" she shouted from the back prep-room in her thick Sicilian accent. "Timer's going off!"

"I heard it!" I yelled back while handing the customer their change. In a softer tone, I told them, "Your pizza will be out soon."

Another customer was coming in the front door, but I turned and pressed the button on the oven timer to halt the incessant beeping. Then I grabbed the huge pizza blade and opened the oven. A blast of heat buffeted my face. By the time I scooped the pizza out and dropped it into a cardboard box, new beads of sweat were already forming on my temple and forehead.

I never really wanted to work here. I did it back in high school because it was easier than finding my own job, and because Dad needed the help. Then I went to college and spent four blissful years nowhere near a pizza oven. The only time I came close to a cash register was when *I* was the customer buying something.

But then I came back home after college, more out of guilt than out of any real desire. It was just supposed to be a few months to help Mom get on her feet after Dad's funeral.

A year had gone by, and I was still here. And the restaurant was still called *Tony's Pizza*, even though dad was just a lingering memory.

"Thank you, enjoy the pizza," I told the first customer while handing him the box. I turned to the new woman and said, "Welcome to Tony's Pizza, what can I get for you?"

While I was taking her order, the phone rang twice. Mom answered it from the back, where she was prepping pizzas. After I had taken the woman's order, my mom poked her head around the corner.

"Delivery," she said. "Pizza will be ready in five."

I groaned. The only thing I hated more than working in the kitchen was doing deliveries. There were some real creeps out there, the kind that would make a joke about offering me a big *tip*, wink wink. There was a reason most pizza deliverers were dudes.

Most restaurants had a digital order system, but mom still insisted on doing everything by hand. Every order was written on a little slip of paper and clipped to a wire above the prep area. I grabbed the delivery slip and scanned the address. The street was legible, but the number was just a few scratches.

"South Henderson..." My heart skipped a beat. "On the corner?"

There was one place where I loved to make deliveries: the fire station. Those guys were amazing. And not just because they were the kind of heroes who rescued people from burning buildings. The guys who worked at the Riverville, California firehouse were *yummy*. Hunks in baggy pants and tight white T-shirts. Charming smiles and bulging muscles.

I'd like two servings of that with extra sauce, please.

But my mom shook her head. "Not on the corner. Six twenty-three." She wiped her forehead with a sleeve. "A few blocks south."

Damnit, I thought. We usually got an order from the firehouse on Friday night, but it hadn't come in yet. Maybe they were switching up their food routine.

"Why can't Dan take the order?" I asked.

"Dan's still out on the last delivery," mom replied impatiently.

"Because he stops to smoke on the way back," I muttered.

She gave me a look.

"Yeah, yeah. I'm going."

Mom mumbled under her breath in Italian.

I was still sweating from working in the kitchen, but there wasn't any time to change. I moved two pizzas into a heat-insulated transportation container and carried them out to my car.

Riverville, California was a quaint little town just outside of Fresno. To the west were sprawling suburbs and endless strip malls, and to the east were farmlands all the way to the mountains. Riverville was in that weird middle-ground. Not quite out in the country, but not really suburban, either.

The delivery was only five minutes away. Everything in Riverville was about five minutes from everything else, depending on the traffic lights. The location for this delivery was a house one block off the main road. There were no cars in the driveway, but the lights were on.

I knocked on the door, and a scrawny kid about twelve years old answered. "Delivery from Tony's," I said.

"About time," the snotty little kid said. Behind him in the hallway I saw a gaggle of other pre-teen boys all snickering to themselves. "Don't we get it for free if it takes you a while?"

I smiled politely and looked at my watch. "It took me exactly six minutes and forty-five seconds to get here. Your total's twenty-five dollars even."

The kid handed me two twenties. I dug into my pocket and came out with a ten dollar bill and five ones. He took the change and the pizzas and started to close the door.

"You know, I work on tips," I said.

He sneered. "Shut up, boomer."

"Boomer? I'm twenty-four!"

"Whatever." He slammed the door in my face.

Yeah. It was going to be that kind of night.

I drove home in a bad mood, and not just because of the asshole customers. The crappy thing about working at a pizza restaurant was that the busiest nights were weekends. My Friday, Saturday, and Sunday nights were always spent working. After a while, it wore a girl down.

Mom was ringing people up when I walked into the restaurant. "Another delivery," she told me.

I groaned. "Dan's still not back yet?"

"He's back, but I saved this one for you," she replied. She tried to keep her face still, but a small smile crept into her lips.

I hurried to the back and looked at the order slip.

South Henderson.

Firehouse.

I tried not to do a fist-pump. "How long until their order's ready?"

"Two minutes," mom said over her shoulder.

I hurried into the back bathroom and frantically tried to make myself presentable. I dabbed the sweat off my neck, then untied my ponytail and re-tied it a little tighter to keep the extra strands from coming loose. There was a red sauce stain on my left breast, so I dabbed it with a wet paper towel.

"Let's go!" mom yelled from the kitchen.

I ran out of the bathroom and collected the food from the prep table. I still didn't look the way I *wanted* to look around the firehouse guys, but at least I was somewhat presentable.

"Don't take so long this time," mom told me.

"I don't know what you're talking about."

Mom smirked at me as I hurried out the door.

2

Clara

I tried to put on some makeup in the car ride over to the firehouse. For the first time in my life, I was grateful for every red light I hit since it gave me a little extra time.

Fire Station 31 was on the corner of South Henderson and Jackson Street. I didn't know why it was number thirty-one, because Riverville only had a population of six thousand, and it was the only station in town. I parked out front, taking care not to block the driveway up to the station itself.

It was a nice night, and the big firehouse doors were open. The two red fire engines had been washed to a reflective shine, and in the garage between them sat three firemen. They were sitting in folding chairs, watching a baseball game on a small laptop screen. They turned and smiled broadly at me when I approached.

I've never really bought into the idea of a "happy place." Like, the kind of place people tell you to go to in your mind when you need to feel good about yourself, or relax. "Stressed out at work? Go to your happy place!"

But if I had a happy place, it was definitely the firehouse. The guys were *always* happy to see me—not surprising since I was delivering delicious food. But I couldn't help but swoon whenever they smiled at me, or invited me to hang out with them for a little while, or gave me a friendly clap on the shoulder when I left. No matter how crappy of a day I'd had, spending a few precious minutes with the Riverville firemen always put a smile on my face—and it had nothing to do with the generous tips they always left. They just had that effect on me.

They weren't just nice guys, either. The three firemen working tonight were gorgeous. Like big teddy bears of muscle and strength. But I was most drawn to Jordan. Broad-shouldered and tall, he was the kind of guy who looked like he could pick me up with one arm easily. He had an aquiline nose and a silky puff of dark hair. His full, kissable lips broadened in a smile when he saw me, and his green eyes were warm and bright.

"Clara!" he said happily. He exuded charisma, like a fireplace radiating heat. "Right on time. We're *starving*."

He knows my name, I thought with an internal smile. I definitely knew him, but I wasn't sure if he knew me as more than *the girl who brings the pizza*.

"If you're starving now, then you should've ordered an hour ago," I replied smoothly. "Your Friday order usually comes in around five o'clock. You're slacking tonight."

"Had a call," said Derek Dahlkemper. He only had the rank of Captain, but everyone called him *Chief* since he was in charge of the firehouse. He was even bigger than Jordan, clean-shaven, and with a quiet intensity about him. He wasn't *unfriendly*, but I rarely got more than a few words out of him at a time. I got the impression that's just how he was with everyone.

"Oh? Anything exciting?"

"Carbon monoxide detector went off at Jan Karsh's place," Taylor Heath chimed in. The other two worked full-time, but Taylor was a part-time *Probationary Firefighter* while he finished taking college classes. He brushed back his blond hair and grinned. "Just a false alarm. Better than the alternative, right?"

"Yeah, totally," I said while unloading the food on the table next to the laptop. Two large pizzas and an aluminum tray of pasta. "Get it while it's hot. Mom put some extra meat sauce in the pasta, just how you like it."

"You're sweet," Jordan said, even though I hadn't been the one to do it. Suddenly my cheeks felt red, like I had opened the pizza oven.

I cocked my head at him and pointed at his thin beard. "You guys run out of razors or something?"

"Hah!" Taylor barked a laugh. Even Derek chuckled.

"Hah hah, very funny," Jordan said.

"I didn't think firefighters were allowed to have beards," I said.

"Used to be that way," Taylor answered for him. He bit into a piece of pepperoni pizza and continued with a full mouth. "Modern respirators are positive-pressure systems. They provide a constant flow. That way, no smoke gets in, even if there's not a *perfect* seal."

"Can't let it get too long, though," Derek grumbled. "And I think it's ugly as hell. Might as well wear a ferret on your face."

Jordan rolled his eyes. It sounded like this was not the first time they had argued about this.

"Oh, I don't know," I said. "I kind of like it. A thin beard suits you well."

Jordan was focused on opening the container of pasta, but he smiled to himself.

"Don't let it go to your head," Derek said dryly. "She's just trying to flirt with you."

Even with the dark beard on Jordan's face, I could see his cheeks redden. His blush made *me* blush even harder. Taylor turned away and pretended like he didn't notice.

To change the subject, I gestured at the laptop. "How's the game going?"

"Giants are up four," Jordan said.

"Damn," I replied.

All three of them frowned at me.

"Don't tell me you're a Dodgers fan," Jordan asked.

I gave an awkward wince. "My grandpa lived in Brooklyn after immigrating here. My family has been Dodgers fans since before the team moved to California."

Derek grunted in disapproval.

"I thought you were cool," Taylor said with a playful glare. "But now I'm not so sure."

"You definitely lost some cool points," Jordan agreed.

Despite their friendly teasing, I couldn't help but beam. *I didn't know I had cool points to begin with.*

"Watch this at-bat," Taylor insisted, gesturing with the hand that wasn't holding a slice of pizza. "Posey's going deep. I can feel it."

I scoffed. "Against Kershaw? No way."

"You would be a Kershaw fan," Jordan said.

"Of course I am. He's not just the best pitcher on the Dodgers —he's the best pitcher *in the league.*"

"Little league, maybe," Taylor said, rolling his eyes. "He's past his prime. Ohh!"

Taylor shouted and jumped up as the batter, Buster Posey, crushed a ball toward left field. It was high and deep... but then curled foul at the last minute.

"See that?" Taylor chided me. "A few feet away from a grand slam."

"A foul ball is just a long strike," I replied. "My dad used to say that."

Rather than sit down again, Jordan stood next to me in front of the screen. "Busy night tonight?"

"Yeah, you know how Fridays are," I replied. "But once the

dinner rush ends, it should be slow until we close at nine."

"Oh, cool," Jordan said. "I get off my twelve-hour shift at nine, too."

I looked sideways at him and waited for him to say more. That couldn't have been a coincidental comment, right? Mentioning that we got off at the same time... It seemed like he was thinking awfully hard about something.

Was he going to ask me out?

He turned his emerald gaze on me and rolled the remains of a pizza crust between his fingers. He opened his mouth...

...And then the siren went off in the firehouse.

The three men rushed into action with practiced ease. They hurried over to the lockers on one wall, rapidly stepping into their pants and pulling the suspenders over their broad shoulders. I watched Jordan throw his thick fire jacket on, then carried the rest of his gear over to the fire engine. Derek and Taylor were right behind him.

"I'll put the food away in the kitchen for you!" I shouted over the siren.

"Thanks!" Taylor shouted back, giving me a thumbs-up.

Before the engine could drive away, Jordan suddenly jumped out of the passenger seat and ran back over to me. His face was flushed from running around, an his eyes were wide with adrenaline.

"Hey, do you, uh, want to get a beer or something when we get off?"

"I..." I stammered. A date invitation was the last thing I expected while the fire siren was still going off. "Yeah. I'd love to."

"JORDAN!" Derek roared. "Move your ass!"

"I'll pick you up at your restaurant!" Jordan said before giving me one final, parting grin and hurrying back into the fire engine.

Dazed, I watched them drive out of the station and down the street, lights flashing the whole way.

3

Clara

I smiled as I watched the fire engine disappear down the main street of Riverville. Partly because it was exhilarating watching the firemen rush into their gear and drive away to do something heroic.

But mostly I smiled because *I had a date with one of them.*

Once I shook off my stupor, I packed up their food and carried it inside the station proper. I passed several rooms with bunk beds and a big communal bathroom before reaching the kitchen. First I turned the oven to the *warm* setting. The pasta was already in an aluminum tray, so I threw that inside right away.

The pizza was tougher. Although the cardboard boxes wouldn't burn at such a low temperature, I didn't think the firemen would approve of me putting cardboard directly in an oven. Instead, I found two baking trays in the cabinet and began transferring slices of pizza to them. Then I covered both trays in aluminum foil and threw them in the oven.

Now the guys would have hot food when they returned, and the temperature was too low to be dangerous. Just to be safe, I scanned the bottom of the oven for any crumbs or pieces of loose food. They wouldn't ignite at that temperature, but I figured better safe than sorry.

I found a notepad, scribbled a note about the food, and then left.

On the way out, I paused in one of the bedroom doorways. There was a bunk labeled "Lloyd," which was Jordan's last name. Next to the bed was an art easel holding a blank canvas, and a box of paints were on the floor next to it. Was that Jordan's, or did it belong to the bunk next to his? That one was labeled Heath. Taylor Heath, the blond probationary firefighter.

"I shouldn't be snooping," I muttered, then hurried out of the garage to my car.

"What took you so long!" mom complained when I got back to the restaurant. "There's another delivery waiting!"

"Sorry! The guys got a call and had to run, so I boxed their food up for them." I collected the waiting delivery order and paused. "Mom, I have a favor to ask. Can I get off fifteen minutes early?"

"Early? Why?" she barked from the kitchen.

"I kind of... have a date."

Her head slowly peered around the massive pizza oven. "A date? With who?"

"Jordan Lloyd. One of the firemen."

A huge smile split her face. "My daughter is going out with a fireman!"

I groaned. "Mom. It's not a big deal."

The little Italian woman opened the oven and inserted a pizza. "Not a big deal, she says to me!" She closed the oven and whirled toward me. "Now you will give me grandchildren!"

"Jason and Maurice already gave you a grandson," I pointed out. They had adopted a little boy named LeBron, named after my brother-in-law's favorite basketball player.

"They only have one," Mom said, beaming. "I want *more*. Give me all the grandchildren to love!"

"It's one date. Let's not get ahead of ourselves."

Mom wiped her hands on her apron and hurried to the counter to greet a customer. "Welcome to Tony's Pizza. My daughter has a date with a *fireman*."

I rolled my eyes and hurried out to make my next delivery.

The rest of the night was a blur of activity. I had two more deliveries, and after the last one I swung by the house to get my hair straightener and a change of clothes—nothing fancy, just clean jeans and a blouse. Finally, the dinner rush died down around eight-thirty. I went into the back room, cleaned myself off as best as I could, and changed into my new clothes.

I was straightening my hair when the front door opened at eight-fifty.

He's early, I thought frantically. I wasn't ready yet—I needed more time! But when I poked my head out from the back, I saw a college-aged guy standing at the counter.

"Welcome to Tony's Pizza," I called to him, putting down my straightener and then approaching the counter. "We're closing in ten minutes, but..."

"That's okay," the guy said. He looked stoned. "I need four extra-larges. Two pepperoni, one meat-lovers, and one Hawaiian."

I groaned. *Technically* we accepted orders all the way until nine. But for an order this size, mom would need my help.

"Four extra-larges..." I said, writing it down on an order sheet.

Mom came stomping out of the kitchen. "No! We are closing!"

"Uhh." The stoner guy looked at his phone. "But it's, like, not even nine. And your website says you close at *nine*."

"The website is not the owner!" Mom scolded. "I am the owner! And I am telling you we are closing early! My daughter has a date!"

"Mom..." I hissed.

The stoner groaned. "Ugh. Chill out. I'll go to Pizza Hut."

"I could have helped you with the order," I told my mom.

She made a dismissive gesture.

"I know we need the money," I said. "We have to purchase a better grease trap for the flat-top, and replace the fire extinguisher we used in February."

"Money, schmoney," Mom replied. "Your date is more important."

"I don't think Jordan would approve of us putting off fire safety expenses."

She pulled my head down toward her and kissed my forehead. "You have not been on a date in too long. It is important."

I appreciated her prioritization, but I couldn't help but feel a little guilty about turning away business. And it didn't help that her excitement was putting pressure on the date itself.

I finished getting ready and then waited by the cash register. I drummed my fingers on the counter while scanning the street outside, hoping that every car that drove by would be Jordan. I didn't know what he drove, aside from the big fire engine. And I doubted he would pick me up in that.

Although it would be funny if he did.

Finally, a grey pick-up truck pulled into the parking lot and pulled into a spot facing the door. "Okay, bye!" I called to Mom.

She came running out of the kitchen and kissed me goodbye. "Have a good time! And think *grandchildren!*"

I felt her eyes on me while I walked out of the restaurant. I was only twenty-four. I had no idea what I wanted to do with my life, but kids didn't factor into it at all. At least, not for a *long* time.

One thing at a time, I thought while going outside. *Focus on tonight's date first.*

4

Clara

Jordan climbed down from his truck to greet me. He was wearing jeans and a faded grey T-shirt that showed off his muscular frame nicely—especially his shoulders and arms. I breathed a sigh of relief. I wasn't sure what to wear, so I had erred on the side of casual too.

"You look beautiful," he said while opening the passenger door for me.

"I look like I spent ten minutes getting ready in the restaurant bathroom," I said.

"It must be a hell of a bathroom, then," he replied with a grin.

I smiled to myself and climbed into the truck. It smelled faintly of smoke—not cigarettes, but *actual* smoke. He closed the door behind me, then went around to climb into the driver's side.

"So what's the plan?" I asked. "You mentioned getting a beer?"

He started the truck and twisted to face me. "I've got an idea. But only if you're cool with it."

God, he's sexy. Jordan's smile was so intoxicating, especially when it was aimed only at me, that I wanted to agree to whatever he had planned. But something in the way he said it made me hesitate. Like his idea involved something *really* out there.

"Depends what it is," I said carefully.

"There's a movie I've wanted to see for a while, and it's only in theaters for another week. It's the one with Emma Stone and Timothy Chalamet, and the theater serves beer..."

I blinked at him. "The new rom-com? Seriously?"

His smile faded. "If you don't want to see it, we can do something else..."

"No! I definitely want to. I'm just surprised you do. I would have taken you for an action man."

He put his arm across the back of my seat and twisted to look back while reversing. "I deal with fires all day. On my time off, I want to see something lighthearted."

I laughed. "Hey, no judgment here!"

There was no theater in Riverville, but we were only twenty minutes outside of Frenso. On the drive there, Jordan talked about his day at the station and about the call they received—it turned out to be a small kitchen fire that never got out of control.

We grabbed beers at the concession stand and some snacks—popcorn for him, and Peanut Butter M&Ms for me—and went into our theater. It was totally deserted.

"Good," Jordan said as we selected seats in the middle. "I can make comments without worrying about annoying other people."

I squinted at him. "Wait a minute. You're a movie-talker?"

He sat down and raised the armrest divider between our seats. "What's wrong with that?"

"I demand absolute silence during movies," I replied. "Even comedies. No laughing allowed.'

Jordan raised a dark eyebrow, leaned toward me, and said, "This isn't going to work out."

"At least we figured that out at the start!" I stole a handful of popcorn. "Now I don't feel bad about mooching on your snacks."

I grinned as he laughed at my stupid joke. Jordan was remarkably easy to be around. Normally I was all awkward and quiet whenever I was in the presence of a really cute guy, but I felt at ease with him. It was strange.

But in a good way.

The previews played, and then the movie started. Without the divider between us, Jordan was able to spread his legs wide and get comfortable. His knee was a mere inch away from mine, so close that I could feel the heat radiating off him. He was such a big, lumbering guy that his elbow brushed against my arm every time he grabbed a handful of popcorn.

I took a bigger gulp of my beer and was grateful that the lights were too low for him to see my blush.

Like most rom-coms, the movie was predictable. It was a second-chance romance where old high school sweethearts meet up ten years later, once they're adults. The first twenty minutes were full of sexual tension and awkward encounters between the two protagonists.

"I don't know what she's thinking," Jordan said in a not-so-soft whisper. "I wouldn't take him back. Not after what he did."

"But he's changed!" I whispered back.

He shook his head doubtfully. "No way. He's just putting on a show for her. He's still a bad boy at heart."

"Girls like bad boys," I pointed out.

"Only if they can change them."

"She's going to!" I insisted playfully. "Just watch!"

"She's going to get hurt again..."

Jordan made disapproving noises throughout the movie. Every time the female protagonist smiled, he grunted. When the male protagonist said something cheesy, he snorted.

"You're starting to sound like a buffalo," I said.

Jordan responded with an extravagant animal noise halfway between a groan and a cow's moo. I almost spit out the last gulp of my beer from laughing so abruptly.

"Another?" he asked, reaching for my cup.

"Yes, please!"

I savored the sight of his huge, chiseled frame as he walked down the stairs to get more beer. He returned a few minutes later.

"What did I miss?" he said while handing me another plastic cup of beer.

"They just had sex," I replied, deadpan.

He sank into his chair and stared at me. "No way!"

"Yep. It was super hot. Emma Stone showed full-frontal. And you missed it."

Jordan sighed. "I'm going to need both beers to drown my sorrows." He reached for my drink.

"Hey!" I slapped at his hand.

Rather than pull back, he deftly slipped his hand down between my legs, snatching my box of M&Ms. He didn't *actually* touch me, but the cardboard scraped against my inner thigh as he pulled the box away and dumped some candy in his huge palm.

A tingle of naughty excitement went up my spine.

It's been a long time since I felt anything like that, as innocent as it was. Sometimes the smallest gestures meant a lot.

"Please?" I said, referring to his lack of manners.

He chewed the candy and glanced at me. "Please what?"

I mimicked what he should have asked: "Please, may I have some M&Ms?"

"Sure, but there's not many left." He tipped the box over and allowed a single piece to slide into my palm. He gave me a silly grin.

I tried to snatch the box out of his hand, but he quickly pulled it back.

"Gimme!" I climbed over him to reach for the candy, which he held back like Michael Jordan keeping a basketball away from a defender. I grabbed his arm and tried pulling it toward me, but it was like grasping onto a chiseled statue. A *warm* statue.

Realizing I had climbed over his thigh and was half in his lap, I slowly sat back down in my own seat. "I didn't want any more candy anyway."

Jordan looked sheepish as he handed the box to me. "Fine. You win. But save a few for me."

This time he let me snatch the box out of his hand. Feeling silly, I tilted the box at my head and dumped the remainder into my mouth. It was *way* more than I expected, but at that point I was committed to the scene. By the time the box was empty, I looked like a chipmunk who had collected enough acorns to last the entire winter.

"Having trouble there?" he asked casually.

I turned toward the screen and pretended like I was fine. "No trouble at all," I tried to say, but it came out all muffled.

"What's that? All I heard was *mo gruffle ah ahh.*"

Unable to speak, I flashed him a thumbs-up. He roared with laughter that had nothing to do with the movie.

It was really nice having the theater to ourselves. I generally didn't like people who talked during movies, but it was different on a date with a guy I barely knew. We were having so much fun teasing and joking with each other.

I can't remember ever having such a good time on a first date.

The theater was chilly, and Jordan must have known I was cold, because he put his arm around me. I tensed as his fingers rested against my back, touching my bra strap through my shirt. I didn't think he meant to do that.

I like the way he holds me, I thought.

I chanced a glance over at him, and he immediately looked at me. Electricity passed between our gazes for a moment, his eyes illuminated by the glow of the theater screen. I found myself pulled into his stare, hypnotized by his easy charm. Did he want to kiss me? I knew what I wanted *him* to do to me.

Here? I thought. We were alone in the theater. Nobody would know if we made out. I had never done anything like that, and the thrill of being naughty with someone—a first date, at that!—filled me with excitement.

But then he returned to watching the movie, although his arm remained around me. I sighed and spent the last twenty minutes of the movie snuggled up against him, savoring his warmth.

"That was pretty good," Jordan said as we walked out of the theater.

"I had a good time," I said. "But the ending was dumb. It was a convoluted problem, and then they got back together anyway."

"Duh," Jordan replied. "Rule number one of rom-coms: there has to be a happy ending."

"I know. But they could have done it better," I said.

He glanced sideways at me. "You mean you didn't enjoy staring at Timmy Chalamet for an hour and a half?"

"He's pretty to look at," I admitted, "but he's kind of scrawny. I like my men to be a little more, I don't know, *manly.*"

"Like a fireman?" Jordan said hopefully.

I raised an eyebrow at him. "Maybe. Put in a few months at the gym and maybe you'll bulk up to that point."

He barked a laugh, which made me grin. It was ridiculous to imply that Jordan was anything other than a huge, hulking, burly man. He must have been two hundred and fifty pounds of pure muscle.

"Regardless of my opinion of the ending," I said, "I had a great time watching it with you."

He slipped his hand into mine and squeezed. "Even though I'm a movie-talker?"

"Everyone is allowed one huge flaw," I said. "I just hope you don't have another one."

"Guess I'd better cover up my third nipple, then," he muttered.

I gave him a playful little smack on the arm. "You do *not* have a third nipple."

"Of course I don't." He winked dramatically. "How many nipples does this guy have? Just two! That's what my buddies say whenever they see me. There goes the guy with the totally normal number of nipples."

We laughed and held hands all the way back to his truck.

The drive home was spent discussing our favorite rom-coms. I thought Jordan had chosen the movie tonight for my benefit, but it turned out he really *did* like romantic comedies. He knew his stuff.

"*Love Actually* is not a rom-com," he argued. "There's hardly any comedy in it. Also, it's a bad movie, regardless of genre."

"I watch it every Christmas!" I shot back.

"Remind me to avoid your house around the holidays."

I scoffed loudly in faux-offense. "It's better than *Ten Things I Hate About You*. That movie is just a rip-off of *Taming of the Shrew*."

"Rip-off? It's a *retelling* of it! It's intentional!"

"Intentionally *bad*," I muttered.

"Keep this up," he said, "and I'm not showing you my third nipple."

"You don't have a third nipple." I hesitated. "Do you?"

"You'll never know."

He pulled the truck into the restaurant parking lot. My car was the only other one still there. Before I could say goodnight to him, he hopped out of the truck, came around the side, and opened my door.

"You could have parked right next to my car," I said, pointing.

Jordan grinned. "But then I wouldn't get to walk you to it."

We slowly crossed the parking lot together. He didn't hold my hand—he shoved his hands in his jeans pockets.

Is he going to kiss me goodnight? I wondered. *I hope he does.*

"So is this the reason you guys order food every Friday?" I asked. "Just to see me?"

He shook his head. "Sorry to burst your bubble, but Tony's has the best Italian food in town. We've been ordering from here for five years, since Tony himself was around."

My smile slowly faded at the mention of my father. Time had healed the wound, but it still hurt if you pressed on it.

Jordan seemed to realize he had said something wrong, so he added, "He was a great guy, your dad."

"Thanks. He really was." I stopped next to my car and turned toward him. "I'm glad you asked me out."

"Me too, Clara."

He was smiling like he wanted to kiss me. I could feel the tension in the air, just like in a scene from the movie. The moment before *the moment*.

But there was a question on my mind, and I was too curious not to ask it.

"What made you finally do it?" I asked. "I've been delivering to your firehouse for a year now, since we lost our other two delivery guys. You've had plenty of times to ask me out before now."

Jordan shrugged his massive shoulders. "I dunno. I finally worked up the courage, I guess."

"Come on," I said. "What's the real reason? Were you dating someone else before now? Is that why?"

"Nah, I haven't been in a relationship in about a year. I..." He trailed off as if searching for the right words. "You want to really know why?"

"As long as it doesn't have to do with your third nipple," I replied.

He smiled for a moment, then grew serious. "The guys I work with? They have huge crushes on you, too."

I gave a start. "Really?"

"Yeah, Taylor and the Chief. Derek. We've kind of had a running joke about who was going to ask you out first. Well, I'm pretty sure they were both *really* close to asking you out, so I jumped in before they could."

I could hardly believe what he was saying. Going out with one heroic fireman was great, but finding out that *three* of them had crushes on me? It was overwhelming.

I thought about the other two for a moment. Taylor was the cute blond guy, who was just a probationary firefighter at the moment. And Derek was ruggedly handsome—despite being close to forty. I'd never had a thing for older men, but an exception could *definitely* be made for him.

Jordan was waiting for my response to this information, so I made myself grin up at him. "Well, in that case, give me Taylor's number so I can call him."

Jordan chuckled. "Not interested in the Chief, huh?"

"I'll save him for last, after I go out with Taylor. You think he'll try to steal my M&Ms?"

"Taylor doesn't share food," he replied with a laugh. "If you tried to take a handful of his popcorn, he'd probably make you walk home from the theater!"

"Good thing I went out with you tonight then, huh?"

"A very good thing," he agreed.

We smiled widely at each other. Jordan leaned a little closer, the fingers of his left hand twitching. I saw everything that was about to happen in my mind. He was going to cup my cheek and give me a long kiss. His thin beard would feel nice and rough against my smooth skin. I would lean into him, pressing my body against his warmth.

Do it, I begged him with my eyes.

Suddenly his phone rang. He flinched, ignored it, then let out a long sigh.

"I've got to answer that. Technically, we're all on-call in case... Yep, it's the station."

I tried not to let him see me groan.

"Hey Chief, yeah, I'm here. Sorry, I must have missed the others because I was in a movie, and... Okay. I'll be there."

He hung up and gave me an apologetic wince.

"I've got to run. Some sort of emergency at the firehouse. If the other shift can't handle it..." He started to turn away, then abruptly leaned back into me. He gave me a soft, respectful kiss on the cheek. For a split second, I savored the sensation of his beard against my skin, even though it wasn't the kiss I *really* wanted.

"I'm so sorry," he said as he began to jog away. "I'll call you!"

Damnit.

I gave him a little wave as I watched him go.

5

Jordan

Man, talk about the *worst* luck.

Generally, I preferred to take things slow with women. Nothing was ever gained by rushing into something, or getting too physical too fast. It was better to take your time, get to know the other person, and draw it out. That way, when things *did* start getting hot and heavy, it was even better.

Yet something about Clara Ricci made me want to abandon that mindset and dive right in. We clicked on our first date in a way I had never felt before. We had a connection that was tough to explain. Even though we only exchanged a few pleasantries whenever she delivered our food, it felt like I had known her much longer than that.

It was the kind of spark I thought only existed in cheesy rom-coms.

But it was real. It was so, so real.

As I walked her back to her car, I didn't know what I should do. Normally, my go-to move on a first date was a kiss on the cheek. But I wanted to do so much more with Clara tonight. I wanted to *really* kiss her. I wanted to fold my arms around her and feel her curvy body against mine.

I want to take her home and...

Then my phone rang.

Any other time, and I would have ignored it until I was back in my truck. But it was pushing midnight, and there was a short list of people who would call me this late. Sure enough, the name on the screen said *Captain Dahlkemper*.

"*Get down here,*" he told me. "*We've got a situation.*"

I was tempted to joke about him intentionally torpedoing my date, but something in his voice had me on edge. "Okay, I'll be there."

And that's how I ended up giving Clara Ricci a polite kiss on the cheek.

"Stupid, stupid, stupid," I berated myself in the truck on the way to the firehouse. It was a crummy ending to an otherwise perfect night. I could have taken a few seconds to end the date properly. A *real* kiss, full of warmth and promise. The way Clara deserved.

But I knew that Derek wouldn't be calling unless it was an emergency, and every second might count.

When I got to the firehouse, the first thing I noticed was that both fire engines were still in the garage. That was strange. If there was an emergency, at least one should have been gone. I walked through the garage and into the living room. The three guys from second-shift were sprawled out on the couches and recliners, watching a replay of the Giants game.

Firefighter shifts varied from firehouse to firehouse, and state to state. In big cities, the most common shift schedule was twenty-four hours on, then forty-eight hours off. Another popular shift schedule involved twelve-hour shifts, four days a week.

For a small town like Riverville, we didn't have the luxury of those kinds of schedules. Instead, we did four days on, then three days off. My shift started at 9:00 PM on Monday and ended at the same time Friday night. Then, the backup shift took over for three days while we were off.

In a major city center, this would be a grueling schedule. But around Riverville, we just didn't get a lot of calls. It was mostly false alarms or quality-of-life responses. For example, in the past week, the most excitement we'd gotten was when little Jeffrey Parker got his head stuck in his fence.

"What's going on?" I asked the second-shift guys.

"How the fuck should we know?" Billy replied.

I liked most of the other firefighters in town, but Billy Manning was a grade-A asshole. Thank goodness I got matched up with Derek and Taylor rather than his crew.

"Chief called me," I replied. "Said it was an emergency."

Billy rolled his eyes and turned his attention to the game. One of the other guys jerked his thumb and said, "Chief's in one of the bunks."

I gave him a grateful nod and went that way.

The hallway between the garage and living area had six bedrooms. All of them were open except the one marked *Captain Dahlkemper,* which was closed. I gently knocked, then opened the door.

Unlike the other rooms, which contained bunk beds, Derek's room boasted a single queen-sized bed. Derek and Taylor were standing over the bed with their backs to me. There was a strange sound, one I couldn't quite place.

Taylor looked over his shoulder at me. He gave me a look: *Holy shit, dude.*

"Chief?" I asked. "What's going on?"

Derek looked at me with a grimace, then stepped aside. Taylor did the same.

On the bed was a small laundry basket. The kind used for bath towels and nothing else. I stepped forward, not sure what I was going to see.

A baby was the *last* thing I expected.

It was wrapped up in a bunch of plush towels. Like a little white nest. A tiny bundle of human was buried inside, with only its face and one hand exposed. It blinked at me, mirroring my own confusion.

"Uh," I said. "There's a baby on the bed, Chief."

"Thanks," Derek replied. "I didn't notice."

Taylor wordlessly handed me a handwritten note.

> *Please find a good home for my boy. He deserves more love than I can give. I'm so, so sorry.*

I read the note twice, then glanced at the baby. He was staring up at me expectantly, as if to say: *you're the adult, not me. I'm just a baby.*

"I stayed late to shower, because I was planning on heading straight to Tracy's Bar," Taylor told me. "When I left, I found *it* sitting in front of the door to the station."

"Him," I corrected. "The note says it's a boy. And leaving a baby on a doorstep? I thought this kind of thing only happened in old movies."

"I know, right?" Taylor said. "This is nuts. You can't just abandon your baby like that."

"Safe Haven laws are still on the books in most states," Derek lectured. "Anyone can legally surrender an unwanted newborn without fear of arrest or prosecution. It hasn't happened in Riverville to the best of my knowledge, but it's not unheard of."

"We brought him inside," Taylor said. "I haven't told the other shift about him yet. Billy would probably want to eat him or something, weirdo that he is."

The baby made a cooing noise, and began to wriggle in the

basket. I reached inside and took him in my hands. He was so small that when I wrapped my hands around his belly, my fingers touched.

Cradle the head, I remembered from when my nephew was born a few years ago. I kept one hand underneath his little head and lifted him into my arms. He was wearing a diaper and nothing else.

"Look!" Taylor said. "There's an envelope underneath him."

Derek opened the envelope. "It's a birth certificate. His name's Anthony."

"Anthony," I whispered to the little guy. His eyes moved around like he was trying to examine every part of my face at once. I grinned at him, and he returned the smile.

"Shit," Derek sighed. He gestured with the birth certificate. "He was born two months ago."

"Why's that a problem?" Taylor asked.

Derek clenched his jaw. "In California, you're required to surrender a baby within seventy-two hours."

Taylor glanced at the birth certificate. "He was born in Texas." He pulled out his phone and started typing. "How much you want to bet the law is different there... Yep. Texas Safe Haven laws allow for the surrender of a baby up to sixty days."

"The mother could get prosecuted for this." Derek sat on the bed and sighed. "She thought she was doing the right thing, but didn't realize the law is different from state to state."

"Okay, so there are laws surrounding this," I said. "What do we do now, Chief?"

He crossed his arms over his chest. "My sister works in Social Services over in Fresno. I left her a message asking what the procedure is."

"There's nobody else we can call?" I asked.

Derek narrowed his eyes. "I'd rather talk to her than whichever bureaucratic idiot is on-call tonight. Which is why it's best if we keep this from the guys on second-shift. The last thing I want is Billy causing trouble."

Taylor and I nodded immediately. Neither of us wanted *him* involved.

Suddenly, little Anthony's face twisted in concentration, like he was trying to solve a math problem. He relaxed, then began to cry softly.

The firehouse bedrooms were all heavily soundproofed, with individual alarm speakers in each one. That way, the people who weren't on shift could sleep soundly if they needed to, while those who were on-call could hear the alarm. Taylor slipped behind me and closed the door so the second-shift guys wouldn't hear the crying.

"Aaand, you're not so cute anymore." I held the baby out to Derek.

He kept his arms crossed. "Why would I take him?" he demanded.

"I don't know. What am I supposed to do?"

We both turned to Taylor.

"Don't look at me, I'm the youngest child! I never had to change anyone's diapers."

"Is that the problem?" Derek asked me. "He needs to be changed?"

I pulled open his diaper an inch, and immediately recoiled. "Ugh. Yep. It's a diaper problem. Oh my God. How can something so cute create a smell so *terrible?*"

"Do we have diapers?" Taylor asked. "There's no way we have diapers lying around the station, right?"

Derek grabbed his keys from the bedside table. "Sal's General Store is closed at this hour, so I'll have to drive up to the Walmart in Fresno. I'll be back with supplies." He pointed at me. "Keep the baby in here, and don't let the others know about him."

When the door closed behind Derek, I stared at the whimpering baby in my arms. Suddenly I was the one in charge of the situation. It was an unnerving feeling. The most experience I had with babies was holding my sister's kid for about thirty seconds at a time before handing him to someone more maternal.

And right now, Anthony was still crying. The sound triggered something in my brain, like nails being scratched on a chalkboard.

"What do we do?" Taylor asked me.

I looked around. "Chief has a private bathroom. Let's get this little guy cleaned up."

The next ten minutes were a comedy of incompetence. I peeled the dirty diaper off Anthony and tossed it into a trash bag, which Taylor quickly double-tied and hid inside the bathroom cabinet. Then we used normal toilet paper to clean up the poor baby. That wasn't really adequate, cleanliness-wise, so we got the water from the sink faucet nice and warm. Using four hands, we flipped Anthony over and stuck his butt under the drizzle of water.

Anthony liked this, and let out a flurry of giggles while we moved him back and forth until his little baby tushy was clean.

"Acting as a baby bidet wasn't what I expected when I left the movie theater," I muttered.

"Oh, yeah! How'd your date go?" Taylor asked.

"It actually went *amazing*," I replied. "Clara is... She's something special. We *clicked* in a way I've never clicked with someone before."

"Aw, man. That's awesome." Taylor gave me a pat on the shoulder, realized his hand was wet, and then shrugged. "Man. I'm still kind of jealous you asked her out first."

"You snooze, you lose."

"Did you mention..." Taylor hesitated. "You know. What the three of us talked about?"

My stomach sank. I'd had such a good time with Clara that I

had forgotten all about it.

"No, I didn't," I said.

"What do you think she would say?" Taylor insisted. He was younger than Derek and me, and his eyes were wide and excited. "I know that's a weird thing to suggest to a girl, but... Do you think she'd go for it?"

"I have no idea," I said, which was the honest truth. I wasn't even sure if *I* wanted to go for it. "But for now, we have more important things to worry about."

I hefted Baby Anthony and dried him off with a towel. He squirmed a little bit in my hands, but he wasn't very strong. Not yet, at least. We wrapped him in one of Derek's T-shirts and did our best to tie it securely. It wasn't a diaper, but for now it would have to do.

It's just for tonight, I told myself. *We can handle a baby for one night.*

6

Clara

My mom was not a night owl. She typically went to bed the moment she got home from work, and rose at four in the morning. But when I got home from my date with Jordan, I found her waiting in the kitchen with a mug of coffee in her hands.

"There's my daughter!" she said happily. "How was the date? It went well, did it?"

I told her about my night. The events poured out of me because I was excited to tell someone. Mom practically vibrated on the kitchen stool.

"This man, Jordan, will give me big firefighting grandbabies!" she declared.

I rolled my eyes. "Again, Jason and Maurice already gave you a grandson."

"One is wonderful," she said, "but more is better!"

I replayed the evening in my head while getting ready for bed. One thing that stuck out was what Jordan had said at the end of the night, about how his two firefighting colleagues also had crushes on me. How Jordan had beaten them to the punch of asking me out.

I didn't think I would go out with either of them. Not when the first date with Jordan had gone so well. But it was nice to know I was *desired*. Curvy girls like me didn't always get so much attention. It made me feel like I was the belle of the ball.

I can't wait to go out with him again.

Weekends were always busy at the restaurant, and I didn't have much free time. I knew all about the "two-day rule," but I ignored it and texted Jordan on Saturday.

Clara: I had a great time last night! Hope we can hang out again soon.

Jordan: Totally

Clara: Was everything okay at the firehouse?

Jordan: Why wouldn't it be? Is there a rumor that something weird is going on?

Clara: No, I'm referring to the phone call you got at the end of our date.

Jordan: Oh, right. Yeah, everything is fine.

Jordan: Gotta go, talk to you soon!

It seemed like Jordan was acting weird, but I tried not to overanalyze it. Our date had been fantastic, and I wasn't going to let anything ruin the giddy afterglow that I felt.

The restaurant was closed on Mondays, so it was pretty much the only day I had off. I allowed myself to sleep in, ate a lazy lunch, and then went for a jog.

It was a gorgeous day in California, mid-eighties and almost no humidity. I wasn't a very good jogger, but I still tried to make an effort once or twice a week. Even if it felt impossible to lose weight, the exercise did a good job of flooding my body with wonderful hormones that brightened my mood.

It also cleared my mind.

I did some of my best thinking while out for a run. Today, my mind drifted to the future. I didn't really know what I wanted to do with my life. I had *never* known, if I was being totally honest. I majored in English Literature in college, and there wasn't much I could do with that. Not much that interested me, at least.

When dad got sick, coming home helped give me a sense of direction. It was the easy thing to do. But now that he was gone, I felt rudderless again. Drifting along in the ocean of life, with no idea where I was supposed to be going.

I believed that things happened for a reason. Life would give me a sign. When I was debating where to go to college, a bus with a UC Irvine advertisement drove by the restaurant. I took that as a sign and applied the next day. When I was choosing my major in the library one day, a biography about Emily Bronte fell off the shelf and hit me on the head. Another sign.

A week before graduation, when I was trying to decide what to do next, we got the news about Dad. That wasn't a *good* sign, but it decided things for me.

I desperately needed a sign right now. I had been home for a year, first working in the kitchen at the restaurant, and now doing a little bit of everything. Too much time had passed. I needed something *new*.

I gazed up at the billowy white clouds, wishing they would spell out my next move for me.

When I got home, mom was grinning at me. "What's up with you?" I asked.

She casually nodded at the kitchen counter. "You got a phone call. While you were gone."

I ran to the counter and grabbed it.

"It was from Jordan!" she said before I could even check my phone history.

"You were snooping!"

"I happened to glance at the phone when it rang," she said with her Italian-American bluntness. "This is not my fault."

I rolled my eyes and called Jordan back. As it rang, I began to fear that he might not answer. But then he picked up on the fourth ring.

"*Hello?*" came his sexy voice.

Goosebumps covered my arms, and the words poured out of my mouth excitedly. "Hi! Jordan, it's me, Clara. I saw that I had a missed call from you, which is perfect, because I was going to call you and ask if you wanted to hang out today. I know your shift starts tonight, so maybe you would like to get an early dinner before then?"

"*Oh,*" he replied. "*I'm, uh, actually kind of busy later. Things are crazy around here.*"

I didn't know where *here* was since he wasn't working, but I was too disappointed to think about that. *He turned me down.*

"Okay," I said awkwardly. My stomach sank, but I ignored it and pushed on. "Maybe another time. So, uh, why did you call me?"

I heard him whispering on the other end. Talking to someone while covering the receiver. "*Clara, can you come over to the station? Right now?*"

"The firehouse?" My heart surged with hope that maybe I would get to see him after all. "Yeah! Sure! I mean, I can come over if you want me to."

More whispering on the other end. "*Great. See you soon.*"

I hung up and beamed at Mom. "He wants to see me!"

"This is wonderful! He—"

I held a finger up to her. "If you say *grandchildren* to me one more time, I'm getting my tubes tied."

She clamped her lips shut so quickly I'm surprised a shockwave didn't echo through the house.

I ran upstairs and took a shower. When I got out, I realized I was still sweating—I hadn't given myself enough time to cool off after my jog. So I took a *second* shower, then stood in front of my closet and agonized over what to wear. This wasn't a date; he was only inviting me over to the firehouse. So jeans and a T-shirt were probably best.

Come to think of it, why was he at the firehouse? His shift didn't start until tonight. Maybe he switched with someone, and that's why he couldn't hang out with me later.

I drove to the firehouse and parked on the street, once again taking care not to block the fire engine doors. There was a hideous lime-green Mustang in the parking lot, with the license plate: FIRMAN.

I knocked on the front door. A few moments later, someone I didn't recognize answered. He had a shaved head, but patches of dark hair were starting to grow back on his scalp. His head was round and large—a little *too* large, if I'm being totally honest—with small ears on the sides. Maybe the small ears were what made his head look too large by comparison. His dark, beady eyes didn't help.

He whistled to himself. "Why, hello there. It's not my birthday, but suddenly I wish it was. I'm Billy, and I'm *very* happy to meet you."

His comments, and the way his eyes raked over my body, made my skin crawl. I ignored his outstretched hand and said, "Yeah, okay. Is Jordan here?"

Billy's wormy smile faded. "What're you doing with him? I'll treat you much better."

I didn't know how to respond to that, so I just sort of stood there.

Jordan suddenly appeared next to him. He gave Billy a not-so-friendly shove and said, "Why do you have to be an asshole to everyone you see?"

"Asshole? I was giving the lady my compliments." He turned his gaze back on me and gave me an even *creepier* smile.

"That's what I'm talking about. Stop it." Jordan blocked Billy's body and gestured. "Come on in."

"You're a real loser, you know that?" Billy told him. "First you crash here all weekend, and now this..."

Jordan put a guiding hand on my back and led me down the hall. "Thanks for nothing, Billy."

I felt the other fireman's eyes on my back as we walked away.

"Crash here all weekend?" I asked.

"Long story," Jordan replied. "Thanks for coming."

Something in his tone confused me: it was like I was doing him a favor. "No problem. What's going on?"

"You'll see in a minute," Jordan said wearily. Now that I got a good look at him, he appeared exhausted and disheveled, like he hadn't gotten any sleep. His shirt had a pale white stain on it, like ranch dressing. And his beard had gotten longer.

"I thought Derek didn't want you to let your beard get any longer," I said with a friendly finger-wag.

"Been kind of busy," he replied.

I frowned. "Did you end up working all weekend? Your shifts are already crazy, but making you work a week straight like that..."

"No, no, it's not that."

"Then what's going on?" I asked, alarm growing. "Why did you invite me here?"

He guided me into a room marked *Captain Dahlkemper*. Inside, Derek was standing in the corner. He turned around and scowled when he saw me.

But I ignored the look on his face, because there was a *baby* in his arms.

Jordan gestured. "*This* is why I asked you to come over."

7

Clara

I gawked at the baby cradled in Derek's muscular arms. My brain took a few seconds to reboot. A baby was the *last* thing I expected to see when Jordan invited me over to the firehouse.

Then my maternal instinct took over.

"Aww! What's your name, little girl?"

"He's a boy, actually," Taylor chimed in. "I don't know why the Chief bought a pink blanket."

"Because it was on clearance," he replied dryly.

"His name is Anthony," Jordan said.

I froze.

Anthony was my father's name. Anthony "Tony" Ricci.

A memory from a year ago flashed in my head, still painful after so long. I was in the hospital with Dad, and I complained to him that I didn't have a clue what I wanted to do with my life.

Even on his death bed, Dad was good at dispensing wisdom. "Clara," he had told me, "if you don't know what you want to do, then settle down with someone and start a family. Raising you and Jason was the most fulfilling part of my life. It's what I'm most proud of."

"Maybe," I had said. "I have to find the right guy, first."

"As long as you give your mother grandchildren," he said. "Lots and lots of grandchildren!"

I remember smiling at him. "I promise, Dad. And the first boy I have? I'm going to name him Anthony."

Dad smiled at me. "A little baby named Anthony? With a promise like that, I might beat this cancer after all."

I blinked, and suddenly I was back in Captain Dahlkemper's room at the firehouse, staring at a pudgy little baby. I felt dizzy, so I sat on the edge of the bed.

"He was dropped off on Friday," Jordan explained. "The mother's identity is protected due to Safe Haven laws."

My heart felt like it was being twisted into knots, first because of the promise I had made to my dad, and then because I realized this baby had been abandoned. His parents didn't want him.

As if he was equally upset about the situation, Baby Anthony's face twisted into a grimace and he began to wail. I took him from Derek and made comforting noises while rubbing his tiny little back.

"This is why I said I was too busy to hang out," Jordan explained.

"We've been watching him all weekend," Taylor said, dropping down onto the bed next to me. "None of us have gotten much sleep. We're kind of clueless when it comes to babies."

I had no experience at all when it came to babies, either. My older brother Jason had changed plenty of my diapers, and he had a child of his own now, but I didn't have younger siblings. I had never helped raise anyone. I was just as clueless as these three firemen.

But they were all looking at me with hopeful expressions, like I was the savior who had come to help them.

And I really, *really* wanted to help them.

"I know some," I said, which was a lie.

"Did we put the diaper on correctly?" Jordan asked. "We watched a few YouTube videos, but I can't tell if it's too loose or too tight..."

Baby Anthony was still crying, so I gently laid him on his back on the bed. I opened the diaper—which took several confusing moments before I found the fastening tape—and then re-sealed it. I had no idea what I was doing, and was totally going by instinct alone.

But the crying stopped, and Baby Anthony squealed happily and wiggled his arms and legs on the bed.

"See?" Jordan said to Derek. "I told you it was a good idea to invite her over."

I picked Baby Anthony up. "Yeah, that's much better, isn't it?" I bounced him in my arms. That's what you're supposed to do with babies, right? Bounce them?

"You said you've been watching him since Friday," I said to Taylor. "Isn't there someone you can call to take him?"

Derek crossed his arms over his broad chest and sighed deeply. "I called my sister. She works for the California Department of Social Services. Turns out they're *severely* underfunded right now. They don't have the money or manpower to handle their current responsibilities, let alone additional children. If we hand him in, he'll be placed in an overcrowded foster home."

"I don't understand," I said slowly. "I thought there are lots of people waiting to adopt babies."

"Usually, yes. But apparently adoption agencies are experiencing a lull in demand," Derek said bitterly. "My sister says it will be better when the fiscal year is over, because they'll have a brand new budget and more resources. But until then..." He shrugged.

"We can't give the baby up until we know he's going to be properly cared for," Taylor insisted.

"Not to mention the mother," Derek added. "She surrendered

the baby too late, by accident. Under California law, she'll be prosecuted for abandonment. My sister is working on a way to slip the baby into the system and change the back-date, so the mother isn't liable."

"So," I said, "you're taking care of the baby until then?"

Jordan and Derek answered at the same time.

"Yes," Jordan said.

"No," Derek said.

They looked at each other.

"You said you would consider it!" Jordan said.

Derek shook his head. "I *am* considering it. But no matter what we choose to do, there are no good options."

"Then let's choose the least shitty option," Jordan insisted.

"This is a firehouse, not a nursery," Derek shot back. "I have no idea what I'm doing. Neither do either of you. And even if we did, how are we supposed to do our jobs while watching a child? What happens if we get a call? You think we can strap him into a baby seat in the fire engine and take him with us?"

"Oh, totally!" Taylor said. "We can get him a matching uniform and everything. Cute baby overalls. He'd be, like, our mascot..."

He trailed off at a glare from the Chief.

"Oh, nevermind. I was just joking."

"Chief, come on..." Jordan said.

While they argued, I stared at the baby, and he stared right back at me. Jordan had brought me here because they needed help. The problem was that I didn't have any experience with kids. Hell, I didn't even feel comfortable around them. I don't know why—I just didn't have that maternal gene. I was holding Baby Anthony in front of me like he was a bomb that might go off at any moment.

I was the last person who should be helping the firemen.

I opened my mouth to say as much, then hesitated. These guys were helpless. If I didn't help them, someone else would. I liked Jordan —I *really* liked him—and wanted an excuse to keep seeing him. I wanted to be useful.

And beneath all that, I couldn't shake the feeling that the baby sharing a name with my deceased father was the sign I had been looking for...

"I can watch him!" I said.

All three men turned toward me.

"Are you sure?" Jordan asked. "We don't want to impose..."

"Absolutely," I lied. "I know what I'm doing, and the three of you clearly need help. I'll take him back to my house and watch him until Social Services has the budget to give him a proper home. That's only a month or so, right?"

Sitting next to me on the bed, Taylor suddenly enveloped me— and Baby Anthony—in a big hug. He was leaner than the other two men, but still covered with corded muscle.

"Thank you," he whispered into my hair. "You're such a sweet person, Clara."

"You guys are sweet for making sure he goes somewhere good," I replied. "It would be easier to turn him over now."

Taylor pulled away and looked awkward about the hug. Baby Anthony blinked in confusion as well.

"You can't take him back to your house," Derek said. "There are legal complications."

"What do you mean?" I asked.

"First of all, we're doing this off the books. We're required to turn in any surrendered child immediately. Every day we *don't* do that, we run the risk of getting in bigger trouble."

"I understand, but doesn't that mean you want him *away* from the station? So you don't get caught?"

Derek grimaced. "One would think so, but no. I spoke with a lawyer friend of mine about the situation. She says that if we take the baby to one of our houses, and we get caught, it might appear that we intended to abduct the child for ourselves. However, if we have kept him at the firehouse for the majority of the time, then we can make the case that we still had the child's best interests at heart. That we always intended to turn him in when the time was right. My lawyer friend is adamant that we keep the baby here, that it will be much easier convincing a judge of our good intentions. We don't need to keep him here *one hundred* percent of the time, necessarily, but a majority of the time."

"Okay. I might be able to make that work. Let me talk to my mom..." I winced. Mom was relying on me to work at the restaurant. I might have been able to scrape by if I could bring the baby to the restaurant with me, but if I had to be at the firehouse...

"Is there a problem?" Jordan asked. "Because if you can't do it, we'll understand."

"No problem at all," I said without hesitation. "I just need to rearrange some things on my schedule."

Derek nodded slowly to the group. "All right. It appears we have the beginnings of a plan. The most important thing is that we don't tell anyone else about this. *Especially* not Billy Manning." He turned to me. "He's the bald shitbag on second-shift..."

"I had the pleasure of meeting him already," I replied.

"Billy has a beef with the Chief," Jordan explained. "He's looking for any excuse to get Derek fired."

"And the last thing we need is to hand him the ammunition he needs," Derek said dryly. "We've managed to keep the child's presence a secret all weekend, thanks to the soundproofing in my bedroom. But I don't know what we're going to do next weekend. The last thing I want is to stay locked in my bedroom all weekend with an unhappy baby."

"The other shift didn't get suspicious about the three of you staying here?" I asked.

"We crash here sometimes, when we don't feel like going home," Taylor said. "The soundproofing is great when I need to study for exams."

"But if we do it two weekends in a row, it'll raise some eyebrows," Jordan said.

"We'll worry about that problem when we come to it," Derek said. "For now, we're grateful to have your help, Clara."

I looked at my watch. "If I'm going to be staying here, I need to run home and get some things. Can you guys watch him until I get back?"

Jordan took Baby Anthony from me and cradled him against his chest. The sight of the tiny baby cuddled up against the big, burly fireman was so cute that I think I felt one of my ovaries twitch.

"We survived this long," he said. "We can last a little longer."

*

I was in a daze as I drove home. It felt like the encounter at the firehouse had been a dream—a silly, implausible one at that.

Had I really done that? Offered to watch the baby for them?

As the gravity of the situation sank in, I began feeling overwhelmed. I didn't know what I was doing. I couldn't do this. This felt like I had lied on my résumé and had just accepted a job that I was totally unqualified for. Except the stakes were much higher, because a *human being* was the one hanging in the balance.

I also felt vaguely disappointed that Jordan invited me over to the firehouse to ask for help with the baby, and not because he was excited to see me. But he needed me, and this was a great excuse to see a whole lot more of him.

Then there was the baby's name. *Anthony.*

I had been waiting for a sign, something to point me in the

right direction in life. Was this it, or was it just a massive coincidence?

Regardless, the three firemen needed me. Baby Anthony needed me. I had agreed to help them, and I had to see it through to the end.

"Home so soon?" Mom asked when I walked through the door. "Oh no. He broke up with you, didn't he?"

"We're not even *together*, Mom. We went on one date. But no, it's not that."

I explained the situation to her. She reacted not with shock or surprise, but with excitement.

"A baby!" she exclaimed, clapping her hands together. "I want to see him. Bring him to me!"

"Maybe next weekend," I said. "Once we get into a groove. But Mom... I need to take some time off. I won't be able to help around the restaurant for a while. *Maybe* I can help on the weekends, if the other guys can watch the baby when they're not working, but..."

The little Italian-American woman pulled my head down so she could kiss me on the forehead. "Take all the time you need!"

"Really? But the restaurant..."

She waved a hand. "Angelina will help me. She owes me a favor after I catered her son's graduation party."

"This might be for a while, though..."

"She is a stay-at-home mom with no children to watch. What else is she going to do? Sit around the house all night? Pfft."

I hugged her. "Thank you, Mom. I have one more favor to ask."

She smiled at me with all the love of a mother to her daughter. "Anything."

"I need to know the basics of taking care of a baby."

8

Derek

I didn't like this one fucking bit.

"I said invite her over so she could show us the basics," I growled at Jordan. "I didn't mean bring her over to be the fucking nanny."

"Come on, Chief!" Taylor said. "This is great. We need the help—badly, if you couldn't tell—and she's qualified. She handled the baby like a natural."

"Still, though..."

"If you have a better plan, let's hear it," Jordan said to me. "Because out of all the crappy solutions, this one is the least crappy."

I wanted to keep arguing, but they were right. We needed someone to help, and Clara was the only person we knew.

It's better than handing the baby over to Social Services, I thought bitterly. No matter what happened, I didn't want to send Baby Anthony to an overloaded system. I knew better than anyone that that was a bad way to grow up.

He deserved better than that, even if it meant hanging out with us for a little while.

"We'll need more supplies," I grumbled. "I'll look at the budget and see what I can do."

I opened the door a crack, paused to make sure the coast was clear, and then slipped out into the hallway. We had been lucky to keep the baby a secret over the weekend. If this was an older fire station, rather than one that had been built new six years ago, we wouldn't have the soundproof sleeping quarters. We were lucky.

I must have used up all my luck, because I ran into Billy in the kitchen. He sneered at me while stirring creamer into a mug of coffee.

"Hanging at the firehouse all weekend. You must have a boring life, *Chief*."

He wasn't exactly insolent, but he always said the word *chief* like it was a curse. Technically, I wasn't a Battalion Chief—I had the rank of Captain. But everyone called me Chief because it just sort of fit.

"I'm doing my taxes," I said dryly.

"You do your own taxes? With your salary?" He scoffed. "I'm surprised you don't pay someone."

I gritted my teeth and forced myself not to engage with him. "Something you need, Manning?"

He shrugged. "Just wanted to know if you're planning on retiring any time soon."

"There are plenty of other stations with upward mobility," I replied. "You should transfer to one of them."

"I like it here in Riverville. I'm close to my ex-wife and kids. They're in Fresno."

"Then transfer to one of the Fresno stations."

"Riverville is quieter. I can relax, watch the game without having to respond to a lot of calls."

"Most of the guys here treat the job as a responsibility, not an annoyance," I said dryly. "If you worked on your attitude, maybe you'd get promoted."

I started to leave, but Billy moved to block my way. "You're cocky now. You won't be when I catch you slipping up. Then your cushy job will be *mine*, along with the rest of the station."

"Get out of my way," I growled, "before I permanently rearrange the teeth in your mouth."

Billy gave me a shit-eating grin and stepped aside. I felt his sneer all the way to the administrative office.

This job only looked cushy to outsiders. Being a leader meant always having the weight of responsibility on your shoulders. Following orders was easy, but giving them? It was so much harder. If I made the wrong decision, people died. That kind of stress wore a man down over time.

Not to mention all the other responsibilities I had on a daily basis. Keeping an inventory on our supplies. Assigning fire code inspection duties to the guys.

Taking in a helpless baby.

Now there was a responsibility Billy Manning would never understand. If he were in my place, I knew exactly what he would do: turn the baby over without a second thought. He wouldn't care what happened to little Anthony, so long as it didn't get in the way of his own selfish priorities.

Billy was no leader. I knew that in my gut. I would sacrifice everything I had before I would let him take over as Captain.

Baby Anthony was definitely a liability, though. He was the ammunition Billy had been waiting for, the reason to get me fired and take my job. Keeping the baby safe was the right decision, but it was not without its dangers.

We need to protect him, I thought emphatically. *Until my sister lets us know they have the manpower to take him in.*

I spent an hour with my station budget, moving money around so we could afford extra supplies and take care of the baby. We didn't have much wiggle room, but if need be, I would pay for everything out of my own pocket. If it came to that.

Second-shift ended promptly at 9:00 PM. Billy left without saying goodbye—like he usually did—but the other guys on his team all popped into the office to let me know they were leaving.

They were a good group of guys. It was a shame they had to work with Billy.

Clara arrived five minutes later. She hurried through the front door with her suitcase in hand, closing the door behind her and then peering out the window nervously.

"I parked down the street and waited for them to leave. Then I waited some more, just in case they came back."

My eyes skimmed down her body involuntarily. Clara had a gorgeous curve to her hips and full breasts. A voluptuous figure that was accentuated by her tight jeans and blouse. Her blonde hair was usually pulled up in a ponytail when she made deliveries, but now she wore it down, a curtain of silk around her neck. It suited her that way.

I had been admiring Clara from afar ever since she started delivering food to the firehouse. All of us had admired her, as a matter of fact. But we knew she was only in town because her father had gotten sick, and then passed away. Surely she would eventually leave again.

Except she hadn't left. She was still here. And so Jordan had finally been the first to ask her out.

"I'll call Officer Balmer and let him know not to give you a ticket for parking there too long," I said, locking my eyes onto hers. "Thanks, uh, for doing this, by the way."

She had such a warm, welcoming smile, and she gave it to me then. "Of course. Anything for the baby."

"I moved some money around in the budget. I should be able to pay you as a consultant. I'll figure out the exact verbiage later, when I submit the expenses up the chain. But the point is, you won't be doing this for free. We know your time is valuable."

"Oh. You don't have to—"

"This isn't a discussion," I said firmly. "You're essentially doing a full-time job for the foreseeable future. You need to be paid accordingly."

She nodded. "Yeah. Okay. Is there anything else I need to know?"

I hesitated. There was something else I needed to talk to her about. And it was an awkward conversation, both because I liked her, and because she was helping us.

But I had to talk to her about it, no matter how uncomfortable it was.

"The other night," I said. "When you delivered our food, and then we had to run out on a call. There was something you did..."

"Oh, I wasn't snooping!" she suddenly blurted out. "I glanced in one of the bedrooms, but only for a minute. It probably looked awkward on the security cameras or whatever, but I didn't do anything weird. I stayed in the hallway the entire time."

I shook my head. "What? No, it's not that. You put the food in the oven."

"Oh, yeah," she said, visibly relieved. "I wanted to keep it warm. Don't worry—I checked for food crumbs to make sure nothing would catch fire."

I clenched my jaw. "You can't leave an oven on while nobody is here, Clara. It's careless. Carelessness leads to fires, and fires lead to *deaths*."

Clara's mouth hung open. "The oven was barely on. I used the *warming* setting. They wouldn't have those settings if they weren't safe."

Fire safety was a big deal. I had seen homes burned down and lives lost thanks to the logic she was using right now. It pissed me off that she was acting so flippant about it when confronted on the matter.

"You shouldn't have done it. It was a mistake. If you're going to be living in this firehouse, you need to acknowledge that. Because I need to know you won't do something careless again."

"Careless? I was trying to help..." She trailed off and shook her head. "Nevermind. I'm sorry. It won't happen again."

She rolled her suitcase down the hall past me, tears welling in her eyes.

I sighed. Shit. I didn't mean to make her feel bad about the whole thing. I just wanted to make her aware.

If some hurt feelings are what it takes to make her understand the importance and take it seriously, I thought, *then so be it.*

The weight of responsibility was heavy indeed.

I followed her down the hall to the bedrooms, annoyed that I had gotten off on the wrong foot with a girl I liked.

9

Clara

I ran from Derek with tears welling in my eyes. Somehow, I managed not to actually start crying. That was a small victory, at least.

I was just trying to be helpful! The three of them were heroes, rushing away on their screaming fire engine to risk their lives. The least I could do was ensure their food stayed warm.

So much for Jordan saying Derek had a crush on me.

I shook it off when I reached the room with the baby. I may not have been a natural at this, but nothing brightened up a person's mood like a giggling, smiling baby. Taylor was peering into the laundry basket where Baby Anthony was wriggling around. When he saw me, he smiled and brushed back his blond hair.

"I put him down an hour ago," Taylor said, "but he woke up again. I think he likes all this attention."

"I can't blame him," I said, picking the baby up and holding him to my chest. "Is he on a feeding schedule yet?"

"According to the Internet, a two-month-old should be fed every four or five hours. About six ounces per feeding." He gave me a wry look. "I don't usually believe everything I see on the Internet, but that sounded right. And in our short experience, he *has* been waking up to eat about that often."

Across from the bed was a tall dresser. Taylor opened the top drawer and revealed a big canister of baby formula in powder form, and a bunch of empty bottles.

"We've been using warm water to mix it up," he added, "but now that we have access to the kitchen without the second-shift guys here, we can heat it on the stove if we need to."

I nodded. "He has a lot of toys in his basket."

Taylor grinned. He had a bright, cheerful smile. "Oh, yeah! I bought them at the thrift store. Whole big tub of them for, like, five bucks. Snuck them into the station in my backpack." He chuckled. "We wanted to sneak *him* out of the firehouse. We even had a couple of chances when the second-shift guys were asleep."

"I was going to ask about that," I said. "Do we really need to keep him here? It would be easier to keep him at my house. There's less chaos, and less chance of him being discovered..."

Taylor grimaced. "I said the same thing. Great minds think alike, huh? But Chief was insistent. Guess that lawyer buddy of his knows what he's talking about. I'm not a lawyer, so I just go along with whatever the experts say, you know?"

"Yeah, I guess so," I said. I was keenly aware that I wasn't the one risking her job to temporarily keep the child.

Baby Anthony hadn't been fed in two hours, so Taylor showed me how to mix a bottle. I cradled the little guy in my arm and held the bottle to his mouth. He closed his eyes and sucked the formula down eagerly.

While the baby ate, Taylor and I went out to the living room. Jordan and Derek were sitting on the couch, speaking quietly.

"Looks like you're doing a good job," Derek told me gruffly. It felt forced, like he was trying to make up for scolding me earlier.

"It's just a bottle," I replied. "The baby's doing most of the work."

"He's a hungry little guy," Jordan agreed. "He's going to be big."

I looked around the room. "Should I be out here? If the sirens go off, I don't want it to disturb the baby. Or worse: damage his hearing."

"No chance," Derek said. He ran a hand through his dark hair, which was thick despite having a few silvery strands mixed in. "We have variable-volume alarms. I turned down the volume on everything in the station. They'll get your attention if you're in the public areas, but it won't damage anyone's ear drums."

I breathed a sigh of relief. I was still jumpy after being in the garage on Friday night when the alarm suddenly went off.

"So what's the living situation... I mean, where should I stay? Do you want me with the baby at all times, or...?"

"You and Baby Anthony can sleep in my room," Derek replied. "I'll bunk with Jordan."

"You don't have to do that," I said. "I'm fine sleeping anywhere, honest..."

He pursed his lips. "I'm not doing it out of the kindness of my heart. It makes the most sense, logistically. There's a private bathroom, which you'll need while taking care of the baby. There's also more space for your things. The other bunks are cramped."

He looked at his watch. "All right, it's after ten. I'm going to hit the sack while I can."

"Same here," Taylor said.

I blinked. "Your shift just started an hour ago. You're sleeping already?"

"We just made it through the *hot zone*," Taylor replied. "That's the busiest time of day for us—between six and nine o'clock at night. Everyone's getting home from work, turning on electronics, cooking food. That sort of thing."

"There's another hot zone in the morning, for the same reason," Derek said. "Don't worry: I already disabled the sound alarm in my quarters. If we get a call in the middle of the night, it won't startle you. Thanks for being here, Clara. We do appreciate it."

He looked like he didn't know what else to say, so he nodded gruffly and walked away. Taylor grinned, gave me a little wave, and then followed him down to the bedroom hallway.

"You're not going to bed, too?" I asked Jordan.

"I usually stay up a little later. We've got flexibility, so long as we're jumping up and ready to go if we get a call."

I sat on the couch next to him and shifted the baby from one arm to the other. He made an unhappy noise when the bottle wasn't in his mouth, which immediately ceased when I gave it back to him. There wasn't much left in the bottle, but he seemed happy to nuzzle at the rubber nipple.

"Wow, look at that," I said, nodding at the TV. "The Giants are losing to the Diamondbacks."

"It's early," Jordan replied curtly.

"It's the seventh inning."

Jordan glared over at me, but his expression softened when he saw the baby in my arms. "It's been a crazy few days. When you texted me on Saturday, I was kind of busy learning how to change a diaper. I hope my short answers didn't come across the wrong way."

"Actually, they kind of did at the time," I admitted. "But I understand the situation now."

"It's crazy. It's all so crazy." Jordan shook his head in wonder. "I just can't believe this happened on Friday night, the night I finally worked up the nerve to ask you out."

"Bad timing indeed."

Or good timing, depending on how you look at it. After all, I'm here with Jordan, and will be spending a lot more time with him.

"Speaking of timing," I said, "you should switch to the Dodgers game. They're tied going into the ninth right now."

"I'm perfectly happy watching the Giants, thank you very much."

"Come on. The Dodgers are playing the Brewers. It's a series with playoff potential." I took the baby's bottle away and put him over my shoulder, then gently rubbed his back. "I'm here, helping take care of this little guy, and you won't even let me watch the Dodgers..."

Jordan glared at me again. "How long are you going to milk that?"

"For as long as possible! Besides, the Giants suck."

Jordan clutched his chest like he had been shot. "Keep talking like that and you can kiss a second date goodbye."

I raised an eyebrow. "Does that mean you *do* want to take me out again?"

"Maybe," he said. "Depending on how much Giants trash talk I have to endure."

"The Giants are a very respectable team," I said diplomatically. "Even if they have silly Halloween colors."

I realized that baby Anthony was asleep on my shoulder. I slowly got up from the couch and carried him back to Derek's room—my room, for the foreseeable future.

As I laid him into his basket of towels, Jordan whispered, "It's kind of pathetic putting him in a laundry basket, huh?"

I swaddled the baby in a towel and said, "I think it's cute. You're doing what humans have been doing for all of time: trying to get by with whatever they have at their disposal."

Jordan loomed over the basket and brushed Baby Anthony's cheek with his thumb. "Don't worry, little guy. We'll get you some blankets and a proper bassinet the next time we go out."

"That's a lot of money to spend for a child you're only keeping temporarily," I pointed out.

Jordan responded without taking his eyes off the baby. "Whatever he needs. Besides, we can donate what we have when we're done." He sighed and finally looked at me. "Can I ask you something?"

"Of course," I replied softly.

"Are we doing the right thing?"

Up to this point, I thought the whole situation was crazy. I had taken it in stride, but it was still totally out of the ordinary for someone like me. I was *still* struggling to make sense of it all.

But seeing the way Jordan cared for the baby, and understanding the risks to their careers they were accepting, I felt different about the entire situation.

"Of course you're doing the right thing," I replied. "If you turned him over to Social Services, he'll just be another name in a database. He'll be part of a system that's stretched too thin, and likely given to a foster family who is only in it for the money. Baby Anthony is *much* better off with the three of you. I can see that already."

I touched his bearded cheek to comfort him. Jordan's hard face relaxed at my words and my touch. He let out a relieved breath. "I think I needed to hear that. Thank you, Clara."

"Thanks for putting the baby's needs first," I said. "It's selfless."

We smiled at each other, and suddenly it felt like that moment outside my car on Friday night. The sexual tension between us had disappeared in the past few hours, but now it had returned twofold.

And seeing the way the big, burly fireman tenderly touched he baby? It made him about a billion times sexier to me.

Jordan reached up and cupped my hand, which was still touching his cheek. He gave it a squeeze, enveloping my fingers in his much larger hand. He was warm and strong and tender all at the same time, and my body tensed with anticipation.

He touched my cheek, much in the way I had touched his, and

then he leaned in and pressed his lips to mine.

There was no phone call to interrupt us this time. I raised my head and accepted his kiss eagerly. My body came alive as he churned his lips against mine, fingers still cupping my cheek with growing strength.

I was panting when he finally pulled away, and Jordan smiled down at me. But then his smile wavered.

"Maybe we shouldn't be doing this."

I jerked my head toward the baby. "I don't think *he* minds, as long as we're quiet."

"I mean because of... My teammates. Taylor and Derek both really like you..."

I scoffed. "Derek? Are you sure? He yelled at me for putting the food in the oven the other night."

"That's just how Derek is," Jordan replied. "He's a hard-ass with everyone. Taylor and I are like family to him, but he still chews us out when we deserve it."

"Okay, but so what? Taylor's nice, but I haven't even gone on a date with him. I've gone out with *you*. If they liked me, they should have asked me out first. It's that simple."

Jordan grimaced. "It's more complicated than that, actually..."

"How?" I hissed, keeping my voice quiet. "Tell me how it's complicated."

He shook his head and pinched the bridge of his aquiline nose. "There's just a lot going on, especially with the baby in the mix. You know? Maybe we should take it easy until things settle down."

I wanted to argue with him, but I also didn't want to seem too eager. If he was saying we should wait, there probably wasn't anything I could say to make him change his mind.

"Yeah, sure," I said. "When things settle down, maybe we can pick things up."

He nodded gratefully, gave Baby Anthony another loving smile, then bowed out of the room. His broad-chested, massive frame was silhouetted in the door frame for a moment, and then the door closed with a resounding click.

I fell back on the bed and groaned. I didn't think I was moving too fast with Jordan. We had *almost* kissed after our date, and the kiss we just shared felt natural. It wasn't awkward. And *he* had been the one to initiate it!

I got up and went to the baby basket. Anthony was nestled in his towels, sleeping quietly with a smile on his tiny face.

"I'd be happy too, if I was a baby," I whispered. "You don't have anything to worry about, especially now that the four of us are watching you."

I turned to grab my suitcase so I could change, and the door opened again.

Jordan's silhouette was huge, hulking, and unmoving. He stepped inside and closed the door. There was a quiet intensity to his movements.

"I can't," he said, crossing the space between us. "I can't just drop things now."

I closed my eyes as he took me in his arms.

10

Clara

Jordan folded me in his arms and crushed his lips against mine. The earlier kiss was soft and tender and warm, but this? This was a kiss of desire.

It was a kiss of *need*.

In his arms, all my worries disappeared. The restaurant, my mom, even Baby Anthony—all of them faded away in the presence of Jordan's embrace. For now, for however long this moment alone lasted, nothing in the world mattered except the two of us.

His broad chest was as hard as chiseled rock, and I pressed all of my body against him. My body came alive as the kiss deepened, opening like a flower toward the rays of nurturing sunlight. Jordan walked me backwards until I felt the bed, then pushed me down onto my back. He wasn't forceful, but I could sense his tremendous strength. He could manhandle and maneuver me any way he desired, if he so chose.

That turned me on in a way that I had never experienced.

"Clara," he murmured while his hands laced into my hair. He planted a knee on the bed and climbed on top of me, covering me with his warmth and protection.

"I'm glad you came back," I breathed. "I couldn't wait either."

"I don't know what I was thinking."

"Well, you *are* a Giants fan."

Jordan dove into me with renewed enthusiasm, grinding into me with his entire body. I wrapped my arms around him, savoring the touch of the muscles in his broad back as they flexed and contracted.

This is so much better than a kiss by the car.

His hand dove between us, sliding down my body and moving lower. I spread my legs wider for him and he flicked open the button of my jeans, fingers exploring their way into the waistband of my panties. The teeth of the zipper clicked as his palm pushed deeper, and I tensed as he found my mound and then my soaked lips.

As soon as he touched me, all the tension melted away. I let out a soft moan as he curled his fingers up into my wet heat.

Jordan broke the kiss long enough to say, "Shh. You can't be too loud, or..." He glanced in the direction of the baby basket.

"If you want me to be quiet, you'd better stop doing *that*," I replied.

His grin deepened. "Not a chance."

I closed my eyes and sighed as he delved back into me. His fingers corkscrewed in and out of me, twisting in just the right way to touch all of my inner walls. I drove my hips up into him, demanding *more* of his thick fingers. Heat built inside of me, a pressure that had to be released.

I reached between us and found the bulge in his pants, hard and hot. Jordan made a rumbling noise deep in his throat as I ran my fingers over him, stroking him through the fabric and wishing there was nothing between us.

The faster I rubbed, the quicker his own fingers pistoned in and out of me. I went tight like a wire as the pressure built, nearly too powerful to withstand. The only thing keeping me from crying out with pleasure was his tongue rolling against mine inside my mouth, but that sensation was only heightening everything his fingers were doing...

Finally the pleasure between my legs could no longer be contained. Like someone suddenly opening the pizza oven, a blast of heat and pressure filled my body, so intensely pure that it almost felt painful. I shook with release and opened my mouth to scream in bliss, but Jordan clamped his free hand over my mouth.

I finally let loose and unleashed my cries of pleasure, which were properly muffled beneath his strong hand. My eyes clenched shut and everything vibrated with a soft hum, like the world had been reduced to its barest atoms.

As the ecstasy faded, Jordan's tongue forced its way into my mouth, conquering and claiming me. I took hold of his face, his beautiful face, in both of my hands and pulled him into me, demanding that he *never* stop kissing me.

I don't remember him taking off his pants with his free hand. I only remember the endless kiss and the orgasm aftershocks that trembled inside me. His fingers were still locked inside my pussy, like he was holding onto me and didn't dare let go. That was just fine. I liked the way he felt inside me.

Only when he finally removed them did I open my eyes. Jordan broke the kiss and stepped out of his pants, which were now on the floor. The only thing covering his junk was a pair of grey boxers, which were so tight they might as well have been painted on.

They're only tight because of what's inside...

In the soft light of the room, his bulge looked massive. Bigger than it felt underneath my fingertips. But my attention was quickly diverted as Jordan reached up and pulled his shirt over his head, revealing an armada of muscle. The bumps of his six pack appeared first, then his chest muscles, and finally the bulging muscles of his shoulders and arms. One arm flexed deliciously as he reached out, tossing the shirt to the ground.

"I can see why some people start fires," I breathed. "If it means *you* come to rescue them."

He favored me with a small smile. "Fortunately, you don't have to."

Jordan yanked on my jeans, pulling me toward the edge of the bed with them. He resolved this problem by planting a hand—such a strong hand!—on my chest to keep me still, then using his other arm to pull the jeans the rest of the way off. I leaned up and kiss his bare arm, feeling the corded muscles taut underneath my lips. He slid his own boxers off, and a shiver of excitement went up my spine as I caught a glimpse of the thick ridge of his cock.

I shimmied out of my panties and kicked them aside. I tensed, waiting for him to sink into me, this time with more than just his fingers.

I've never wanted anything so badly before in my life.

Instead, Jordan sat on the edge of the bed. He pulled me up and into his lap, my knees on the bed and our foreheads pressed together. I let out a moan—a *soft* moan—as he nuzzled at my neck.

I could feel him beneath me, his crown brushing against my wet entrance. Every near-touch sent electricity through my bones. I wanted desperately to reach between us and guide it into me, but Jordan was holding me against his chest too tightly for that. I loved the way he embraced me, an arm around my waist and holding on for dear life. It made me think of the way he might hold onto someone while carrying them from a burning building.

He's not just some guy, I thought while his lips kissed down my neck. *He's a fireman. He's a hero.*

Finally his hand slid down my lower back and cupped my ass cheek. But he wasn't just groping me—he was positioning me in just the right spot.

He thrust up into me, and used his grip on my ass to push me down onto him.

The entire length of his cock filled me, from tip to base. I arched my back and bit my lip to keep from voicing my pleasure. I felt Jordan's skin tighten against my neck; even he had to clench his powerful jaw to suppress his groan.

We remained like that for a long moment, both of us simply savoring the flawless sensation of finally being joined.

"I've been thinking about this since Friday," he gritted out.

I ran my fingers into his hair and down the back of his neck, exploring every inch of him. "You wanted to do *this* on Friday?"

"What if I did?"

"I'd tell you the thought crossed my mind that night, too."

He vibrated with laughter, something I felt throughout his body rather than heard with my ears. "Glad we're on the same page."

Jordan used his strong thighs to gyrated up into me slowly. I craned my head back and sighed, allowing him to lead, but soon I was flexing my own hips in time with his erotic movements, meeting him stroke for stroke.

For the first time in the past year, I allowed myself to forget about everything going on in my life. There was no career that I was trying to discover, no future path that I was trying to navigate. The restaurant, the overbearing—but loving—mother, even the now-absent father, all of it dimmed away to background noise.

The only thing that mattered was the gorgeous, chiseled man underneath me, and the way he smiled lustily at me with his green eyes.

For the first time since I could remember, I was truly *present* in the moment.

And it's a hell of a moment to be present in.

He kissed me again, gently at first but growing more forceful along with the speed of our bodies. I took over most of the movements, pulling up off of Jordan and then impaling myself on his hard ridge, again and again, as our kiss deepened and his arms grew tighter around my body. Sweat covered his chest in a sheen and beaded on my own temple, but neither of us cared.

Tonight, I was his, and he was mine.

There in the soundproof firehouse bedroom, we made love until neither of us could breathe, losing ourselves to the mindless drive of our bodies.

11

Jordan

As I held Clara in my lap, kissing and grinding into each other, I thought to myself: *I can't believe I waited so long to ask her out.*

I'd been crushing on her since the first day she delivered pizza to the firehouse. After that, I always looked forward to ordering dinner on Friday night, the last meal before our shift ended. Anything to see Clara Ricci. Even on nights where they were slammed, she always delivered the food with a smile and chatted us up before leaving. She made us feel like we were more than just a customer she was being friendly to for tips.

She was certainly much more than a delivery girl to me.

I waited so long to ask her out because I didn't expect her to stay in town. Everyone knew what had happened to her dad, Tony, and she was only here to help out in the immediate aftermath. Soon, I knew, someone different would arrive to deliver the pizza on a Friday night, and we would learn that she had left town.

I wasn't the kind of guy who had flings or one-night-stands. I'd tried that before, and I knew it wasn't for me. I couldn't keep things casual. I always fell for the girls I was with, and sometimes I fell *hard*.

So I didn't ask her out, even though I *really* wanted to.

Now, that felt like such a waste. We'd been flirting for almost a year. I could have asked her out *months* ago. Why had I waited so long?

Shut up, brain, I thought while Clara ground her hips into me. *Stop thinking and enjoy it.*

Clara felt so good underneath my palm. Her skin was smooth, and I couldn't get enough of her curves. I wanted to grab and squeeze every part of her body, and never let go.

She rode me faster, arching her back to take as much of me as possible. When she shook and shivered with release, I couldn't hold it any longer. Her pussy lips clamped around my length like a vice, squeezing the last remnants of constitution out of me.

I grabbed hold of her waist and drove up into her, as hard as I could for those final few strokes. Clara started to cry out with ecstasy but then bit her lip to silence herself, eyes clenching shut as she rode the wave of pleasure with me.

And then my own orgasm arrived like a backdraft blowout in a burning building, with little warning. One moment I felt it building, and the next I was overwhelmed with lust. My vision went bright as I exploded inside her, pulsing with rope after rope. I didn't trust myself not to cry out with torrid waves of pleasure, so I pulled her head down to mine and kissed her. Both of us moaned into each other's mouth, using our tongues to muffle the otherwise deafening cries of our climaxes.

I fell back onto the bed, bringing her with me. Our bodies were slick with sweat, and our chests heaved as we caught our breath in the afterglow of the physical workout.

It feels good to give in, I thought. *I'm glad I came back after all.*

"So," she said after a while. "You really thought about *this* on Friday?"

I gently stroked her hair. It was silky smooth everywhere except her temples, where it was damp. "You said it crossed your mind, too."

I felt her smile against my chest. "I don't want to sound like I'm too *easy*, but yeah. It did cross my mind when you walked me to my car."

"Rom-coms make the best dates," I said.

She twisted to frown up at me. "Wait a minute. Is *that* why you chose that movie? To get me in the mood?"

"Not precisely. But I did wonder if Timmy Chalamet would warm up your engine, so to speak."

She leaned forward to brush her lips against mine. It was a sweaty, salty kiss, but neither of us minded. The moment was too perfect.

"I told you. He's too skinny for me. I prefer a *real* man. One who can carry me out of a burning building."

"Is that why *you* agreed to go out with *me*? Because I fulfill your fireman fantasy?"

"I've actually never had a fireman fantasy," she admitted. "But after tonight, I don't think I'll ever have anything *but* fireman fantasies." She raked her fingernails across my ribs, sprouting goosebumps everywhere she touched. "I'm also glad to see you don't *really* have a third nipple."

"Maybe I do, and you just didn't look hard enough."

She looked up at me, then we busted out laughing together. Moments later, we realized we were being too loud. We both froze and glanced over at the baby basket. There was no sound.

"I'm glad we didn't wake him," I said. "One thing I've discovered this weekend: a crying baby is like nails on a chalkboard to me."

She giggled and rested her head against my chest again. "Me too. Believe me, there were several times I wanted to *scream*. These soundproof rooms will come in handy if we can ever pawn the baby off on one of the other guys."

I chuckled, but the mention of the other guys suddenly

reminded me of a conversation we'd had a week ago. A conversation that was spawned after a few pitchers of beer on our night off, but slowly built momentum as the days went on, leading up to me actually asking Clara out.

I promised Taylor and Derek I would mention it to her. They were my teammates, and my best friends. I trusted them with my life, and I knew they trusted me with theirs. In fact, that loyalty had been proven on more than one occasion when we ran into a burning building together.

Yet I hadn't done what they had asked.

Clara seemed to realize that her comment had changed my mood. She folded her arms underneath her chin and looked down at me with concern.

"Should I have not mentioned them? Do you feel guilty about, um, sleeping with me? Since they have a crush on me?"

"Sort of. It's... complicated."

She frowned. "You said that earlier, when we first kissed. What do you mean by that?"

I wanted to bring it up. But I had never said something like that to a woman before. It wasn't the kind of thing you just blurted out to a girl, either.

But if there was ever a time to tell her, a blissful post-coital moment might be it. I certainly didn't think I could say it at any other time.

So I took a deep breath—which caused her to rise and fall on my chest—and said it.

"Taylor and Derek don't just have crushes on you. We kind of had a plan to *all* ask you out."

She furrowed her brow. "Like, all ask me out at once? And see who I picked?"

I hesitated. "Not quite. We wanted to see if you would go out with *all* of us. At the same time."

She stared at me, so I kept talking.

"We were going to ask if you wanted to date all of us at once. We would share you."

She stared at me some more.

"Our shift schedule makes it tough to date normally," I explained. "The last girl I dated complained that it was like dating *half* of a man, and the other half was married to the firehouse. So, Taylor and Derek and I talked it out. We figured that maybe if we all date the same girl, we can give her the full attention that she needs. That she *deserves*."

Again, that vacant, shocked stare.

"I know what you're thinking," I said.

"I doubt it," she said, deadpan.

"You're thinking that we all have the same schedule right now," I said. "What's the point in sharing a girl if we are all busy at the same time? But shifts changes often. It won't always be that way. The next time things are shuffled around, we'll be perfectly set up for... Yeah. What I just told you."

Clara stared at me for so long that I began to wonder if she had been transformed into a wax statue. She didn't even blink. She just kept staring at me with those big, round eyes.

Finally she sat up into a sitting position. "The three of you... want to share me?"

I gave her a shaky smile. "That's right."

She let out a nervous laugh. "Is this a joke? Am I being punked right now?"

"I'm serious."

She shook her head and began blinking rapidly. "This doesn't make sense. Three guys like you should have *no problem* finding Tinder dates. I didn't have a fireman fantasy before tonight, but I know for a fact that plenty of women do."

"You'd be surprised," I said. "Sure, women want to hookup with firemen. But dating us is another story, through the crazy schedules and long hours."

She cocked her head. "You're serious, aren't you?"

"I'm as serious as a five-alarm fire," I confirmed. "*We* are serious. All three of us. We've been toying around with the idea of sharing one woman, and, well... We wanted to see if you would be interested in that."

"Okay. Wow." She swallowed. "This is, uh..."

"I know it's a lot. If you're not comfortable with it, then we'll understand. But I promised Taylor and Derek I would bring it up to you. So you could at least consider it."

I saw the internal struggle in her eyes as she *really* thought about it. Weighing the pros and cons.

Before she could give me a response, the LED light on the speaker next to the door began to flash red. There was no sound in here since Derek had disabled the audio alarm in the roof, but I knew that the siren was going off through the rest of the firehouse. I felt a heavy *thud* as Derek—or Taylor—jumped down from one of the bunks in the room next door. Vibrations sensed through the floor rather than audibly heard.

"I have to go." I kissed her goodbye, grabbed my clothes, and hurried to the door. With my fingers gripping the doorknob, I could *feel* the pulse of the siren through the wall. I waited three seconds, then timed it perfectly so that I ran out into the hall and closed the door between siren blasts, so the baby wouldn't be disturbed in the room.

Derek and Taylor were running down the hall. Derek did a double-take when he saw me in my underwear, but then hurried toward the engine room. I hopped into my clothes while following them.

Despite coming from the bedrooms, we were only about thirty seconds off our typical response time. I shimmied into my gear and jumped into the passenger seat of the fire engine a heartbeat behind Derek, and before Taylor jumped onto the back.

I grabbed the radio receiver. "What's the address?"

"*Eighty-four Sycamore Street,*" the dispatcher replied. "*Another carbon monoxide alarm.*"

"Jan Karsh's place again," I said to Derek.

"Copy."

He drove the fire engine out of the station and down the street, lights flashing but not using the siren. We bounced along in silence for the first few blocks.

"Saw you coming out of my room," Derek finally said. "You were in a state of... undress."

Derek wasn't just my boss—he was like an older brother to me. I wasn't going to lie to him, even if I wanted to keep this from him. Which I didn't.

"We slept together," I said.

Derek let out a half-sigh, half-groan. "Really? In there?"

"Don't worry: we were quiet," I replied. "The baby slept through it all."

He glanced over at me. "I was more upset about it happening in my bed."

"Oh." I winced. "Yeah, sorry about that, Chief."

"It's all right," he grumbled. "I take it you haven't brought up our... *idea*, to her?"

"Actually, I did bring it up."

Derek looked at me with surprise and hope. "What did she say?"

"The alarm went off before she could really say anything. But she seemed shocked. It might take some time for it to sink in."

"Fortunately, time is something we have plenty of," he said. I knew the truth of that: one thing about being a fireman was that we had a lot of downtime between calls.

Derek rounded a corner and pulled up to a small bungalow, where a frail Jan Karsh was standing on the front yard, waving.

"Evening, Mrs. Karsh," I said while hopping out. "Same problem with the carbon monoxide alarm?"

"It keeps going off!" she said. "I'm sorry to bother you so late, but..."

"Don't apologize," Derek told her. "We're just doing our job. You stay out here while we check it out."

"That's a lovely robe, Jan!" Taylor said to her. "Is it new?"

She beamed. "Oh, you always notice, Taylor. My granddaughter gave it to me for my birthday. Don't you have one coming up soon?"

"In a few weeks!" he said cheerfully. "What'd you get me?"

"Oh, you're such a rascal," she said with a laugh.

Derek and I shared a wry look as we went into the house.

12

Clara

It had been a while since I'd had sex. Since college, in fact. Before I moved back home to Riverville.

I had forgotten just how *good* it was. Arms and legs wrapped around each other, grunting and squeezing and moving our bodies together in perfect harmony. Maybe it was the afterglow of sex talking, but Jordan was better than anyone I had ever been with. That was only a handful of guys, but it was true. My long-term boyfriend in college was awkward and nervous in bed. And Jordan was *certainly* better than Peter Abraham, the boy I lost my virginity to in tenth grade, who *finished* on practically the same stroke he entered me in.

This is much better than taking care of myself, I thought while laying in bed.

Sex aside, Jordan was the kind of guy I'd always wanted. Big and strong, but not a bully. Kindhearted. His job was to *help* people. The kind of guy that ticked all of my boxes. I never expected to find someone like him.

Let alone *three* of them.

Jordan's offer hardly seemed real. He and the other two firemen wanted to *share* a woman? And they had considered me? It kind of felt like someone offering me a winning lottery ticket. It was too good to be true. There had to be a catch.

Did I want that? Jordan and I had only just started seeing each other, but it seemed like we had a good thing going. I was attracted to Taylor and Derek, that was certain. But there was a difference between appreciating a guy as eye-candy and wanting to be shared by them like a Netflix password.

I shook it off. I didn't want to think about it right now. I was too happy after sleeping with Jordan. My lady-parts ached wonderfully, like leg muscles after a really good run. I would sleep well tonight.

At least, I might have if not for the baby.

Anthony woke up a few minutes later, whining softly in his basket. "I'm here, little guy," I said while picking him up. "You're loved."

He was wet, so I retrieved a clean diaper from the drawer and set about changing him. It was tougher than I expected. Just remove the old one and strap on the new one, right?

Nope.

Baby Anthony squirmed and squealed. Despite being an infant, he had a surprisingly strong kick. Eventually I got the new diaper on, but it wasn't a cakewalk.

I expected him to go back to sleep now that he was changed, but he was wide awake and ready to *party*. It was too soon to feed him again, so I bounced him on my shoulder and hummed him a song.

Eventually he went back to sleep. I crawled into bed and tried to do the same, but he woke again an hour later. I prepared a bottle, fed him, and then put him down again. Hopefully that would be the last time.

It wasn't.

I could see why the guys struggled with him this weekend. He woke several more times in the night, once with a dirty diaper, and two other times for no apparent reason. I sat up in bed with my back against the headrest and let Baby Anthony sleep against my chest, but whenever I carried him back to the basket, he woke right back up again and started crying.

All in all, I got about two hours of uninterrupted sleep *total* that night.

I never heard the guys return from their call. Jordan didn't check on me—probably because he assumed I was asleep—and the soundproof walls in the bedrooms did a good job of muting all sound. It *would* have been a perfect environment for soundless sleep if not for the infant I was sharing the room with.

Baby Anthony was wide awake—because *of course* he was—so I carried him out of the bedroom and into the kitchen. The guys were putting away their breakfast dishes, but all of them brightened when they saw me and the baby.

"There's our little station mascot!" Taylor said happily. He came over and squeezed Baby Anthony's cheek. "You must have slept through the night."

I scoffed. "What makes you think that?"

"I checked on you half an hour ago," Jordan told me. "You were *passed out.* You didn't even respond when I told you breakfast was ready."

"That's because he *didn't* sleep through the night," I said wearily. "He kept me up all night."

"He's got a set of lungs on him, that's for sure," Derek muttered.

I frowned at them. They were wearing their boots and blue fireman pants already ."Are you guys going somewhere? The alarm isn't going off."

"We're giving a presentation on fire safety at the Clearlake Summer Camp," Jordan explained. "We'll be back in a few hours."

"I made you extra breakfast!" Taylor said. He pointed. "Scrambled eggs, bacon, and toast. There's a plate in the oven to stay warm."

"You'll note the oven is *off*," Derek said dryly. "It keeps plenty warm inside without the risk of burning the place down."

I was too tired to say anything back. But Jordan came to my defense instead.

"You made your point about the oven last night," he said to his chief. "Drop it."

Derek gave him an even look, as if wondering whether or not he should be taking orders from one of his subordinates. But then he put the last dish away in the dishwasher and said, "We'd better go."

He and Taylor left, but Jordan lingered long enough to give me a kiss on the cheek. "We'll be back. Call me if you need anything."

"Is that all I get?" I replied. "Not a proper goodbye kiss?"

He hesitated. "Well, with the baby in your arms..."

"He doesn't mind. I promise."

Jordan grinned, then folded me into his arms and lowered his lips to mine. For five long, glorious seconds I was entranced under the spell of his kiss and his embrace.

"Better?" he asked softly, face still close to mine.

"Much better." I sighed happily. "Last night was much better, too."

"Better than what?"

"Um. Better than *not* doing it?" I said. "It was good, is what I'm trying to say."

"It was." Jordan pointed at me while backing away. "Let's do it again sometime."

I smiled as he disappeared into the engine room. When I heard the fire engine rumble away, I twisted Baby Anthony around to face me.

"Looks like it's just the two of us, little man."

He blinked as if he wasn't sure what to think about that.

Throughout my life, I was close to my dad. *Really* close, more than just your typical daddy's girl. I told him everything. Which boys I liked, what school subjects I was struggling in. I even told him about the seventh grade girls who picked on me for being big-boned. That was something I didn't even tell *mom* about.

Dad was a good listener, and always had some sage advice to impart on me, no matter the subject.

I could use some of that advice right now.

Growing up, I was never close with my older brother Jason. But once dad died, we leaned on each other for support, and were much closer than before. He didn't exactly fill the role dad had played in my life, but as far as substitutes went, he wasn't too bad. He was downright acceptable. And he was always there for me, with little-to-no judgment.

After feeding Baby Anthony, I gave him a call. He picked up on the second ring. "*There's my favorite little sister.*"

"I'm your *only* little sister," I pointed out.

"*Both of those statements are true. How's it going, sis?*"

We spent a few minutes talking about him. How Maurice—his husband—was doing, and their baby LeBron. Eventually, the subject naturally segued to me.

"I kind of need some advice about taking care of an infant."

He hesitated. "*Why? Are you babysitting on the side, or something?*"

"Or something..."

I explained the situation to him. He made sad, sympathetic sounds when he heard about the surrendered baby. But by the end, he was laughing uproariously.

"*You're babysitting at a fire station? Don't tell Maurice. He'll insist on coming down to visit. I think being surrounded by a dozen sweaty firemen is one of his all-time fantasies.*"

"There's not a dozen of them. Just three."

"*Three is plenty. Are they cute? Could this turn into a romantic relationship with any of them?*"

"Well, funny you mention that..." I lowered my voice, even though I was alone in the fire station. "I slept with one of them. His name is Jordan."

"*That's fantastic! Just don't tell mom. She'll start bugging you about grandchildren. She mentioned that the first time I told her about Maurice, and we had only been dating a month at that point.*"

"It's already started," I said with a laugh. "Mom was talking about grandchildren before the first date. But... that's not all. The situation gets weirder."

"*Weirder than taking care of an off-the-books child for a bunch of firemen?*"

There was no easy way to segue into it, so I just blurted it out. "They want to share me. The three of them."

I expected Jason to laugh in my face, or accuse me of making it all up. But the reaction I did get was much weirder.

"*No kidding?*" he said. "*Small world.*"

"Small world? What do you mean by that?"

"*Well... You know my old Navy buddies? The ones down in Los Angeles?*"

"Yeah, I met them at your wedding."

"*Did you see who they brought to the wedding? They brought the same date. A woman that they were sharing, too. She started out as their nanny, then started dating them... Now they're serious. Like, really serious. It's been going on for a few years now, and they're happier than ever.*"

"Wait," I said. "Is that the same woman Maurice gave a toast to at the rehearsal dinner? The one who is responsible for you two meeting in the first place?"

"Yep. She was pregnant with their child at the wedding. Her water actually broke in the bathroom, before Maurice tossed the bouquet. Anyway, yeah. She has that situation going on with her three men."

My mind raced. "So this is something people actually do? It's not crazy?"

"*Maybe it's a little crazy,*" he replied. "*But some of the best things in life are crazy. It's not for everyone, that's for sure. I would never want to share Maurice with anyone. We're monogamous to our core. But other people... Who am I to judge? Love is rare in this world, Clara. No matter how you find it, it's precious.*"

"I'm not sure we're talking about love, here," I said with a chuckle. "I got the impression they were talking about a physical relationship. Plus, I've gone on one date with Jordan. Let's not get ahead of ourselves."

"*Even if it's just physical, that's great too,*" he insisted. "*You could use the attention, especially after the dry spell you've had.*"

"Jason!" I hissed.

"*Tell me I'm wrong. How many dates have you been on since moving back to Riverville?*"

"It's a small town," I said defensively.

"*Next to Fresno, a bigger town. There's no reason a smart, attractive woman like you shouldn't have a date every weekend.*"

"I work weekends at the restaurant. At least, I did before this new thing came up."

"*Weekends, weekdays. It doesn't matter. My point stands. Maybe you should enjoy this opportunity.*"

"Maybe." Baby Anthony was squirming in his basket, so I said, "Back to the reason I called. I have an infant here, and I need some pointers. Can you help me out?"

"*You're in luck. I made a spreadsheet of all the things we learned taking care of LeBron, so we would remember when we eventually adopt a second child. I'll send it to you."*

I snorted. "A spreadsheet? You're such a nerd. I can't believe they let you into the Navy."

"Love you too, little sis. And try to have fun in the situation, all right?"

"We'll see," I said, still unsure about what was going to happen next.

13

Clara

Jason's spreadsheet was a lifesaver.

It wasn't just a jotted-down list of things they learned. It was practically an encyclopedia of baby knowledge. There were five tabs, each one with its own heading and subject. Feeding, sleeping, changing, play time, miscellaneous. There were also sources cited and links to YouTube videos and baby books.

For example, under *feeding*, one of the lines said: "You don't need to warm up his formula. This is an old wives tale. Plenty of babies prefer their formula to be room-temperature or chilled. Whatever the baby prefers is best."

At the end of the note was a link to a YouTube video with a maternity expert explaining the point.

"I've written college papers that were less thorough than this," I muttered while reading it.

Having something, *anything,* to reference made taking care of Baby Anthony exponentially easier. It was like I had a cheat-sheet to motherhood.

We got into a routine over the next few days. Baby Anthony

preferred his formula to be room-temperature, and he guzzled it down more eagerly than when it was warm.

Regarding diaper changes, there was one piece of advice that became a game-changer: "Always keep the baby distracted." Now when I changed Baby Anthony, I recruited one of the guys to help me distract him with a toy. Taylor made silly noises and waved Anthony's noisy rattle back and forth, transfixing the child while I cleaned him up and put on a fresh diaper.

I was clueless about the basics when I first arrived, but within two days I felt like an expert. My confidence seemed to transfer into the three firemen, who began to relax and trust that I had things under control.

The one problem was that Baby Anthony was still struggling at night. Even with the spreadsheet tip recommending that I over-feed Anthony a little bit before bedtime, Anthony was waking up almost every hour.

Unfortunately, there was one tip under *sleeping* that was bolded and highlighted in yellow: "If baby is restless, there's nothing you can do. Just keep comforting him when he wakes and he will eventually grow out of it."

So I suffered his moods at night and tried to sleep whenever I could. Soon I was an expert at falling asleep practically the moment my head hit the pillow, although that had more to do with my severe exhaustion rather than any particular skill.

"I think he's nocturnal," I said one morning while bouncing the baby in my arms around the kitchen. "He sleeps more during the day than he does at night."

"He's a baby," Jordan said while pouring me a mug of coffee. "He's still figuring it out."

It was weird being around Jordan while also taking care of a baby. It was kind of like the two of us were playing house. Except that we were in a fire station. And two other guys were around all the time. And the baby wasn't ours.

Okay, maybe it was nothing like playing house. But it was weird all the same. We had been on one date, and had slept together once, and suddenly we were *living* together. It felt like we had skipped a whole bunch of steps in the process.

Kissing him was kind of awkward around his two firemen teammates, too. Jordan was more comfortable with it than I was, but slowly I started getting used to it. Neither Derek nor Taylor seemed to mind, and tried to give us some space whenever Jordan was affectionate with a warm hug or a peck on the cheek.

Even though I was the one taking care of the baby, the guys had weird sleep schedules. Occasionally getting an emergency call in the middle of the night would do that, I supposed. Derek seemed to fight through his sleepiness with extra coffee, while Jordan and Taylor grabbed cat naps whenever they could. It wasn't unusual to walk into the living room and find one of them asleep in the recliner and another stretched out on the sofa, no matter what time of day it was.

I started learning their routines and getting a deeper appreciation for what it took to be a firefighter. The guys went out on Tuesday to get groceries, taking the fire engine and their gear in case they got a call while they were out. They returned with more baby supplies, too: diapers, wipes, formula, and even a baby monitor. I really appreciated the latter, because it meant I could let Baby Anthony sleep in the soundproof bedroom while I hung out in the kitchen or living area.

Breakfast was the biggest meal of the day, I learned. Taylor went all out: every day was some combination of eggs, bacon, sausage, toast, English muffins, French toast, waffles, pancakes, and fruit. They had sandwiches for lunch—Derek and Jordan preferred sliced turkey, while Taylor made himself a peanut butter and jelly sandwich every day.

Dinner was almost always some sort of casserole meal. The firehouse kitchen had six different casserole dishes, and Taylor put them to use.

"Not that I mind," I said on Wednesday evening while watching Taylor make dinner. Jordan was napping, and Derek was watching Baby Anthony in the other room. "I've loved everything you've made so far. But do you ever have anything *other* than casseroles?"

Taylor's back was to me while he mixed the ingredients together in a bowl. The motion made his butt—a butt that was *very* cute—jiggle back and forth. I found myself not-so-subtly admiring his body while he cooked. I was too exhausted to pretend not to.

"It's a strategic food," Taylor said over his shoulder.

"Strategic? How can a food be *strategic?*"

"The busy time of night is between six and nine," he explained. "It's when we're most likely to get a call and have to leave suddenly. If I'm grilling a fancy meal—let's say steak, and a bunch of sides. What happens if I'm halfway done cooking the steaks when we get a call? I have to turn off all the pans, and the food gets ruined. Steak isn't very tasty when it's half-cooked, sits out for an hour, and then is re-cooked. Trust me—I've had to do that before."

He turned and poured the bowl mixture into a glass dish. There was chicken, gravy, and a bunch of vegetables mixed in. "But casseroles? It's much easier to fix. If it's in the oven when we get a call, all we have to do is turn the oven off and remove the dish. It doesn't matter if it sits out for a while—when we get back, we just throw it back in the oven and cook it. Generally speaking, of course."

"That makes sense," I admitted. "Especially the oven part. I know how important it is not to leave that on while you're gone, even on the lowest setting."

Taylor gave me a rueful look and lowered his voice. "Don't take it personally. Chief is real particular about that."

"Don't I know it," I muttered.

Taylor covered the dish with a healthy sprinkling of shredded cheese and popped it in the oven. He then ran his hand through his silky blond hair and sighed. "Chief likes you. He just has a weird way of showing it sometimes."

"That's what Jordan told me," I said glancing into the other room. I didn't think he could hear me, but I still kept my voice low. "That Derek has a crush on me. It just doesn't really feel like it after getting chewed out by him."

Taylor crossed his arms and leaned casually against the oven. "What else did Jordan tell you?"

Here it was. The awkward subject that I had been semi-avoiding all week. It had been easy to not think about it while taking care of the baby and trying to get what sleep that I could, but now I was faced with it directly. Taylor was staring intently at me, and I found it difficult to meet his gaze.

"He told me all three of you had crushes on me," I said. "And that you... Um. That you wanted to..."

I took a deep breath to collect myself. "That you wanted to *share* me."

Taylor smiled softly, and his blue eyes sparkled with mirth. "Yep. That's about the gist of it." He held out a hand. "I'm not going to pester you about it, asking if you've made a decision or thought about it or anything. But I will say one thing. We don't want you to agree to anything you're not comfortable with. You probably feel overwhelmed by all of this, right?"

I chuckled and met his gaze for a moment. "That's exactly how I feel."

Taylor shrugged. "That's all right. Heck, that's probably the normal way someone should feel about such an offer. Think it over and make a decision whenever you're ready—whether you agree to it, or decline."

"You make it sound like I'm accepting a job offer."

Taylor laughed. It was a light, carefree sound that set my mind at ease in a soothing way. "It kind of does seem like that, huh? It's new to me, too. That's why I'm kind of awkward about it."

You're awkward about it? I thought. *You seem smooth and*

charming compared to my awkwardness.

A question popped into my head, and I voiced it before I could chicken out: "Do you think you could do that? Share a woman with two other guys, I mean."

He shrugged. "Heck if I know. I *think* I can. I'm willing to try! Especially for..."

Especially for you, he was about to say. As if I was someone special, someone worth sharing. I had never felt that way in my life before, but for a brief second, I felt like the most beautiful woman in the world.

"...especially for the right woman," Taylor finished instead.

"I'll be honest," I said. "I like to get to know a guy first before we... take things further. Usually, I mean. Jordan and I kind of jumped into things, but we had a *really* good first date, which made it feel like we had been dating longer. Does that make sense? I feel like I'm babbling."

Taylor took a step forward and put a reassuring hand on my arm. "You don't need to explain yourself. I get it. There's no pressure, so just consider the offer. And in the mean time, we'll all take care of Baby Anthony."

I smiled at him, and he smiled back in a way that was totally disarming. Like he really *did* mean there was no pressure on me at all. I could take all the time I needed.

His comment about the baby made me frown. "I haven't heard any baby noises in a while..." I said.

Taylor furrowed his brow. "It's definitely *too* quiet. Better check on that while I throw a salad together."

I walked out of the kitchen and into the living room. Derek was stretched out in the recliner, watching TV. Baby Anthony was asleep on his chest, limbs splayed out in all directions on Derek's white cotton T-shirt.

My heart swelled at the sight. There was nothing sexier than a big, muscular man with a baby. It was a primal part of my brain, the same part that handled most of a woman's core instincts. Just like knowing that chocolate was one of the main food groups, that part of my brain told me that Derek would be a good father, and that I should mate with him.

I pushed the feeling down and approached. Derek turned and smiled at me.

"He's calm around you," I whispered.

"Yeah." He looked puzzled. "It's strange. I don't think I've ever been good around kids."

I sat on the arm of the couch next to him. "I don't think it's strange at all. You're the one protecting him. Risking your job to make sure he goes to a good home, rather than being tossed into an underfunded system. He can sense that."

"Maybe. How's dinner coming?"

"Taylor says the casserole will be ready in twenty minutes. And don't worry—if you guys have to suddenly leave on a call, I'll keep an eye on it. Wouldn't want to leave an oven unattended."

His lips pursed together and his eyes studied me. He looked like he was trying to decide whether to laugh it off, or scold me for making light of a serious situation.

"I know I'm extra sensitive to fire safety," he said.

I held up a hand. "You don't need to explain it. I get it."

He went on in a quiet voice as if I hadn't spoken. "We got a call to a dorm about ten years back, when I was working in Fresno. Before I got transferred here. Some college kids put a pizza in the oven and then passed out drunk. Pizza burned, then caught on fire, and eventually spread. Entire dorm went up. No fatalities, thank God, but those were some of the worst burns I've ever seen in my life."

I put my hand over my mouth. "Oh wow..."

"Most ovens are safe," he went on, gently stroking Anthony's tendrils of black hair. "Even if there's a fire inside the oven, they keep it contained, and don't let it spread. But this was an old oven, and someone opened it and tried to pull the burning pizza out. Point I'm trying to make is that it's a risk. That's a big part of our job: educating people to minimize these kinds of risks, because they add up. Maybe I'm too sensitive to that kind of thing, and if so, I'm sorry."

The last two words sounded like they had been yanked out of his mouth with pliers, but he had still said them. And as I looked at the mature, experienced man, I could tell he didn't say them lightly.

"I understand," I said. "I would be sensitive if I had experienced that, too."

"All right, then." Derek nodded down at the baby on his chest. "I've had to pee for the last half hour, but I didn't want to disturb him."

"I'll take over until dinner." I scooped up Baby Anthony gently. As I did, my fingers brushed against the hard muscles of Derek's chest. I felt another tingle run up my spine, the same kind that had entranced me when I saw the baby on his chest in the first place.

This is a real man, I thought, tearing my eyes away from him. *All three of these firemen are.*

Feeling better about my relationship with Derek, I carried Baby Anthony back to the bedroom.

14

Clara

When I arrived at the firehouse on Monday night, I felt out of place. I was a visitor. An intruder. Someone who certainly didn't belong with the three hulking, broad-shouldered men who occupied the station.

By Thursday, I felt like one of the guys.

Everyone was friendly. Even Derek, once we broke the ice about the oven incident. He wasn't as cheerful as Taylor or as caring as Jordan, but he was friendly in his own way.

For the first time since moving home to Riverville, I was excited about what I was doing. And not just because it meant hanging out with the three sexy firemen. I actually enjoyed taking care of Baby Anthony. It was fulfilling in a way I had never experienced before. A maternal program in my brain had clicked on, and it was running around the clock now. Even when one of the guys had the baby, I found myself thinking about him in a protective way.

Mom called that afternoon. *"When can I come see your baby!"* she demanded.

"It's not *my* baby," I replied. "And you can't come see him. We're trying to keep this a secret, Mom. Just for the time being."

"*You have the baby, so for now? It is your baby!*" she insisted. "*Which makes him my grandson, even just for now! I want to see him!*"

I started to tell her that seeing him would make it difficult for her when we had to turn him over to Social Services. That's when I realized it might be tough for *me* when we got to that point. I had only been around him for a few days, but I was already attached to the little guy. I smiled sadly at him in his basket, and he grinned back at me and wiggled his pudgy little toes.

"How's the restaurant?" I asked Mom instead. "You're getting by without me?"

"*Is no problem,*" Mom replied. "*Angelina works very hard. Harder than you. She is very fast on deliveries! No flirting with firemen, hah!*"

"Gee, thanks for that, Mom," I replied. "I don't know what's happening this weekend, but I'll probably swing by to get more things."

"*Swing by with baby!*" she said happily.

The thought tormented me as I changed Anthony's diaper that evening. What happened if I grew too attached to the little guy? When I was ten years old, Mom let me adopt a kitten from the animal shelter. I got to keep him for two weeks. Then Jason came home from summer camp, and we discovered that he was *deathly* allergic to cats. I was certain that we should give Jason up instead of the kitten, but I failed to convince my parents.

Giving up that cat was one of the hardest things I had ever done. Sure, it seems like no big deal now, and I know that he went to a good home, but I remember how *devastated* I felt at the time. Like someone had ripped out a chunk of my heart.

Deep down, I knew that giving up a baby would be much, *much* harder. Even though I knew little Anthony wasn't really mine, and even though I had known from the start that this was only temporary. After three days with him, I truly felt like I loved him.

I can't think about that now, I told myself while mixing baby formula into a bottle. *All I can do is focus on the task at hand.*

We fell into a routine with the baby. I watched him most of the time, but the guys chipped in plenty of other times. "We brought you in to *help* us, not to do all of the work by yourself," Jordan told me that evening. "I don't mind watching him while you jump in the shower."

I brushed my lips against his. "I promise not to take too long. I'm not washing my hair."

"Really?" Jordan asked, confused. "Then what's the point?"

"You're not supposed to wash your hair *every* day," I said.

His confused expression deepened. "You're not?" He ran his hands into his hair as if expecting it all to suddenly fall out.

I gave him a playful shove, then went into Derek's private shower. It was nice being able to bathe in there rather than the communal shower in the hall. Not that there was anything wrong with it—they kept it very clean. But the individual shower stalls in one big room made it feel like I was back in college, and I preferred to have some privacy while I showered.

When I opened the door, I expected to have the room to myself. The guys had given me plenty of privacy in the room, and not even Derek had come in here without knocking. But Jordan was laying on his side on the bed, propping his head up with a flexed arm.

I felt a moment of prudishness. I was only wearing a towel around my waist, and it *barely* covered my privates. Sure, Jordan and I had already slept together, but I still felt awkward about it. There was a certain level of comfort a girl needed to reach with a guy before just flashing the goods around.

"I thought you were watching the baby," I said.

"Taylor took him," he replied. "He wanted to teach him the alphabet."

"The alphabet? He's only a couple of months old. I don't think he's able to process any thoughts beyond eating and pooping."

Jordan shifted until he was sitting on the edge of the bed in front of me. "That's what I told Taylor. But he insists on trying. Which, lucky for us, means we have some alone time together..."

"Oh."

He rose to his feet until he was looming over me with a hungry look in his eyes. He snatched the corner of the towel and whipped it to the side, leaving me standing there, nude. For a long moment he drank in the sight of me. I felt his eyes raking over my skin like a caress.

We had been sharing kisses around the station all week, but we always remained reserved since Derek and Taylor were around. But the kiss Jordan gave me now? It was a *real* kiss, given with his entire body. He held nothing back, and I could feel how much he needed me as his fingers danced over my damp skin. It was a reflection of my own desire for him that had been building since our sizzling night together on Monday.

Jordan lifted me into his arms, spun around, then dropped me on the bed. It was a totally unnecessary movement since it transported me about two feet, but I didn't mind the excuse to be carried in his arms, even for a few brief seconds.

He smothered me with another deep kiss, beard scratching wonderfully along my cheek, and my body came alive underneath him.

"Relax," he breathed. He favored me with a mischievous smile, then kissed a trail down my neck. I squirmed as his lips brushed against my nipple, nose digging into the flesh of my breast, but down he kept moving, hands raking over my skin as he went.

I had never really enjoyed having a guy go down on me. It wasn't a self-conscious thing, at least not primarily. Getting eaten out was *nice*, I guess, but it just didn't do much for me. I would much rather be filled while in their arms, kissing and moving together in the dance of lovemaking.

"I want you," I said to him, reaching for a handful of his hair. "Come back up and kiss me."

"Oh, I'm going to kiss you," he replied, dodging my grasping hands. "Like I said: relax. This is just about you right now."

Despite his words, I remained tense as he edged closer and closer to my lady parts, breath whispering across my core. His strong hands gripped the inside of my thighs and pushed them apart, exposing me to him. Self-conscious thoughts ran through my head, thoughts about the amount of shaving guys prefer down there, and if he would *enjoy* doing it or if he was just trying to be nice.

All those thoughts disappeared as his chin tickled over my clit. He buried his nose in between my pussy lips, nuzzling at me rather than going right to work. He inhaled deeply, then sighed as if he had just smelled the perfect bouquet of flowers.

He thinks I'm sexy. He likes how I smell.

Slowly but surely, I began to relax.

Jordan pulled me closer to the edge of the bed, then wrapped his massive arms around my thighs. I felt myself quiver with excitement as he finally began sliding his tongue up and down my wet heat. His movements weren't tentative or reluctant—it was like he was licking an ice cream cone, eager to get *every* single drop of me.

Oh, I thought. *That feels goooooood.*

The last remnants of self-doubt disappeared and I surrendered underneath his firm grasp. Now I *preened* as he worshiped me with his tongue.

"You're soaked," he rumbled into me, deep and dark, barely words at all.

Jordan's voice set my body on fire. He must have sensed my desire because his tongue wedged deeper into me, wriggling up and down as he pushed further into my lush heat.

I closed my eyes and savored the way he felt. This was *totally* unlike the other experiences I'd had with a guy going down on me. Like the difference between watching Tee-Ball and professional baseball.

His tongue swirled out and around my clit, then back inside of me. He ran a figure-eight like that, intensifying the pressure with every loop, before eventually enveloping my entire clit in his mouth. Two fingers caressed my entrance then, getting nice and coated in my juices before sinking deep into me while he gently sucked on my clit.

I couldn't get enough of the way he made love to me. Jordan made me feel like a goddess he was worshiping, rather than *me* being the lucky one to be with him. I arched my back, relaxed into the bed, then arched it again as his speed increased.

What did I do to deserve this?

My orgasm built slowly, brick by brick. Jordan took his time and never grew impatient, allowing the pleasure to grow. Soon it felt like an impending hurricane, gathering strength out in the distant ocean. I could sense it drawing near, preparing to smash into the shore.

Destroy me, I thought as his fingers moved faster. *Wipe me out and leave nothing behind.*

My groans grew louder, and I bit my tongue to silence them. Then I remembered that I didn't *need* to be quiet this time. It was just the two of us, and we were in a nearly-soundproof room.

"Ohh," I moaned, back arching violently. "Just like that. Oh Jordan..."

I was close. So close. Jordan's tongue was swirling around my clit, and the hurricane of my orgasm was whipping at the shore, about to destroy me with ecstasy...

And then his tongue abruptly stopped moving.

"What are you doing? Don't stop!" I begged.

I felt his mouth curl into a grin against me. "I like teasing you."

I grabbed his head and pushed him back into me. "Keep going, I'm right there..."

His tongue resumed licking around my clit, and the storm picked up right where it had left off. His fingers curled upward, just *barely* touching my G-spot, and new electricity spread through my body as I reached the edge and began to fall over...

And once again, he abruptly stopped *right* before I came.

This time he rumbled with laughter. I pushed my hips into him and tried grabbing his head, but he pulled back this time. All I could feel was his hot breath on my pussy.

"You're torturing me!"

His green eyes gazed up at me form above my mound. "It will be worth it in the end. Trust me."

"If you don't finish what you started I'll never trust—*ohh.*"

I cut off as his tongue swirled around my clit twice. *Only* twice. Again, I could sense my orgasm just out of reach.

Back and forth Jordan went, bringing me right to the edge of my climax and then pulling away before it could ravage me. Each time, the sensations were more intense and powerful than before. If it was a category two hurricane at the beginning, it was now a category five.

After a few minutes of edging, I was like putty in Jordan's hands.

"Please," I begged. "Don't stop. Give it to me."

"You want it?" he crooned up at me.

I bobbed my head and gazed down at him. "I need it so bad."

His tongue slowly returned to my clit, pushing it back and forth like his own personal punching bag. The two fingers inside me began moving again, and the orgasm gathered strength once more. I clenched my inner muscles around him, begging him to keep going. I would have signed over my life to him if he would just *finish me.*

His tongue swirled, and his fingers pistoned faster. They curled upward in a *come here* motion, brushing against my G-spot again and reigniting the nuclear bomb that was armed between my legs. As the pleasure ramped upward I wanted so badly to believe it was going to happen this time, that he would *finally* push me over the cliff and give me release, but I knew it wouldn't happen.

And then he gave me what I wanted.

My orgasm swirled and intensified, bringing me back to that edge, and this time Jordan didn't stop.

The hurricane slammed into my shore, more powerful than I had ever imagined.

I gasped and drew a ragged breath. My body totally fell apart under Jordan's touch, fingers tapping against my G-spot and mouth sucking on my clit. The fire of a million suns scoured my body from head to foot in white-hot, toe-curling pleasure. I screamed at the top of my lungs and squeezed my thighs around his head, holding him against me as I came again, and again, wave after wave of it as I arched my back on the bed.

I cried out until my lungs were empty, sucked in another breath, and then cried out some more. I thrashed and bucked against Jordan's face as the pulses of pleasure surged through me, and then my entire body shook and shivered with one final release.

When I finally became still, he was gently kissing my inner thigh and laughing to himself.

"What's so funny!" I asked in a hoarse voice.

"I've never seen a girl do that before," he replied.

"I've never had it done to me!" I reached down and found his hair, my fingers tightening in it. "Get your sexy face up here and kiss me, damnit."

He covered me with his warm body and obeyed. I could taste myself faintly on his lips, but rather than gross me out, it turned me on even more. An erotic reminder of the wonderful things he had just done to me.

"That's my first time edging a girl," he admitted.

"Edging?"

"That's what it's called, bringing someone *right* to the edge of orgasm, then stopping, then starting again. It's supposed to make the climax that much more powerful."

"Wait a minute." I pushed up onto one elbow. "That was your first time doing that to a girl?"

He smiled hopefully. "It was that good, huh?"

"It was *amazing*, but it was torture up to that point." I bit my lip and reached down between him, finding his hard length in his pants. "I wonder if you'd like it if someone did that to you."

I gave him a squeeze through his blue fireman pants, and his cock *leaped* with excitement.

"I wonder the same thing," he grinned. "Maybe we need to... Aww. Fuck."

"What?"

I twisted to look over to the door. The LED was flashing. The alarm was going off.

"Thank goodness that happened *after* I was done," he said.

"But what about you? I feel bad that you're missing out..."

"I don't mind." He pecked me on the cheek and then hurried to the door. "I enjoyed that just as much as you did."

Somehow I doubt that, I thought as I hurried to get dressed so I could get the baby.

15

Clara

"*Is this about the baby again?*" Jason asked on the phone.

"Yes! But it's important this time, I promise," I replied.

"*Did you check the spreadsheet?*"

"The spreadsheet has been a huge help, but this isn't on there."

I heard my brother sigh. "*Okay. What's up?*"

"Baby poop."

"*Baby poop.*"

"It's a really weird color," I said.

My brother exhaled. "*I was eating lunch, but I guess that's over now. What color is the baby poop, Clara?*"

"Sorry! It's a weird mustard color. Like, dark yellow. That can't be normal. Right?"

"*There's a tab on the spreadsheet about this,*" Jason said impatiently.

"The spreadsheet says that *gray* poop is a cause for concern, because it means the baby isn't digesting food properly. But it doesn't say anything about yellow."

"*Yellow is fine. Gray, or chalky poops are the only concerning ones.*"

"Are you sure? I feel like you're just trying to get me off the phone so you can get back to your lunch."

"*Trust me: lunch is officially over. Maurice? Will you talk to my sister, please?*"

There was a pause, and then my brother-in-law's chipper voice took over. "*Why hello there, sweetie! Why is my husband rolling his eyes right now?*"

"I had a question about baby poop. Yellow. Thoughts?"

Maurice laughed. "*Oh, sweetie, that's totally normal. Gross, but normal. Little LeBron had demons living inside his tushy, I swear. You have nothing to worry about.*"

I breathed a sigh of relief. "Thank you. I just wanted to make sure, and I didn't trust the internet."

"*As you shouldn't. Now, on to more important matters: how are your firemen? Are they sweaty right now? On a scale of one to ten, tell me how sweaty they are presently.*"

"Ugh, Jason told you?"

"*He tells me everything, sweetie. And now you have to tell me everything. There's a polyamorous situation going on? Ooh la la!*"

"Nothing is going on yet," I replied while tossing the offending diaper. "Jordan suggested it to me. I haven't really been thinking about it since then."

"*Three firemen make you the offer of a lifetime, and you haven't thought about it?*" Maurice asked, incredulous.

"I've been kind of busy with the baby. You know. The one I'm taking care of without any experience?"

He ignored me and continued on. "*Do you like the other two guys?*"

"I think so," I said. "Taylor is a sweetheart. And the Chief is nice too, once you get past his gruff exterior."

"*Chief? Oh, sexy. Working your way up, huh?*"

"Technically he's just a Captain. But everyone calls him Chief."

"*Okay, so we've established that you like them both. Are you attracted to them?*"

I laughed. "Derek's a big, burly fireman. And Taylor is leaner than the others, but he's still *shredded* with muscle. I saw him coming out of the bathroom the other day with just a towel on and... mmm."

"*Then give it a try! What's stopping you?*"

I held Baby Anthony to my chest and moved the phone to my other hand. "I'm afraid it might get in the way of what I have with Jordan. It's new and exciting and has *potential*, and I don't want to mess that up."

"*How about this,*" Maurice said. He sounded like a hostage negotiator. "*Go out with the other two. Give it a try. And if you don't like it, you can always fall back to going out with Jordan exclusively. Best of both worlds!*"

"Maybe," I said doubtfully.

There was a rumble in the station. By now, I knew the sound meant that the fire engine was pulling into the garage.

"Maurice, I have to go," I said. "Give Jason and little LeBron my love."

"*Good luck, sweetie!*"

The guys undressed in the gear hallway and then came into the kitchen. Taylor grinned widely at me, then frowned and sniffed the air. "What's that smell?"

"Did something die?" Jordan asked right behind him.

"That's Baby Anthony," I explained. "We had a few diapers that could qualify as nuclear waste."

"Glad we missed it," Derek said with a grimace.

Taylor leaned in close to me and caressed the baby's cheek. "We should call the United Nations, because you're a weapon of mass destruction."

"Considering where it came from, we should call him a weapon of *ass* destruction," Jordan said with a huge grin.

Everyone laughed, including Baby Anthony. He kicked his legs in my arms, giggling with his entire little body.

"He's feisty today," Jordan said.

"Yeah! He's getting used to this place," I said. "He's a happy little boy."

Derek leaned against the kitchen wall and cleared his throat. "We need to talk about the situation."

"The guy from Jersey Shore?" Taylor asked.

Derek silenced him with a stare, then went on. "I talked to my sister. The wait list for fostering infants is slowly progressing. Depending on next quarter's budget, we might be able to hand him over to Social Services as early as next week."

"That's great," I said.

"It is," he agreed. "But it means we have a problem about this weekend. What to do with the little guy, and how to keep him from second-shift."

Jordan crossed his arms and frowned. "Walk me through it. What happens if we turn him over to Social Services today? It can't be that bad, right?"

"There are three foster families in the area who could take him," Derek said. "My sister says none of them are ideal. They all have multiple complaints on their record, and they're already fostering other toddlers. My sister does *not* like the idea of handing an infant over to any of them."

"What about other adoption agencies?" I asked. "Surely we could contact some of them..."

"Already considered that," Derek said blandly. His face was hard, but his dark eyes were sympathetic. "All adoption agencies would require time for processing. Baby Anthony would still be turned over to a local foster family in the interim." He shook his head. "I would rather keep him ourselves than allow an overworked, exhausted foster family to take him. I trust Clara with him above all else."

I swelled with pride at the compliment. He said it so matter-of-factly, without even looking in my direction, that I knew it was the truth. He wasn't just saying it to be nice.

"Not to mention the mother," Derek added. "We need to give my sister time to find a way to slip Anthony into the system without implicating her for surrendering him too late."

"Okay, so we're keeping him," Taylor said. "Why not get *us* approved as, like, a real foster family?"

"Us?" Jordan asked. "A family?"

Taylor shrugged. "Clara, then. I don't know. I'm just trying to think of other solutions."

Derek shook his head. "It takes time to get licensed as a foster family. Weeks, or months, even in the best of circumstances. Considering how backed-up the Social Services department is right now..." He spread his hands doubtfully.

"There has to be another option," Jordan muttered out loud.

"Well..." Derek clenched his jaw. "If we contact Anthony's biological mother, we could get her to legally sign over guardianship to us, even temporarily. That would skip all the red tape."

"Then let's do that!" Taylor said excitedly.

Derek's grimace deepened. "Couple of problems. One, she surrendered the child. She probably doesn't want to be contacted. Two, she surrendered him *after* the Safe Haven period. If we track her down and she puts her name to paper, it might increase the chances she faces prosecution. And three," he added, "she'll find out that we've been keeping him off the books this past week. She might report us. It's just too risky to involve her at this time."

"Okay," Jordan said slowly. "Then we keep doing what we're doing. What do we do about this weekend?" He looked at his watch. "Second-shift will be here in a few hours. If Billy Manning finds out about him..."

"There aren't any good options," Derek said wearily. "If we stay here for a second weekend in a row, holed up in our rooms the entire time, Billy will get suspicious. I think we have no choice but to take Baby Anthony out of the firehouse for the weekend."

"But you said it was important to keep him here," Jordan pointed out. "For legal reasons."

Derek crossed his arms over his chest stubbornly. "I know what I said. Even if we take him home for this weekend, he'll have spent the majority of his time in the station. Seven days here, and three days elsewhere. If we get caught and have to argue our case before a judge, I think we can show that we didn't intend to keep him. That we had his best interests at heart."

I had remained mostly quiet up to this point, but now I realized I could be useful. "I can take him back to my place! I'll watch him there. Away from you guys, so nobody gets suspicious."

"That's nice of you to offer," Derek said, "but I think we should keep him at my house. It has four bedrooms, and it's secluded on the north-east side of town. I don't get a lot of visitors. Nobody can know we have him."

That's a good point, I thought. Mom got lots of random visitors at our house: neighbors, friends, and other locals checking in on her. She was a pillar of the Riverville community, and even though it had been a year since Dad died, there was still an outpouring of support for Mom.

"All right!" Taylor cheered. "Sleepover at Chief's house!"

16

Clara

If I was going to stay somewhere, I needed to get more clothes and a few other things. It was risky leaving Anthony with the guys since they might get a call at any moment, but we decided to risk it. If they *did* get a call, they would text me immediately and I would rush back to watch the baby.

With that in mind, I raced home and collected a bunch of new clothes. I didn't bother dumping out the dirty clothes from this past week—I figured I could wash them at Derek's place. If this nannying thing went on any longer, I would need to wash and reuse clothes, anyway.

The restaurant was on the way back to the firehouse, so I decided to stop in and make sure Mom was doing okay without me. Angelina, one of our neighbors, was behind the counter taking an order from a customer."

"One extra large with pepperoni and half pineapple. One large with olives, peppers, and mushrooms. It'll be about fifteen minutes." She jotted the order down on a piece of paper, then saw me. "Clara! You're back!"

"Hi, Angelina. Getting the hang of things?"

"I think so." She put the order on a wire and slid it back to the kitchen, then turned her head to shout to her son. "Delivery order is waiting, Marcus! What's taking you so long?"

"I'm going," the teenager complained. He took the order and went out the back.

"Sorry about that," she told me, wiping her hands on a towel. "How's your project going?"

"Project?"

"Your mom said you're working on a creative project for a week or two. That's why she needs help here at the restaurant. What kind of project is it? A painting?"

"Um... Yes! It's a painting! I'm just learning, so it has been tough, but I'm, uh, having a great time."

She gave me a quick hug. "You've been working so hard here since your father passed. You deserve some time off. Your Mom is in the back."

I smiled at her and went back into the kitchen. I was actually kind of surprised that Mom hadn't blabbered about the baby. When it came to secrets, she usually couldn't last a few *hours* without telling everyone she knew.

Her face lit up when she saw me come around the corner by the pizza oven. "There's my daughter! Where is the baby?" She looked behind me, as if he might be hiding there. "Are you done? Is the baby gone now?"

"We're still watching him," I explained. "We're taking him away from the firehouse for the weekend, though."

"You are staying at home?" Her eyes lit up. "Or at Jordan's?"

"Actually, the baby and I are staying at the Chief's house."

She squealed with excitement. "Chief Dahlkemper! So much more handsome than Jordan. Are the two of you..."

"No! The *four* of us are staying there. We're taking care of the baby together. It's not a big deal."

Mom shifted subjects gracefully. "And where is baby? I want to see him!"

"He's back at the station."

"Bring him to me tonight!" she insisted. I had never seen my mother so excited before. "On your way to Chief Studmuffin's house! Only a minute! Very quick!"

"We'll see," I said, but I knew I couldn't do that. It was Friday night, and the restaurant would be busy. Someone would see me with the baby, and questions would be asked.

I kissed Mom goodbye and rushed back to the firehouse. Fortunately, the guys hadn't received any calls while I was gone.

"It's seven o'clock," Derek said. "You should probably take Anthony now, in case any of the guys from second-shift get here early."

He gave me the keys to his house, which were on a little red fire extinguisher keychain. I pulled my car around to the back of the station, and they discreetly brought Anthony's little basket out to me. We placed him on the floor of the front passenger seat, but then Derek lingered outside my door.

"I didn't think about getting a car seat," Derek grumbled.

"Don't worry—I'll drive as slowly and safely as possible," I replied.

He ran a hand through his dark hair and scowled. "Maybe I should carry him to my house. That would be safer."

I glanced at the GPS on my phone. "Your house is four miles away!"

"I can jog," he said stubbornly. "I ran seven-minute miles at the fire academy. I'll be back in an hour."

"I promise I'll keep him safe," I said.

He didn't look happy about it, but he finally nodded. "We'll see you later tonight," he said while closing the passenger door.

As I drove to Derek's house, taking the back roads and never going above ten miles per hour, I thought about how protective he was of the baby. He was willing to carry him in his arms all the way across town just to avoid him being in an unsafe car for a short period of time. It was endearing.

Not to mention how he was risking his job to make sure Anthony was given the best possible care, rather than becoming a number in a system. Firemen probably had a pension program for retirement, plus other benefits. Derek was thirty-seven, I had learned, and had been doing this for fifteen years. He had accumulated a lot of service time toward that pension.

And he was risking it all for the tiny bundle of joy on the floor of my car.

He's more than just a big, burly, grumpy fireman, I thought. *He's a good man.*

Anthony wiggled happily in his little basket, unaware of what was going on.

Derek's house was on a big corner lot on the north-east edge of Riverville. None of the lots around him were developed, so it was just his house surrounded by empty land. It was a big two-story Craftsman, painted electric-blue with crisp white trim all around. A white picket fence surrounded the big yard, and I had to get out of my car to swing open the fence gate so I could pull up the driveway. Four newspapers were scattered around the front porch, the ones he had missed while being at the firehouse.

"Derek's got a really nice place," I whispered to Baby Anthony while carrying him inside.

Despite being an older house, the interior was clean and well-maintained. It was a four-square house on the first floor, with four bedrooms upstairs. The wooden steps creaked as I carried the baby up there, exploring the house that would be my weekend residence. The first two rooms I checked were guest rooms, adorned with old wooden furniture and beds that were topped with quilted comforters.

The third room had a bed and its own bathroom, but half the room was filled with typewriters. Six of them were sitting on tables, gleaming and pristine as if on display. There were boxes stacked in the corner, and a quick glance showed that there were more typewriters in there.

"Weird," I said, leaving the room.

The last room I checked was the master bedroom. A huge four-post bed occupied a large chunk of the room, with a stand mirror and an adjacent bathroom. Everything was orderly and tidy. It made me wonder if Derek had a maid.

I was starting to leave the room when I noticed a framed photograph on the bedside table. I took a closer look at the couple in the photo: the woman was wearing a chiffon wedding dress with a transparent veil, and the man was wearing a well-fitted suit with a red vest and a matching red pocket square.

Derek was so young in the photo that I almost didn't recognize him.

He was married? I wondered.

Suddenly I felt like I was snooping, so I put the photo back and left the room. I carried Anthony downstairs, retrieved the rest of the things from the car, and set him up in the living room. I turned on the Dodgers game on the big TV and began feeding Anthony.

"See them?" I told Anthony. "Those are the Dodgers. They're winning, which is a good thing. We like the Dodgers. We *hate* the Giants."

Anthony sucked happily on the bottle.

17

Clara

The guys got home around nine-thirty, their headlights spraying across the house and through the living room windows. They came through the front door quietly, like they were trying to break in without anyone noticing.

I hefted Anthony and met them by the door. "Don't worry. He's awake."

They resumed walking normally. "We wanted to be safe," Derek said. "This house is old and creaky, and unlike the station, it's *not* soundproof."

"Everything go smoothly at the firehouse?" I asked.

Taylor paused to pinch Anthony's cheek. "It was horrible. Some other kid brought us our Friday-night pizza. He wasn't even *close* to a hot blonde." He punctuated it with a wink.

I smiled and felt my cheeks grow warm.

"We saved you some," Taylor added. "It's in the oven."

"I hope the oven is *off*," I said pointedly.

Derek ignored the jab. "Billy Manning acted strange. He said there was a smell in the air. Something different."

"I dumped the trash with the diapers in the dumpster down the street," Jordan said. "The smell must have lingered in the air."

"We can blame Anthony's little tushy on that," Taylor said. "What are the sleeping arrangements, Chief?"

Derek dropped his backpack off by the stairs. "You and Jordan can have the two guest bedrooms upstairs on the right. That way Clara and the baby can have the room attached to the bathroom."

"The typewriter room, you mean?" I asked.

"It's weird, right?" Jordan chimed in. "Who collects typewriters?"

"Lots of people," Derek said curtly. "Tom Hanks has an impressive collection."

"Ohh," Taylor said with fake enthusiasm. "Well if Tom Hanks has one, then that explains it."

Derek ignored him and hefted a bag. "I bought more formula and toys on the way home. If anyone needs toiletries, the hallway bathroom is stocked."

"Thanks, Chief," Jordan said. "I'm exhausted, so I'm going to head to bed."

"He loves sleeping in on Saturdays," Taylor said.

"Yeah, and I didn't get to do it last week," Jordan grumbled. He hesitated, then gave me a kiss on the cheek. "If you need help with the baby tomorrow, my schedule is clear."

"You're sweet."

"I'm hitting the sack too," Taylor said. "I'll be up to go for a run in the morning, Chief, if you want to go with me."

It must have been a joke, because Derek grunted unhappily, and Taylor chuckled. He gave me a friendly little wave, then jogged up the stairs with his backpack.

Derek walked to the kitchen, and I followed him with Anthony. He turned back to me and said, "I'll watch the baby, if you wanted to go upstairs with Jordan and..." He left the rest unsaid.

"I'm fine down here," I said. "Anthony is still awake, so I'm going to keep playing with him until he goes down."

"Good," Derek replied. "Like I said, the house isn't exactly soundproof." As if to prove the point, the ceiling creaked and groaned as the other two firemen walked around upstairs.

"Okay," I said, not wanting to discuss the volume of my sex life any further.

Derek took two beers out of the fridge and offered one to me. I took it gratefully and we went into the living room together. I put Anthony back in his basket and cracked it open. The beer was crisp and cool.

Derek made a noise when he realized what was on TV. "In this house, we watch the Giants." He tapped on the remote to change the channel to the San Francisco game. The Giants were losing, fourteen to three.

I gave him a smug look.

He grunted unhappy. "Tonight I'll make an exception. Dodgers it is."

"Much better," I replied.

The two of us watched the game in silence for an inning while sipping our beers. Derek got up and got two more, handing me another one without a word.

As the silence stretched, I realized there was an awkward elephant in the room. The guys had proposed to share me. I had discussed it with Jordan and Taylor, but I still hadn't talked to Derek about it. I had only heard that he was interested indirectly, through Jordan.

Eventually it became too awkward to bear, and by the end of my second beer, I was ready to carefully broach the subject.

"The three of you want to share a girlfriend, huh?" I blurted out.

Okay, maybe I didn't broach it carefully. But at least I brought it up.

Derek grunted in surprise. "Sure."

"Sure? That's it?"

"Yep."

"You don't seem to have much to say about it."

"The offer seemed pretty straightforward," he replied. His dark eyes flicked to me, then back to the TV. "And you haven't really given us an answer yet, have you?"

"I'm still considering it." I got up to get two more beers, then handed one to Derek when I got back. "Why would you rather share a girl than find one to keep all for yourself?"

"I would have assumed Jordan and Taylor told you the reasons."

"They told me *their* reasons. I'm asking why *you* want to."

The can of beer cracked open, and Derek took a long pull. The veins in his arms seemed to pop out as he put the beer on the table next to the couch. "I was never any good with regular relationships. The schedule is a bitch. Four days on, three off. Women don't like it. Can't blame them."

"Is that why you got divorced?" I asked.

He gave me a look. I held up my hands defensively.

"I wasn't trying to snoop, I swear. I was checking out all the rooms and I saw the wedding photo next to your bed."

Suddenly, an alarming thought came to me: what if he *wasn't* divorced? What if she had died somehow? I waited for his reaction, wincing before he spoke.

"My ex is very much alive," he rumbled. "We were only married two years. She's with someone new, now. They've been together eight. Wait, no. It'll be nine years next month. Time really flies."

He shook his head. "But to answer your question: no. It wasn't the job that did it."

He didn't go on, and I was curious, so I said, "Other relationship problems, then?"

"Our relationship was perfect," he said. "We were perfect in every way. Every way except one, that is." He took a deep breath and let it out slowly. "I wanted kids. She didn't. Eventually, our different expectations became too great to ignore."

I groaned. "Ouch. That really sucks. You didn't discuss it before you got married?"

"Oh, I knew she didn't want kids from the start." Derek leaned back in his chair and smiled sadly. "I thought she would change. All women get that maternal itch eventually, right? Well, not her. She didn't want them, and knew she never would. Which is fine. She was always very clear about that. It's my damn fault for not believing her."

Anthony was fussy, so I carried him over to the couch and sat next to Derek. "Oh, Derek. I'm really sorry."

"Me too." He smiled over at Anthony. "Life sucks sometimes, doesn't it, little guy?"

Anthony gave him a puzzled look, furrowing his tiny little brow.

My heart went out to Derek in that moment, while he and the baby stared at each other. It explained a big part of the entire situation, one that I hadn't quite understood: why Derek would risk everything for this little guy. He wanted children of his own. He wanted to be a father. And that paternal instinct was manifesting in his insistence that we do *whatever* is best for Baby Anthony, even if it risks their careers.

I suddenly remembered Maurice's question on the phone: *are you attracted to them?* Before now, the answer was that yes, I was physically attracted to them. All three of them were undeniably gorgeous, and would have been even if they weren't firemen.

But now I realized I was attracted to more than just Derek's body. He was a good man, which made his chiseled exterior even sexier than it would be by itself.

I should ask him out. We could get one of the others to watch Baby Anthony and get dinner or something tomorrow. If he wasn't going to ask me, then I would ask him.

Before I could, the wooden steps creaked as Taylor walked downstairs. He was wearing red boxers and a white tank top, and his blond hair was disheveled.

"Did you have a nightmare, little guy?" Derek asked in a condescending tone.

Taylor flipped him off, then turned to me. "Hey. I was thinking. Do you want to go out tomorrow? Like, out on a date?"

"Oh," I said. His question totally caught me off guard. "Yeah. That sounds like fun."

"Are you sure?" he asked. "I don't want to force the issue about sharing you. I just figured it was a good time, and we can get one of the other guys to watch the baby..."

I was just thinking the same thing regarding a date with Derek.

"I would love to go out with you," I said.

"Cool. Awesome. Neat." Taylor bobbed his head. "Okay. I'm going back to bed now."

"Goodnight," I said.

The steps creaked and shifted as he walked back upstairs.

"So," Derek said calmly. "You *have* come to a decision about our... offer."

"Maybe," I replied. "We'll see."

18

Taylor

I had a big, stupid, headache-inducing crush on Clara Ricci.

I had the hots for her *bad*.

Since I had been working at the firehouse, I always looked forward to Fridays, because that's when we ordered food from Tony's. Which meant Clara would be delivering the food to the station.

Sometimes Dan, the other guy, delivered the food. Those days sucked. But usually it was Clara.

We knew she was hot. Curvy in all the right ways, with full breasts and silky hair that I wanted to run my fingers through. That was all apparent within a few seconds of meeting her. I tried not to objectify women too much, but shoot, it was impossible not to eye Clara whenever she was around.

But now that we had spent a week pretty much living together, I knew she was much more than a good-looking woman. She was funny, and smart, and caring. So caring! The way she handled the baby put a permanent smile on my face.

To borrow a phrase some of my buddies used: she was *wife material*.

I sat in bed and stared at the ceiling, unable to sleep. Usually, I was a good sleeper. You had to be in this business, catching power naps whenever you could. But tonight, Clara kept running through my mind.

Was she interested in our proposition? Or did she just want to be with Jordan?

It took about half an hour to work up the courage to just go downstairs and ask her out. At least then I would know the answer to the question. But despite my fears, she accepted the date.

I was so happy, I practically jogged back upstairs. I still couldn't sleep after that, though now it was because I was excited.

And because Jordan was snoring in the room next to mine. Derek was right: these walls were *thin*.

Sleep or no sleep, I woke up full of energy the next morning. I threw on my running shorts and sneakers and went downstairs. Derek was sipping coffee in the kitchen while reading the newspaper.

I frowned. "Isn't that Tuesday's paper? The Athletics game on the front was from Tuesday."

"I like to catch up on the news I missed during the week," Derek replied. He flipped the page and then said, "So you and Clara are going out tonight, huh?"

"Yep!" I replied cheerfully. "I'm excited. There's this cool restaurant across town I want to take her to, and then after that..."

I trailed off as I heard someone coming down the stairs. It was Clara, with Baby Anthony in her arms.

"Morning, beautiful!" I pinched the baby's cheek and then glanced up. "Good morning to you too, Clara."

She stuck out her tongue at me. "Very funny. You going for a jog?" She looked me up and down.

"Yep, a quick three miles. There's a trail at the end of this street that looks promising."

"Mind if I come with you?" she asked. "I brought my running clothes just in case..."

"Yeah! Totally! You don't mind watching the baby, do you, Derek?"

He put down the paper and accepted the infant. "I'm the one whose idea this whole thing was. We'll have some guy time, won't we?"

Anthony wiggled happily in his arms.

Clara ran upstairs, changed, and then joined me. She was wearing tight yoga pants, and had pulled her hair up into a ponytail. We stretched a little bit in the living room, then walked outside and headed up the street to the trail.

"What's your typical pace?" I asked.

She grimaced. "I'm not fast at all. I usually average eleven-minute miles. *Maybe* ten forty-five if I'm feeling good."

My typical pace was under eight minutes, but I didn't want to make her feel bad. Plus, I wanted to run *with* her. So I said, "Today's just an easy jog for me. Eleven minutes a mile is perfect."

We reached the trail and began jogging. It was unpaved, and just wide enough that both of us could run side-by-side. Clara's ponytail swished back and forth, just barely brushing against my shoulder as we went.

"How'd the baby sleep?" I asked after a few minutes. "I didn't hear him cry at all last night."

"He slept pretty well!" she replied, smiling over at me. "I've gotten used to the signs that he's stirring. I can get to him *before* he starts crying now."

"So the snoring didn't bother you?" I asked.

"Snoring? No, I didn't hear you at all."

"Not me: Jordan," I clarified. "His snoring sounds like someone firing a machine gun. You're lucky you're in the room across the hall!"

Clara chuckled. "My brother, Jason, snored when we were kids. We shared a room until I was eight. I must have built up a tolerance."

"Lucky you!"

The trail wound its way through some trees, crossed a few fields, and then descended into more woods. At some points, it narrowed and we had to run single-file. Clara sped up and took the lead, and I followed close behind.

And my eyes started to drift.

I couldn't help it. This girl was *fine,* and she was wearing tight spandex. Her ass flexed hypnotically as we jogged along. I felt like I was in a trance, matching her strides while my eyes were locked onto her booty.

Then I started to get a hard-on.

Shit, I thought. My running shorts were thin, and an erection would be embarrassingly obvious in them. I focused on the swaying of her ponytail and tried to think of non-sexy things.

Baseball. The Oakland Athletics. Routine ground ball double-plays. That wrinkly old man we pulled out of the bathtub last week.

I managed to keep the hard-on at bay by the time we got back to Derek's place. "Nice run!" Clara said, high-fiving me.

"You too." I smiled. She was sweating more than me, but somehow it looked good on her. And it made me imagine other ways she might get sweaty, her body moving hypnotically in a totally different manner, without the yoga pants covering her luscious thighs and juicy ass...

"I'm going to shower," I said, hurriedly running upstairs before the tent in my shorts could become obvious.

I spent the day studying in my room. Jordan ordered sub sandwiches for lunch, and that was a nice break, but otherwise my nose was buried in a book until our date at six.

Clara was waiting for me downstairs. She was wearing a crystal-blue maxi dress that was tapered at the waist and had billowy cloth bunched up around the cleavage. It fit her frame wonderfully, especially when she turned sideways to show it off like a model.

My cock jumped at the sight of her, and I had to use all of the willpower in my possession to make it behave.

"Wow," I said. "You look *incredible.*"

"Why thank you," she said. "It was totally unintentional, too. I tossed a bunch of random clothes in my suitcase, and fortunately this was in there."

"Lucky me. I mean, lucky you." I winced, but Clara only smiled more.

Jordan put his arm around my shoulder. "So? Where are you taking the lucky lady?"

"I'm taking her somewhere nice," I replied. "You can hear all about it *after* the date."

Jordan scooped Baby Anthony out of the basket and made his little hand wave. "Say goodbye! Have fun!"

"Be safe," Derek said, giving me a nod.

I drove her to a little Italian restaurant on the other side of town. I don't know *how* I was able to snag last-minute reservations, but we had a table on the patio outside, overlooking the city's namesake river.

As soon as the waitress left, Clara leaned across the table and said, "I can't believe you brought me to one of our competitors."

My heart sank down into my stomach. *Oh no.* How could I be so stupid? Her family owned an Italian restaurant, and I had brought her to a different one...

I must have looked mortified, because she quickly put her hand on mine. "Oh no, I was just joking!"

"Are you sure?" I asked.

"They're not really our competition. We do mostly take-out, while this place is more upscale, and focuses on dine-in."

My heart was still pounding in my chest, so I took a sip of water to try to calm myself. "Speaking of restaurants, how is Tony's doing?"

Clara shrugged. "We're surviving. The restaurant is profitable, but just barely. It's an old building that dad has used for three decades. The pizza oven was manufactured during the Nixon administration." She sighed. "We're always one big repair bill away from going back into the red."

"Ah, that sucks," I said. What did a guy say to something like that?

"But I'm glad I'm home to help," she went on. "Mom really needed the help after dad passed. My brother, Jason, stuck around for a few weeks after the funeral, but Mom needed long-term help. Dad handled *everything* with the business: all the finances, food sourcing, advertising. You name it. I helped Mom understand all of that. I don't know *what* she would have done without me."

"That's so selfless, to put your life on hold and help your family," I said. "She's lucky to have you as a daughter."

"It's *granddaughters* that she wants," she said, accepting a glass of wine from the waitress. "But we don't need to talk about that. What about you? You're technically just a volunteer firefighter, right?"

"Technically, the term is *Probationary Firefighter*. After graduating, I'll be promoted to a full firefighter," I explained. "I'm getting my degree in Emergency Medical Services. As soon as I graduate next year, I'll get promoted and a pay raise."

"That's really cool." Clara leaned forward, showing off the plunging neckline of her dress, and the cleavage within. "What made you want to do that?"

"Mr. Rogers," I replied.

She blinked. "Mr. Rogers? Like, from Mr. Rogers' Neighborhood?"

I nodded. "He used to say that when you see scary things in the news, look for the helpers. You will always find people who are helping. I thought that was such a cool idea. When bad things happen, there are *helpers*. Like superheroes, but real. I wanted to be the kind of person people looked to when they needed help."

I paused to sip my own wine and then went on. "My neighbor, Francis, was in the Army. He was a medic. Growing up, I thought that was so cool. He would come home on leave and walk around in his uniform. I thought that was *so cool.* I wanted to be just like him, spending my life helping people. I figured becoming a firefighter was easier than enlisting in the Army."

"Safer, too!" Clara chirped up. "I mean, relatively speaking. I don't mean to imply that firefighting isn't dangerous."

"Nobody has ever shot at me," I admitted. "So that's definitely a plus."

"How does it work with your schedule?" she asked. "Taking classes, I mean."

"There are classes at the community college which are only on the weekend," I explained. "I can't take a full semester, but I'm slowly getting my degree."

Clara frowned. She was absolutely adorable when she frowned. "Why aren't you at classes this weekend? You're not skipping them just to go out with me, are you?'

I smiled. "It's summer. I only take classes in the fall and spring."

"Oh. Duh!" She shook her head, then paused. "Wait. Then what were you reading today? I saw you studying in your room all afternoon."

"Well, I'm trying to get ahead," I replied. "I have my fall schedule all planned out. For example, I'm taking *Trauma Management* and *Special Populations.* Even though class doesn't start until the end of August, I bought the textbooks and started reading them to get a head start. Because once the semester begins, it can be tough to keep up while working at the firehouse."

"I bet that's hard with such a chaotic schedule," Clara mused.

"You have no idea! One week we'll get almost no calls, and I'll have plenty of time to study. Then the next week I'll have an exam to study for, and of course we'll be super busy and I struggle to find time."

"That's how it works," she said with a rueful shake of her head. Her blond hair swayed around her shoulders. "The calls happen at the most inconvenient time."

"There's no convenient time for a house to burn down," I said.

"Also true."

"Which is why we teach people not to leave ovens on when they're not home," I said, deadpan.

She gave me a glare that could have ignited a fire. "I can't believe you just reminded me of that."

"Reminded you of what?" I casually sipped my wine. "I'm just commenting on one of the *very basic* fire-prevention facts. Never leave an oven unattended, no matter how low the temperature is."

Clara groaned, which made me grin even harder.

"I think it's wonderful that you want to help people," she said. "There's so much bad in the world. It's encouraging to see people like you who want to make a difference."

"It's nice to know it's appreciated," I replied.

"Cheers to that." We clinked wine glasses together and she favored me with a warm smile. My stomach felt all fluttery, like I was on a roller coaster.

Yeah. I definitely have it bad for this girl.

"What about you?" I asked. "What did you want to be when you grew up?"

"Hell if I know!" she said. "I got my degree in English Literature, because I *like* English literature, but it turns out it's not something I can easily make a career out of. Unless I want to teach, which I do not. I'm jealous of people like you who knew what you wanted to do from the start."

I shrugged. "You're great with Baby Anthony. If all else fails, you can make a career out of nannying."

"After the diapers I've had to change in the past twenty-four hours? I'm not sure I want to do *that* for a living."

The two of us laughed and waved to the waitress for more wine.

19

Clara

Before the date started, I was a bundle of nervous energy. I had all the normal pre-date jitters, with the added complexity of this being a totally abnormal situation: I was going on a first date with *Taylor*, the best friend and colleague of Jordan, who I had already slept with.

To say I was a nervous wreck was an understatement.

But Taylor turned out to be a wonderful guy. He was easy to be around—fun and carefree and lighthearted, without any pressure or awkwardness about the situation we were in. Everything felt natural around him, and I soon began to relax.

I found myself wanting to be totally honest with him, too.

"Do you want to know a secret?" I told him after he suggested that I could turn nannying into a full-time profession.

"Depends. Is it a good secret, or a bad secret?" he asked.

"I'll let you decide." I paused to choose my words carefully. "When you first asked for my help last week? You asked if I knew anything about taking care of babies. I said that I did."

Taylor ran his fingers through his blond hair. "Right."

"That was a lie," I admitted. "I knew *nothing* about babies. I had never even babysat before. In fact, I've only *held* a baby once, and that was my nephew LeBron. I held him for about ten seconds before handing him right back to my brother."

"Your nephew is named LeBron?" Taylor asked. "Like, the basketball player?"

"It's a long story," I said with a wave of my hand. "The important thing is that I lied to you. All of you."

Taylor put down his wine glass and grimaced. "That sucks. And here I thought we had a lot of chemistry. Too bad you're such a lying liar."

His chair scraped on the floor as he got up, tossed down his napkin, and began to walk away. I stared in horror as he got halfway across the room.

But then he turned around and came back, grinning widely.

"That's not funny!" I said. "You had me going for a second!"

"I don't care if you lied," he said.

"Really? You don't think it was cowardly?"

"Cowardly?" Taylor scoffed. "If anything, it makes you more courageous."

"Courageous," I muttered. "Now you're just being nice. *Firemen* are courageous. I'm just a girl taking care of a baby."

Taylor leaned across the table, holding my gaze intently. "When we respond to a call, we know what we're doing. We're trained for it. We have experience. But you? You offered to help us with the baby even though you have *no* experience. So, yes. I think that takes courage."

"Or a lot of stupidity," I said.

"Maybe. But I don't think you're stupid, Clara."

I was trying to be self-deprecating, but the way Taylor flipped it around put a smile on my face for the rest of dinner.

We split a dessert—chocolate lava cake, with a scoop of vanilla ice cream—and then left the restaurant. But the date wasn't over. Taylor drove us a few blocks away to a little art studio.

"What are we doing here?" I asked as we walked inside. To be honest, I was surprised it was still open this late.

Taylor grinned. "We are going to take a guided painting class. It's about an hour long."

A memory trickled to the front of my brain. "Wait a minute. Those painting supplies I saw at the firehouse... Those were yours! I didn't realize you were artistic."

Taylor shrugged modestly. "I took an art class as a college elective. And it was fun. I like it. And I hope you will, too."

There was a private room at the back of the studio with individual painting stations all set up. The instructor looked nothing like Bob Ross, but he had the same calm, soothing instructional voice as he guided the class (there were six of us total) through the painting process.

Occasionally, when I looked away from my painting for a split second, I would suddenly notice a new swipe of paint on my canvas that wasn't there before. The third time, I caught Taylor leaning over and swiping his brush across my painting.

"Keep your paints to yourself!" I hissed at him.

This devolved into the two of us giggling and marking up each other's painting. One of the other painters turned and glared at us, but we were having too much fun to care.

"Mine is way better than yours," I said on the car ride back. I was holding both paintings side-by-side.

"Yours looks like *crap*," Taylor said. "Mine is an absolute masterpiece. I'm going to frame it and put it up in the station."

It was all a playful joke: in reality, the two paintings looked nearly identical, except for a few minor differences.

We were still laughing and teasing each other about the paintings when Taylor pulled into the driveway at Derek's house. All the lights were off—everyone was asleep.

Taylor turned the car off, but didn't make any move to leave. "I had a ton of fun tonight, Clara."

"Me too."

"Having two firemen boyfriends isn't so bad, huh?"

I started to make a joke about how lucky I was, then decided to take the conversation in another direction. "Do you *really* want to share me?"

"After all the fun we just had, why do you think I don't?" he asked.

"That means you want to hang out with me, and date me. It doesn't mean you also want to share me with Jordan, and maybe Derek. I bet you only agreed to share me because Jordan asked me out first, and now sharing me is the only way you can go out with me at all."

Taylor frowned. "No."

I turned toward him and poked him in the arm. "Admit it. If *you* had asked me out first, and just the two of us were dating, would you then agree to share me with your two colleagues?"

He got a faraway expression on his face. "Hmm. Good point. Truthfully? I don't know how I would feel if things had shaken out that way." He twisted to face me in the seat. "But I'm not interested in hypotheticals and what-ifs. I'm glad we're here now. Even if it's happening in this weird, totally crazy way."

"Which part is crazier?" I asked. "The baby-watching part, or the sharing me part?"

"Both!"

We laughed, and drifted toward each other in the car. His hand slid up along my cheek, pulling my face toward his before taking me in a soft kiss.

I melted against him, and he pushed into my kiss deeper. Taylor's tongue peeked out to lick at mine, first tentatively, but with growing confidence and lust. Our mouths churned hungrily against each other in the car.

I thought Jordan was a great kisser, but Taylor was on another level. His lips were heady and addictive, and swallowed the soft, mewling sounds I began to make.

I want him, I realized. I wanted him badly. And I could feel the same desire mirrored back at me. Taylor didn't just want to give me a polite goodnight kiss, or a longer make out session in the car.

He wanted *all* of me, a burning need that I could sense in his lips and tongue and chest.

"Do you want to go inside?" I asked, out of breath.

"More than anything in the world," he breathed. His eyes seemed bluer than normal in the moonlight as he glanced at the house. "But..."

"Oh, right," I realized. "The walls are thin. If you can hear Jordan snoring in the room next door, then they can hear..."

"It's not that." He closed his eyes for a moment, collecting himself.

"What is it?" I asked. "What's wrong?"

"I've... never done it before. Have sex, I mean."

I gasped. "You're a *virgin?*"

20

Clara

I looked him up and down. Taylor was only twenty-two, but he was gorgeous. High cheekbones, and an oval-shaped face with piercing-blue eyes. Not to mention his body, lean and strong and totally ripped. Taylor was a freaking *snack*.

How had someone this perfect never had sex before?

For a moment, he looked hurt. "I shouldn't have said anything..."

"No! Wait." I cupped his cheek. "I'm just surprised, is all. I would have expected a guy like you to have been with a dozen women."

"I've dated plenty of women," he said defensively, "but I've never gotten that far. I've always broken it off before feeling ready to, you know, *be* with them."

The fire of lust swirled deep inside me. "And you think you're ready to be with me? After *one date?*"

"I don't know why it's different with you," he said. "But it is."

This time I kissed him, even harder than before.

"But what about the walls?" I asked. "And how thin they are?

Don't you want some privacy for your first time?"

"We're all on the same page about sharing you," he said hopefully. "It wouldn't be *that* awkward."

"That doesn't mean I want everyone to hear us."

Taylor smirked. "Then we'll just have to be *really* quiet, won't we?"

I tingled with excitement at the thought. Moving our bodies together, drowning each other's cries with our lips, muffled grunts and moans and gasps.

But I had done that with Jordan in the firehouse, when we were trying not to wake Baby Anthony. And as fun as it was, I didn't want to hold back with Taylor. I wanted to close my eyes and lose myself in him. And I wanted him to do the same on his first time.

I glanced over my shoulder. "Your back seat is clean."

He looked too. "Yeah, I actually vacuumed it the—" He cut off as he realized what I was implying.

We stared at each other for three long heartbeats. Then we simultaneously opened our doors and scrambled around to the back seat.

Taylor's mouth connected to mine as if drawn by a magnet, and his hands explored my body as we resumed making out. There was nothing holding us back now—just the unrestrained lust we felt for one-another, a lust that was quickly ramping up to ten.

I didn't care that we had only been on one date, or that I had only just gotten to know him this week. I didn't feel awkward about dating his colleague at the same time. I didn't care that as soon as this was over, we would need to go inside and take care of a baby that was only temporarily ours.

As Taylor and I kissed in the back seat, the only thing I cared about was *him*.

In contrast to the slow, sensual way that Jordan had eaten me out in our last sexual encounter, Taylor and I were like teenagers trying to do the deed before our parents came home. He slid his hands up my thighs and I raised my butt so he could pull my dress up around my waist, while I unbuckled his belt and clawed his zipper down. We both shimmied out of our clothes—him out of his pants and boxers, and me out of my panties—and then he fell on me with kisses again, pushing me back until I was resting sideways on the seat.

"I've never had sex in a car," I whispered.

"Me neither," he replied.

After a second, we both chuckled at that.

"Duh," I said.

He grinned. "I don't know why I said that."

"Shut up and kiss me."

He obeyed with enthusiasm, sinking between my legs. I could feel his hard length between us, brushing against my wet warmth. He made a groaning sound deep inside his throat as I reached for him, fingers lacing around his shaft lovingly.

I guided him up and down, coating his crown with my wetness and then positioning him just right. He took over from there, pushing forward and filling me slowly.

The two of us moaned together as he sank his cock into me. I took him eagerly, wrapping my legs around him and holding him inside so we could both savor the moment. It was kind of awkward in the cramped back seat, but it felt right. Like this was how things were *supposed* to go.

"Jesus Christ," Taylor rumbled into my neck, breath hot on my skin. "Clara, I never thought it would feel this *good*."

I kissed him. "You haven't seen anything yet."

I relinquished the vice-like grip of my legs around his waist, and began moving my hips up against him. His body came alive against mine as he moved with me, meeting me stroke for stroke.

It may have been his first time, but he had good instincts.

Taylor rolled his body against mine with perfect rhythm, slow and steady with just the right pace. He fisted my hair, fingers tightening against my scalp, and I surged upward with need.

We lost ourselves in our unrestrained lust as we made love in the back seat. I was grateful for the privacy because soon both of us were moaning loudly, with the freedom of not needing to stay quiet.

Taylor quickened his pace, sending new jolts of pleasure up my spine. I arched my back to take more of him, hands squeezing on his chiseled ass to urge him to go even faster, to give me everything he had.

He began to gasp and groan, and I bucked and thrust against him while clamping my pussy around him. The hard length of his cock drove into me with mindless desire, then shuddered and exploded inside me.

"Clara!" Taylor cried out, meeting my gaze for a split second. "Oh, Clara!"

The sound of my name on his lips drove me over the edge as well, and the two of us shook and shivered with release while he filled me with his seed.

We embraced for a long time after, panting and sweating against the fake leather upholstery, but too satisfied to move.

"Not bad," I said, "for your first time."

He gave me a surprised look. "Really?"

I kissed his sweaty lips. "You're a natural."

"I bet you say that to all the guys."

"Just the ones who are good in bed." I paused. "Or, good in *car*, I should say."

We slowly untangled from each other and collected our clothes. It was no easy task in the cramped back seat, but we managed to get dressed.

We got out of the car and held hands all the way up to the

front door, even though it was only thirty feet. Taylor paused in front of the door and turned toward me.

"I had a lot of fun tonight. During our date, *and* after." He kissed me on the cheek.

I raised an eyebrow. "That's all I get? A little peck?"

"I don't want to get too presumptuous on the first date," he said casually. "Have to leave you wanting more, right?"

The two of us giggled, then shared a *real* kiss.

"Want to sleep together?" he asked.

"Didn't we just do that?" I replied.

"I mean sleep as in *sleep*. Not sleep as in *sex*. Unless you're not a fan of cuddling..."

"Oh, cuddling is the best," I replied. "But I'll have the baby with me. And he's going to wake up several times."

"I don't mind," Taylor said. "It's worth it to fall asleep with you."

It was sweet. And I wanted to say yes. I wanted to feel him drift off to sleep next to me, to watch the rising and falling of his chest as his breathing slowed and he began to dream.

But I knew he needed sleep on the weekend. *Real* sleep, undisturbed by a crying infant. Sure, the walls were thin and he could probably hear the crying across the hall, but I was certain he would rest better if he was in a different room.

"We'll cuddle another night," I assured him. "Or maybe during a daytime nap."

He grinned at me. "I'm a big fan of naps."

We kissed again, then went inside. We continued holding hands at the bottom of the steps, and then slowly pulled them apart.

God, he's sexy, I thought while watching him climb the creaky steps. *I can't believe he was a virgin. And that I got to be his first.*

I found Derek in the study, which was adjacent to the living room on the back side of the house. He was resting in a recliner, with Baby Anthony asleep on his chest.

The maternal part of me twisted up at the sight. There was nothing sexier than a big, strong man holding a baby, and the sexiness was ramped up to a thousand when the baby was sleeping on his chest. Even though I had just had sex—with another guy, to boot!—I felt my lady-parts tingle and my ovaries twitch just a little bit.

His eyes opened and focused on me. "You kids have fun?"

I frowned. Was there a hint of attitude in his tone? The way he said *you kids* seemed vaguely insulting. It made me wonder if he was annoyed at having to watch the baby, or jealous that Taylor got to go out with me.

He wouldn't be jealous of Taylor, I thought. *Would he?*

"We had a very nice time," I said. "You know, it's dangerous to sleep with a baby on your chest. He can smother himself against you if you're not careful."

I only knew that fact from the baby spreadsheet my brother had sent me, but I said it with the confidence of someone stating something that should be obvious.

"I was never asleep. Just resting my eyes." He got up and placed the baby in his basket. His movements were careful and tender, like he was handling something precious. Then he grabbed an envelope from the desk. "This is for you."

I frowned at the envelope, then took it. There was money inside. A thick stack of twenties. "What's this?"

"You're unofficially on the payroll," he said. "That's a week's worth of pay."

I shoved the envelope back at him. "I can't take this. I'm just glad to help the baby."

He refused to take the envelope back. "You gave up working at the restaurant to help us, and I promised to compensate you for your time. You've been well worth it, Clara." He hesitated, then added, "I don't know what we would have done without you this past week."

I lowered the envelope to my side. "Like I said. I'm just happy to help Baby Anthony. Everything else is just a bonus."

One of his dark eyebrows rose. "*Everything* else?"

Even though this room was on the back of the house, I suddenly wondered if he knew what Taylor and I had done in the car. Even though I had nothing to be ashamed of, a shiver of embarrassment ran up my back.

Then Derek stepped up and hugged me.

I was surprised at first, but then relaxed in his arms. He was a bear of a man, huge with muscle, and it was nice to be embraced by him. Deep down, every woman wanted a man to hold them like this. Especially how his hand rested on the back of my neck, and the way he softly inhaled the scent of my hair...

Maybe he is interested in me after all.

"Anthony was last fed about an hour ago," he said, pulling away. "I changed him at the same time. He should be good for a while. Want me to carry him upstairs for you?"

"No," I said. "I can handle him."

Derek nodded. Without another word, he left the room and went upstairs, leaving me confused about what he *really* thought about me.

21

Clara

I carried Baby Anthony upstairs and found someone waiting in my bed. At first I thought it was Taylor, but then I saw the puff of dark hair on his head.

Jordan rolled over and sleepily said, "Hey."

I closed the door behind me. "You're in the wrong room, mister."

He sat up in bed. The comforter drifted down to his waist, revealing his bare chest in the moonlight streaming in the window. "Maybe I wanted to sleep surrounded by typewriters. Did you think of that?"

"*Is* that why you're here?"

"No," he admitted. "I wanted to see you."

I put Baby Anthony down and crossed my arms. "You wanted to see if Taylor and I would come to bed together, you mean."

"Honestly, no," he said. "I was sleeping in my room when I heard him come home. Then, while he was in the bathroom, I snuck across the hall and got in bed here."

"Is it because you want to finish up where we left off the other night, when the alarm interrupted our sexy time?"

He gave me a dour look. "Can't a guy just want to cuddle without getting interrogated? Damn."

I gave him a kiss on the forehead. "Taylor wanted to cuddle with me too. I turned him down."

Jordan grinned up at me. "Good. The bed's not big enough for three."

"I turned him down because I didn't want the baby to disturb him."

"I'm a deep sleeper. I slept through the Loma Prieta earthquake in eighty-nine."

I gave a start. "Wait a minute. You weren't even alive then!"

"No, I wasn't," he admitted. "But if I was? I totally would have slept through the whole thing."

I went through my bedtime routine and then crawled in bed with Jordan. He rolled onto his back, and I curled up against his body and rested my head in the crook of his arm.

"Good date?" he murmured.

"It was," I replied simply.

"Must not have been *that* good. Taylor didn't get lucky."

I tried to laugh at the joke, but it came out awkwardly. Jordan noticed, too.

"What?" he asked. "Did you two do it in the bathroom at the restaurant or something?"

I wasn't sure what to say. Here was another complication of being shared: did we talk about what happened with the other guys? Or was I supposed to pretend like we *didn't* have sex?

But it had been a truthful kind of night—I had told Taylor that I didn't have any experience with babies previously, and Taylor told me that he was a virgin. So I decided to keep the theme.

"We did it in the car," I said slowly. "In the driveway."

I felt him twist his head to look down at me. "You serious, Clara?"

I nodded against his chest.

He barked a laugh. "In the car? Like a couple of high schoolers parked at make-out point?"

"Shut up!" I whispered. "You'll wake Baby Anthony!"

"You could have come inside," he said.

"And let everyone hear what we're doing? No thank you."

"It's not like we don't know. Hell, sharing you was *our* idea."

"That doesn't mean we can't have privacy," I replied. "Especially for Taylor's first time."

Jordan tensed. "Wait, what?"

I groaned. "Shit. Maybe I shouldn't have said that."

"Taylor is a virgin?"

"*Was.* Past tense."

Jordan grunted. "Wouldn't have guessed that."

"I know, right? A guy as sexy and charming as him..."

"Hey, woah, enough of that."

I twisted until my chin was resting on his chest and I was looking up at him. "Uh oh. Are you jealous?"

"No."

"Yes you are." I poked him on the nose. "You're totally jealous."

"Maybe I'm jealous he got to spend tonight with you, while I was stuck at home with the Chief and the baby. I didn't mind Baby Anthony, but the Chief is a boring guy."

"That's how sharing works," I said. "If you wanted me all to yourself, you shouldn't have offered..."

"I know, I know." He rolled me over onto my side and then spooned me from behind. "Goodnight, Clara."

"Taylor told me you're a snorer."

"Taylor is a liar."

"If you snore," I said, "I'm kicking you out."

He vibrated with silent laughter, and then we both sighed happily together under the covers.

It turned out that Jordan *was* a snorer. Within minutes he was wheezing softly, and then it morphed into a deeper, rumbling snore. But it wasn't too bad. And I was so content having his body wrapped around mine that I didn't mind.

A little snoring was worth falling asleep to this.

Baby Anthony woke twice in the night. But both times, Jordan got up and took care of him. I insisted I would handle it, and that he should go back to sleep, but he gently pushed me back onto the bed.

"I've got it covered. Go back to sleep, sweetie."

Sweetie. I liked the sound of that. One date and two sexy-times and Jordan already had a pet name for me.

In the near-darkness of the bedroom, I watched Jordan's muscular frame go through the routine. He checked the baby's diaper, then bounced him on his shoulder and shushed him back to sleep.

Just like when I saw the baby sleeping on Derek's chest, my ovaries gave a big old twitch at the sight. A tiny little human in the arms of an enormous, heroic fireman.

Shut up, vagina, I thought while drifting off to sleep. *I get it. Big men taking care of babies is sexy.*

*

After living with my mom for the past year, it was strange

suddenly being at someone else's place. The fire station was the fire station, but Derek's house felt different. It was like staying at a bed and breakfast, but instead of paying for my room, all I had to do was watch a cute little baby.

It was weirdly stress-free. We hung out, watched TV, and relaxed. On Sunday, I sat in a rocking chair on the porch while Baby Anthony slept and read a book on my phone. It was almost like being on vacation.

Sure, there were periods of chaos where the baby wouldn't stop crying. His diapers were still radioactive. But overall, it was a pleasant change of pace from helping my mom at the restaurant.

Of course, it helped that I had *really* good company.

Taylor and I napped together on Sunday afternoon. We didn't even fool around or anything—we just curled up together on the couch and slept for an hour while Derek watched the baby.

On Monday afternoon, Derek and Taylor went out to run errands. Baby Anthony was sleeping in his basket in the living room, so I snuck up on Jordan while he was pouring himself a glass of milk in the kitchen.

I gave him a long kiss. Then, without another word, I dropped to my knees in front of him on the cold tile floor.

"Hey now, what's all... *ohh*."

Jordan's words devolved into mindless grunts and moans as I gave him a blowjob in the kitchen. I had always doubted my head-giving skills, but I had Jordan coming into the inside of my cheek within minutes. I gazed up at him and devoured the sight of his ecstasy, his face twisting with intense pleasure, while I *also* devoured his come.

It was so much fun being naughty.

"What was that for?" he asked.

I rose and tastefully wiped the corner of my mouth. "Payback for the other night."

"I can't help but notice you didn't torture me the way I tortured you," he said.

I poked him in the chest. "That's because I'm a *nice* person. Also, I don't know how long the guys will be gone, or how long Anthony will stay down."

He grinned and pulled me into a long kiss.

"I'm surprised you want to kiss me after that," I said.

"Why? Because your mouth was just around my penis?" He glanced down at his still-exposed member, slowly going limp through the zipper hole of his pants. "That doesn't gross me out. I *love* my penis. We're very good friends."

"I like it too." I kissed him, and he grinned against my lips. "What?"

"I was just thinking about how you probably haven't done that to Taylor."

I gave him a playful shove. "See? You *are* jealous. You don't want to share me at all."

"I definitely want to share you," he replied, wrapping his arms around my waist and nuzzling his nose against mine. "But we're going to joke about it a little bit along the way."

My own smile wavered. "I still can't get a read on Derek. Just when I think he's about to show some attraction to me, it fades away."

"Like I told you: that's just Derek," Jordan insisted. "He's slow to come around."

I still wondered if he ever *would* come around. And if not, that was okay. I was very happy with Jordan and Taylor. When it came to chiseled fireman lovers, my cup runneth over.

I heard the front door bang open. "We're back," Taylor announced.

Derek came around the corner with a bulky box in his arms. He dropped it to the ground and I saw the picture on the front: it was an infant's car seat.

"Really? You bought a car seat for him?" I asked.

Derek scowled. "I don't care if it's only a three-mile drive. I want him to be safe. I'll donate it to the Fresno Women's Shelter when this is over."

Taylor hefted a bag and grinned. "We got him a bunch of new clothes, too! Now he doesn't have to keep wearing the same two onesies over and over."

"Fun!" I took the bag and sifted through them. My hands froze when I reached one particular onesie that was orange and black. I held it up for everyone to see.

It was a San Francisco Giants onesie.

"I'm *not* touching him while he's wearing that."

All three firemen roared with laughter.

That night, we all packed up our things and prepared to head back to the firehouse for the next four days.

"Are you sure we can't just keep him here?" I asked. "It would make things so much simpler."

"I know, I know," Derek said. "I've gone back and forth about it myself. Ultimately, I'm paranoid about custody issues if we get caught. He needs to stay at the station the majority of the time."

"Also, you'd be all alone here," Taylor pointed out. "At the station, there's *four* of us to help watch this little guy. Isn't that right?"

He wiggled Anthony's little foot, and the baby let out a squeal of happiness.

"We'll text you when it's safe for you to drive over," Derek said. He placed a key on the table. "Lock up when you leave, and make sure the lights are all turned off."

"I'm sure she will, *dad*," Taylor teased.

Derek gave him a heavy scowl as they went out the front door.

I considered that while waiting to get the text. Was that why Derek was so hesitant to show any attraction toward me—because there was an age difference? Derek was thirty-seven, which was older, but it wasn't *old*. He only had a few silvery strands in his otherwise pitch-black hair. And aside from being kind of a grump, he was as energetic and fit as his two younger counterparts.

I was definitely attracted to him. Physically, he was *fine*. Not fine as in "just okay," but fine as in, "damn, that man is *fine*." In addition to a powerful body and ruggedly-sexy face, he had the added benefit of experience. He walked around like a leader, and had confidence in his eyes. That was attractive in a man.

Not to mention the way he handled Baby Anthony. All of his paternal tendencies were just icing on an already gorgeous cake.

I got the "all clear" text from Jordan around nine-thirty. By then I had the new car seat put together and ready to go. It had an arch handle, and could function as a baby carrier even when it wasn't in a vehicle. Baby Anthony scrunched his little face in consternation as I strapped him in, but then accepted his new receptacle without a fuss.

I still drove extra slow and careful on the way to the firehouse. Now I understood why people put those *baby on board* stickers on their cars.

I parked behind the station so we could unload the car and baby without anyone seeing from the main road. Jordan was waiting with outstretched arms.

"Long time, no see!"

But instead of hugging me, he took the car seat out of my hand and began gushing over the baby, tickling his tummy and giving him a healthy dose of baby-talk. Taylor came over and began making faces at the baby, sticking his tongue out and crossing his eyes.

"Good to see you guys, too," I said with a wry smile.

"Shh!" Jordan told me. "We're talking to the baby!"

I drove down the block and parked my car on the street, just so nobody would get suspicious. As I walked back to the station, I felt really good about everything. We were doing a good thing by taking care of Anthony and ensuring he went to a good home. For the first time in my life, my maternal instinct had kicked in and was running at full-throttle in my brain. I had only been around him for a week, but I would do *anything* to protect that little guy.

Maybe Taylor was right: I *could* make a career as a nanny.

More importantly, I knew the guys all felt the same way. All of us were on the same page regarding the baby.

Except for the Giants onesie, of course. I was going to "accidentally" throw that away the first chance I got.

I frowned as I neared the firehouse. There was a lime-green Mustang parked out front. That wasn't there five minutes ago when I dropped everything off...

My stomach sank when I saw the license plate: FIRMAN. I remembered the car now.

Oh no.

I rushed inside, but by then I knew what I would find. My three firemen were standing in the living room, facing a *fourth* man who was wearing street clothes. Derek was holding Baby Anthony protectively in his arms.

The man turned to face me. Billy Manning gave me the same sleazy smile he did the first time I met him.

"Well, well, well," he said. "What do we have here?"

22

Jordan

Billy Manning was a sneaky, piece of shit, asshole, ruthless, slimy fucker. He was *scum*.

Sorry. That's just my honest opinion of the guy.

He left with the other guys from second-shift around nine. He waited for me, Derek, and Taylor to get settled into our own shift. Clara returned to the station with the baby and our other baby-related supplies.

Then, and *only* then, did Billy return to the station and pretend like he had forgotten something.

"Sorry boys, I'll be out of your hair in a bit," he said while hurrying into the station. "Forgot my wallet, I'm so clumsy, and I..."

And that's when he caught the three of us standing around Anthony's brand new baby carrier.

He sneered. "So. You have a baby here. Out of all the things going on, I have to admit, that's the *last* thing I expected. Whose is it, huh? Go on, spill the beans."

I panicked. We were caught. All of our care and planning was for nothing.

Derek and I shared a look. There was nothing to do but tell him, now. What other choice did we have?"

Derek picked up the baby and held him in his arms. "Billy. I'll explain everything. But I hope, once you hear what's going on, that you'll..."

He trailed off as Clara walked into the station.

Billy raked his eyes over her in a way that made me *furious*. I felt my right hand ball into a fist. In that moment, there was nothing in the world I wanted more than to sink my fist into his stupid face.

"What do we have here?" he asked her.

Clara froze. She was just as shocked as we were. But then she did something crazy.

Something *amazing*.

"Thank you so much for helping me," she suddenly said. She took the baby out of Derek's arms and cradled him against her shoulder. "When my poor boy started coughing in the car, I just *panicked*. I thought he was choking. I didn't know what to do! Thank goodness I was driving by the fire station when it happened. And thank *you* for giving him CPR, Captain... Dahlkemper, is it?"

I glanced at Taylor. *Holy shit. She thought of a plausible excuse.* The three of us had frozen when caught, but she came up with a way out on the spot.

Billy looked at her, then at each of us. Then he wagged a finger at Clara. "You almost had me. That's a great story! But I saw what you did. You parked behind the station for a few minutes, then drove down the street and walked back. Your baby wasn't choking at all. You don't want anyone to know you're here."

Shit. The story probably would have worked if the three of us didn't look so guilty.

Derek frowned at Billy. "You were watching the firehouse?"

"No, no, no," Billy lectured. "Don't try to turn this around on me. You were hiding *this* thing." He pointed at the baby. "What's going on?"

Clara sighed. "Okay. You caught me. I'll tell you, but you have to promise not to tell anyone."

Billy narrowed his beady eyes at her. "I'll decide that once I've heard what you have to say."

Clara hefted Baby Anthony and kissed him on the head. "I had him out of wedlock. I was able to hide the pregnancy for a while, but there's no concealing a baby bump. When my mom found out, she was *furious*. Called me every name in the book. When I finally had the baby, she kicked me out. I have nowhere else to go, so..."

Derek suddenly stood up a little straighter as he seized on the story. "There's precedent for using public facilities, such as fire stations and police stations, as shelters for those in need. It's at the Captain's discretion. So I'm allowing her to remain here until she finds a place to stay."

Billy sneered at each of us. "Which one of you knocked her up, then?" He looked at the baby. "Dark hair. Couldn't be yours, Taylor Swift. So he must be one of yours..."

He swung his finger between me and Derek.

"None of us is the father," I said. It was easy to sound convincing because it was true. "We're just helping someone who is embarrassed by her situation, and has nowhere else to go."

Billy's sneer faded. *Holy shit. He might actually believe the story*, I thought.

"You're the pizza girl, right?" Billy asked. "Didn't know you'd been knocked up. Can't remember the last time I was at Tony's, though..."

I could see him doing the mental math. Clara had been back in Riverville a full year. The baby was a few months old. It was possible that he hadn't seen her at the restaurant in a while.

Billy sneered at Derek. "I *knew* the station smelled like baby shit. How long's she staying here?"

"However long she needs," Derek said firmly. "We have the room for her and the baby."

"I don't like the firehouse turning into a hostel." Billy's face twisted with smugness. "Not sure the higher-ups would, either."

Derek took a step forward and aimed a finger at the smaller man. "She's here looking for shelter. She's *helpless*, and has nobody else. Put aside your own animosity toward me and think about that, Billy."

"I could do that, I think," Billy replied. "If I get something in return, of course."

Derek stiffened, and bit off every word. "A commendation. On your next performance review."

"Like the sound of that." Billy extended his hand. "You've got yourself a deal, boss man."

They shook on it, but it wasn't congenial. It felt more like a truce rather than an agreement. Billy turned to Clara and flashed a toothy smile.

"I'm not too busy. Could stay here and play with the runt. Or maybe *we* could play. The three of them could watch your boy while I take you out for drinks, turn your frown upside-down."

I started walking forward without thought, hand squeezing into a fist once again. Taylor put an arm out to stop me. He was trembling with anger too.

Billy never saw either of us because he was focused on Clara. She snorted at him and said, "Tempting, but no thanks."

"Isn't your wife waiting for you at home?" Derek asked Billy.

Billy shrugged. "What she don't know won't hurt her." He fixated his smile on Clara again. "Come on. One drink. I don't bite."

"Thanks, but I prefer my drinks *without* roofies in them," she replied sweetly. "But if I change my mind, I know who to call."

I tensed while waiting for Billy's reaction—he had a temper, and a mean streak. Guys like him didn't react well to women saying no, especially with barbed insults.

But Billy barked a laugh. "I like her," he said to us. "She's got spunk. Just make sure you clean up the baby stink before we start our shift on Friday, yeah?"

He continued laughing to himself while strutting out of the firehouse.

I went to the window and watched him get in his car and drive away. Only then did I breathe a sigh of relief.

"That was close," I said.

Clara made a gagging noise. "That guy is *married*, and he's still acting all gross? Ugh. What a creep."

"Try sharing a station with him," Taylor muttered.

I turned to Clara. "Nice job, thinking up an excuse."

"Twice, too!" Taylor chimed in. "The three of us were like deer caught in the headlights. Chief almost told him the truth."

"Thank goodness I didn't," Derek said dryly. "But he's suspicious, now. Even if he bought our story—which I'm not entirely sure he did—we need to be more careful."

"He must've been suspicious already," Taylor pointed out. "Why else would he hang around and watch the station? He knew something was going on."

I stepped up to my boss and softened my tone. "Maybe it's not worth it, Chief. Maybe we should hand Anthony over to Social Services now. That would be better than letting you get in trouble."

Derek's face hardened. "No."

Taylor stepped up. "But your job..."

"*Fuck* my job," he replied, voice cracking like a whip. "We're the only protection that little baby has in the world. I'm not dumping him off on a bunch of strangers until I know he's going to a *good* foster home, and that's final. I don't want to hear any more discussion on the matter. Is that understood?"

"Yes, sir," both Taylor and I said in unison.

There was an awkward silence. It stretched for a few seconds, and then Baby Anthony started squealing happily in Clara's arms.

She adjusted him, and the two of us shared a look.

How much longer could we keep this up?

23

Clara

I could feel the adrenaline surging through my body after getting caught. It made me twitchy and on-edge. Not to mention the way Billy acted. He looked at me like I was a piece of chocolate cake. And *not* in the good way.

There was also the fact that he was married. Rather than heading home after his three-day shift, he was flirting with a random woman. Screw guys like that.

The first order of business was to bolster our new story: that the baby was mine, and I was kicked out of my house. It would have worked better if Billy didn't recognize me, but since he did, I had to call Mom and let her know.

"*I do not lie!*" she said emphatically.

"It's not lying. It's... fibbing. To protect the baby," I replied.

I heard her grunt unhappily. "*I will do this. I will tell the lie. But only if you let me see the baby!*"

"Okay," I said, surrendering. "I'll let you see the baby this weekend."

She clapped excitedly. "*I see the baby! I lie for you! No*

problem!"

Once that was taken care of, I went back out into the kitchen. Taylor was bouncing Baby Anthony in his arms. There was an empty bottle on the table in front of him.

"My mom is taken care of," I said. "Do you think Billy will accept the commendation you offered him? Or will he still make trouble?"

"I have no idea what he will do," Derek said with resignation. "I'm going to call my sister tomorrow and see if there's any way to expedite the process. Just in case. In the mean time, there's nothing we can do but relax and try to do our jobs here at the station."

*

It turned out there wasn't much of a job for the guys to do. I had my hands full with Baby Anthony, but the firehouse didn't get a single call.

They watched a lot of TV. Derek was in the middle of rewatching *The Sopranos*, but the episodes were intense and they could usually only stand a couple of them at a time before switching to something lighter.

We played board games to kill time. *Monopoly*, and *Sorry*. Derek lost at both, and spent the rest of the day grumbling about how Jordan cheated.

Not receiving any calls made it easy to spend some *intimate* time with the guys. I slept with Taylor again that night while Jordan watched the baby.

"It's weird being with you like this," he whispered while driving into me slowly and tenderly.

I sighed against his neck. "What do you mean?"

"Here. In a bed. Instead of the back seat of my car." Taylor grinned down at me. "It's downright *luxurious.*"

"I don't know," I teased. "You were more *enthusiastic* in the car." I bit my lip.

He raised an eyebrow, then dove into me harder and faster, as if it were a challenge.

The next day, Jordan excused himself to take an afternoon nap. I left the baby with Derek and sneakily went down the hall to the living quarters. But Jordan wasn't in his bed—he was in the shower across the hall.

He yelped with surprise when I pulled back the curtain on the communal shower stall.

"You almost gave me a heart attack!" he said, voice echoing off the tiled walls. Then he realized I was nude. His gaze raked over my body, eyes widening as he took in the sight of me.

"I didn't mean to scare you," I said in an innocent voice. "If you want me to leave..."

I started to turn away, and Jordan grabbed my arm and pulled me under the steamy water. He bent me over the shower and took me hard and fast, not wasting any time while we had our moment of privacy.

The bathroom wasn't sound-proof, but Jordan clamped his palm over my mouth as we came together, drowning out my pleasured cries.

It was strange bouncing between the two of them. One night with Taylor, then the next afternoon with Jordan. It *almost* felt like infidelity to me, sneaking kisses whenever we had some privacy and I didn't have the baby. After all, I wasn't used to going back and forth between two guys.

But Jordan and Taylor were totally on board with it. They joked and teased each other throughout the day, and pretended to be possessive of me. At night, when they were going to bed, they made a competition out of kissing me goodnight, constantly trying to one-up the other.

I didn't mind. After all, I was the one getting all the extra love because of it. Their attitudes took away any awkwardness from the situation and made me comfortable.

I still can't believe it, I thought while falling asleep with Taylor. *I'm being shared by two firemen.* I was the luckiest woman in the world. I never would have believed that this would be my future when I first returned to Riverville a year ago.

But I still wondered about Derek, who showed almost no interest in me. He was polite and cordial, but nothing beyond that.

What was he waiting for?

By Wednesday, the guys *still* hadn't received a single call on their shift. Not even a normal 9-1-1 call that they could respond to for assistance. All was well in Riverville.

"It's a good problem to have," Derek said.

"I guess," Jordan replied.

Derek looked at his watch. "It's almost time to order Chinese. Why don't we run out and pick it up, rather than having it delivered?"

"Count me in," Jordan said, hopping up from the couch. "I'll take any excuse to get out and do *something.*"

The guys gathered their gear, in case they received a call while they were out and had to respond to it without coming back to the station. While holding his helmet, Derek gave me a long look.

"Want to come with us?" he asked. "On a ride-along."

I grunted. "You're joking."

"You can sit in the second row of the cab, with the baby seat strapped in," he replied. "We'll put protective headgear on the baby. It'll be fun."

I shifted Anthony in my arms. "You were super overprotective with him when I was driving three miles in my car. But you'll let him go on a ride-along?"

"As long as he's strapped securely into the baby seat, I'm fine with anything. The fire engines have good shock absorbers. It'll be a smooth ride. But if you would rather stay here and do nothing…"

I was just as bored as they were, so I agreed to go along. The fire engine had a big cab: two front seats, and then a second row that was about the size of a passenger van. I strapped the baby carrier into one seat securely, and took the seat next to it. Taylor sat in one of the two jump seats that faced backwards, while the other two sat in the front.

Baby Anthony looked confused about his surroundings, especially when we put the protective headphones over his little ears. But as the fire engine got moving, he looked around with big eyes, and his little mouth pursed with concentration. I could practically see the gears turning in his baby brain.

"This is fun!" I said over the roar of the engine. "I never got to ride in one of these when I was a kid."

Taylor grinned at me from his jump seat. "I first rode in one on a field trip in fourth grade."

Jordan twisted to look back at us. "So three years ago?"

Taylor flipped him off. "It was *twelve* years ago. And I still never get sick of riding in it."

"You're young at heart!" I replied.

Derek grunted from the driver's seat. "Young of heart, and body, and mind…"

Taylor rolled his eyes.

We stopped at the Chinese restaurant and Jordan ran inside to pick up our food. Before he could return, the radio on the dashboard let out a siren-like burst of sound.

"*Riverville engine, come in,*" said the person who I assumed was the dispatcher.

"This is Riverville engine two, go ahead," Derek replied.

They spoke back and forth in radio lingo that I didn't

understand. The only phrase I recognized was "non-emergency line." Jordan returned from inside with the food, and climbed up into the passenger seat.

"What's going on?"

"Ten-four, we're en route." Derek put the radio receiver down and turned to Jordan. "We've got a stop to make on the way back."

"Murphy's Law," Jordan said while hastily strapping himself in. "Of course we get our only call of the week *now*."

"It's an easy one," Derek replied. "It'll be fun for Clara and the baby. Hold on, everyone!"

I braced myself, but Derek drove carefully and without the siren blaring. Baby Anthony gazed up at me, as if he could gauge the situation based on my reactions. I smiled back at him and waited to see where we were headed.

The destination was a few blocks away from my family restaurant, in a little corner of a residential neighborhood. We parked in front of a house where four people—two adults and two children—were standing on the lawn, waving at us.

"What is it?" I asked. "I'm not squeamish, but I don't like seeing people distressed..."

"Trust me: you're going to be fine." Jordan was already laughing. "Look at that."

"Hah!" Taylor suddenly said while climbing out of the cab. "Been a while since we've had one of these."

I frowned at the family standing on the lawn. What did the guys find so funny? But then I looked beyond them at their house. More specifically, at the *roof* of their house.

A grey husky dog was standing on the roof.

"What the..."

I rolled down the window of the cab so I could hear the conversation.

"Loki got up on the roof again, huh?" Derek asked.

The mother of the family nodded. "Damnedest thing. Must've grown wings."

The dog—Loki—was standing proudly, jaws open while he looked down on the humans. It was a single-story house; there were no upper-floor windows he could have climbed out of.

"Loki?" Jordan called. "You think you're a good boy, don't you?"

"Awrr awrr awrrrah!" the husky replied noisily.

"He's a bad dog!" the mother said, wagging her finger. "Very bad dog, Loki!"

The dog sat on its haunches on the roof and let out a long, argumentative howl.

The sight was so funny that I couldn't stop myself from giggling. Over in his car seat, Baby Anthony joined me with his own infantile giggling.

Taylor and Jordan brought a ladder down from the fire engine and carried it over to the house. They deployed it while the father of the family warned them not to damage his gutters. All the while, the husky continued to howl at everything and nothing.

"Up you go," Jordan said.

Taylor did a double-take. "Why me?"

"Because you're the youngest, and I had to do it last time. Get on up there and wrestle you a husky."

"Awroooooo!" the dog said.

While the family—and neighbors, by this point—looked on, Taylor climbed the ladder to the roof. Loki the husky backed away as Taylor made it to the top and set foot on the slightly-sloped shingles.

"Come here, buddy."

Taylor reached for the dog, but Loki wasn't having any of it. He deftly ran up to the steepled middle of the roof, then walked along the crest to the edge. Taylor grumbled and followed, but right before he reached the dog, Loki turned and trotted to the other side. All the while, the dog howled and talked in that way only huskies can, jaws chomping in the air as he let out a babble of dog-talk.

"Stop playing around and get the dog," Derek ordered.

Everyone was laughing except Taylor, who was trying to maintain his balance on the roof. Back and forth the two chased each other, like some vintage Tom and Jerry cartoon.

"Come here," Taylor grumbled.

"Awr awr awr!" Loki argued back at him.

Finally, the dog went to the edge of the roof and *leaped* over to the neighbor's roof. The gap must have been twenty feet wide, but the dog made it look effortless. From there, he hopped down to a shed roof, then to the ground below. He ran around to join his waiting family, then sat at the base of the ladder and started barking at Taylor from there.

"You're a real piece of..." Taylor started to say.

"There are children around," Derek scolded.

"...cake," Taylor said while descending the ladder. "Real piece of *cake*."

Loki let out a long howl of agreement.

"Another glorious day in the life of a firefighter," Jordan said, sending a grin my way.

I grinned right back at him as they collected the ladder and returned to the truck.

24

Clara

The guys had a good laugh at Taylor's expense the rest of the evening. It was all good-natured though, and even I got in on the fun.

But I made it up to him that night. Jordan watched Baby Anthony while I tip-toed into Taylor's bedroom, silently kissing him as I slipped under the covers. I pushed him down on the bed and straddled him, giving him a long, slow ride until the bed was rocking so much I was afraid the legs might break.

It was nice having a couple of sexy guys who I could do *anything* I wanted with. Like Uber, but for sex rather than cars. And there wasn't an app involved—I just jumped their bones when I wanted to.

The next day was boring like all the others. Taylor seemed like he was in a weird mood, and I couldn't quite place why.

The answer came after dinner, when Jordan suddenly emerged from the pantry with a round chocolate cake in his hands. Seven candles were lit on top.

"Happy birthday!" he said.

Taylor sank into his couch and chuckled. "I thought you guys forgot!"

Jordan scoffed. "We would never miss our teammate's seventh birthday."

"Ha ha. Very funny," Taylor said, but he was grinning from ear to ear. I could tell he was happy with the gesture.

The three of us sang happy birthday to him, and then he blew out the candles. While Jordan sliced the cake, I asked, "Where'd the cake come from?"

"Chief baked it," Jordan replied.

I swung my head around to Derek. "You baked a cake?"

"What?" he asked. "Baking is easy. Just follow the instructions."

"You're sweet," I said. He gave me an awkward little shrug, but as he turned away from me, I noticed he was trying to hide a smile.

So he has a heart after all.

"When are your birthdays?" I asked while we ate the cake.

"March tenth," Derek replied.

"November twenty-fifth," Jordan said around a mouthful of chocolate cake.

I paused with my fork halfway to my mouth. "Seriously? November twenty-fifth?"

He grimaced. "It sucks. It's always around Thanksgiving."

"It's on Thanksgiving Day next year," I said. "I know because it's *my* birthday, too!"

Derek grunted.

"Seriously? No way," Jordan said.

I pulled out my wallet and handed him my driver's license. "There you go. November twenty-fifth."

Jordan gave me a funny look.

"What?" I asked. "Do you think it's a fake ID or something?"

He glanced at it again, then asked, "Your name's *Clarice?*"

I winced. "Oh no..."

Derek took the license from him and barked a laugh. "I'll be damned. Clara is short for Clarice."

I groaned and closed my eyes. "When my mom moved here in the early nineties, she heard that name everywhere. She decided she loved it, so when I was born six years later, she named me Clarice. She didn't realize where it was from."

"Hello, Clarice!" Jordan said in a creepy voice.

I rolled my eyes. "You're not original. I heard that all throughout high school."

"Man, it's a good thing I didn't know this before," he said. "I never would have slept with you if I had known that. I wouldn't be able to stop picturing Hannibal Lecter!"

"It doesn't bother me!" Taylor announced, putting a hand on my back. "Nothing could stop me from wanting to sleep with you."

Derek grunted, and awkwardly turned away.

"Really?" Jordan insisted. "Not even picturing Hannibal dissecting someone, and then eating their liver with fava beans and a nice chianti?"

"The movie came out before my time," Taylor replied simply. "I've never seen it."

Derek whipped his head back around. "You've never seen *Silence of the Lambs?*"

"Seriously?" Jordan added.

"I'm not into horror movies. Plus, I heard it's overrated. The bad guy, Hannibal or whatever, is only in like eight minutes of the movie."

"The bad guy is Buffalo Bill," Derek corrected him.

Taylor scrunched up his face in confusion. "No. I'm pretty sure it's Hannibal. Which, by the way, isn't a very creative name. He's a cannibal, and his name is *Hannibal*? What kind of Dr. Seuss bullshit is that?"

"The movie is a classic," Jordan insisted.

"Classic?" Derek winced. "Thanks for making me feel old. And after I baked everyone a cake, too."

"Regardless, we should watch it tonight," Jordan said.

"Hard pass," Taylor said. "I don't want to watch a horror movie."

"Afraid it'll give you nightmares?" Derek teased.

"Hey, it's Taylor's birthday," I joked. "We should watch something more age appropriate. The new Pixar movie is streaming now."

Taylor jabbed a finger in my direction. "Pixar movies aren't just for kids. They're fun for the whole family!"

We laughed and teased each other. Even Baby Anthony wanted to join in the fun, and let out a high-pitched baby squeal of laughter. Taylor grabbed a piece of cake and pretended like he was going to hurl it, which sent all of us searching for cover.

We never heard the station door open.

"Don't you dare throw that," Derek warned, "or I'm giving you bathroom cleaning duty for the next month!"

"Hello?" called an unfamiliar voice.

All four of us froze.

"Someone's in the station," Jordan whispered.

"Hell—hello?" came the voice again, drawing closer. "I need some help..."

I grabbed the baby carrier and hurried toward the bedroom hallway. I put Baby Anthony down and peered back around the corner into the kitchen.

A man wearing padded bike shorts and a cycling jersey hobbled into the room. One of his legs was scraped up and red, with blood trickling down his ankle. He was cradling his left arm, and his face was twisted with pain.

The three firemen rushed to help him sit down. "Sir, what happened?"

"My tire had a blow-out," he replied in a shaky voice. "I hit the pavement pretty hard. I didn't want to call an ambulance since I was only a block away, to the west—" He started to point with his wounded arm, then let out a cry of agony and let it go limp again.

Taylor grabbed a med kit out of the other room and began cleaning up the man's leg. "How's your head?" Derek asked him.

"Helmet took most of the impact, but I still hit it hard. My ears are kind of ringing. I thought I heard a baby squealing when I came through the door."

"No babies here," Taylor said, deadpan.

Jordan unclipped the helmet and gently removed it. "Might need to give you a concussion test. Just to be safe."

Derek took the man's arm and gently straightened it. "Arm's broken. We'll need to call an ambulance after all."

"Aw, man," the guy said. "I'm sorry to bother you, then..."

"No worries," Jordan said. "We'll take good care of you until they get here."

Derek glanced over at me and raised his eyebrows. *That was a close call.*

I retreated to the bedroom with Baby Anthony before the ambulance could arrive.

25

Clara

I fell asleep quickly that night, but I woke in a cold sweat not long after. I'd had a dream where we got caught. Baby Anthony was taken away from us and Derek lost his job. Billy Manning took over as head of the station, and for some reason—with nonsensical dream logic—I had to remain at the firehouse and do whatever he told me.

I panted in bed while catching my breath. I wish I could dismiss it as a silly dream, but the danger of getting caught was very real. Not just because of the cyclist who wandered into the station, but because of Billy himself. Nothing good could come from him knowing I was at the station with a baby. Eventually, the story might unravel.

I rolled over and expected to see Baby Anthony asleep in his bassinet—which Derek had bought on the same trip when he got the car seat—but the bassinet was empty. It took me three long seconds to realize what I was looking at.

The baby is gone.

I flew out of bed in a panic and rushed down the hall. It took all of my willpower not to scream at the top of my lungs, to warn everyone that the baby was missing.

I skidded to a stop in the living room. Derek was sitting on the couch, holding Baby Anthony against his chest. The baby rose and fell with the bigger man's breathing.

Relief washed over me as I took in the sight. And once again, my heart went out to Derek. The way he cared for the baby was so beautiful.

He glanced over at me. "Why aren't you sleeping?" he whispered.

I walked over and sat on the edge of the couch. "I should ask you the same thing."

"Stress," he replied softly. He gently put his hand on the baby's back. "I was worrying about this little guy."

I smiled sadly. "Me too. The cyclist has me spooked. That and Billy finding out about us."

"Yeah." Derek caressed the baby lovingly. "I've been wondering if I'm doing the right thing. I keep going back and forth on it. Would it really be so bad for one of the foster families to take him? Maybe it would be better than risking my job."

The baby shifted as Derek sighed. "But then I pick Anthony up and bring him out here. And while he's sleeping on my chest, I know I can't turn him over to anyone who won't give him one hundred percent of their love and attention. There are a *lot* of great foster families out there, but the only ones available right now are sub-par. I can't allow him to go to a foster family that is just doing it to collect extra money."

I reached out and put my hand over his on top of the baby. "You're a good man, Derek."

"I'm just a man doing what he knows is right. There's no good or bad about that."

There was something deeper in his comment. A hint of vulnerability. I reached for it while it was available.

"Why are you doing this?" I asked. "The real reason. Why are you so emphatic about making sure the baby goes to a good foster family?"

I expected him to put up some sort of wall. To insist there was no deeper motivation. Instead, he answered bluntly.

"Because three decades ago, I was in his position." He nodded down at the baby. "I was orphaned when I was four. And I was put into an overloaded foster care system. It was awful."

Icy fingers tightened around my heart. "Oh, Derek..."

"Don't get me wrong—there are a *lot* of amazing foster families out there," he said. His voice was wooden and emotionless, presumably from years of practice talking about his pained past. "But the family I was sent to? They weren't one of them. They were doing it for the money. There was no love, no support, no caring environment at all. The father hated us, and never said more than two words to me. The mother was, at best, neutral toward us. There were five of us in that home. We pretty much raised each other." He smiled. "We survived, though. And the experience is the reason my sister—foster sister, technically—went to work for the California Department of Social Services. To make a better place for kids just like us."

I put a hand on his arm. "Derek. I'm so sorry that happened to you."

"Yeah, me too. But it made me the man I am today. And it's the reason I'm willing to risk my job to protect this little guy." His weathered face smiled over at me. "This whole thing is much easier with you here. Thanks for helping us."

"You *are* paying me," I reminded him.

He gave me a long, knowing look. It made me shiver, but not in a bad way. His gaze felt like a caress against my bare skin.

"You're not doing it for the money," he said simply. "You're doing it because you want to help."

I cringed. "You should know that I originally wanted to help for the wrong reasons. When I agreed, I only did so because I wanted to stay close to Jordan."

One of Derek's dark eyebrows rose. "Really?"

I nodded and plowed on with my confession. "It's true. I was only doing it for selfish reasons. And because I thought the baby was a sign."

"A sign?"

"His name is the same as my father's," I said. "It sounds stupid now, I know. Anthony is a common name. But a lot has changed in the past week. This little guy? I care about him *so much*. I feel like so much more than just a babysitter. I feel like a parent, putting his own needs above my own without a second thought. I would do anything for him."

Derek nodded. "I feel the same way." He gently put the baby down in his bassinet. "And you're right. A lot has changed in the last week. You're seeing both Jordan *and* Taylor, now."

I waited for him to say more, but he only focused on Anthony's blankets in the bassinet, tucking him in with care. Why was he bringing it up now? It almost felt like he was judging me for it.

Does he like me, or not?

I was sick of beating around the bush. One day Derek would treat me with respect, and other days he seemed to want nothing to do with me. I was too tired, too exhausted and stressed out, to deal with this. I needed answers.

"Hey," I said, touching his arm to get his attention. "Do you really like me, or not?"

He grunted. "What do you mean?"

"Jordan said you and Taylor wanted to share me," I said. "But when I showed up to help, you were upset at Jordan for inviting me. Then you yelled at me about the stupid oven. Sometimes I catch you looking at me when you think I'm not paying attention, and then other times you give me the cold shoulder. Well?"

"I like you, Clara," he said bluntly.

I snorted out my nose. "Then what's the problem? You haven't made a move or shown me any outright affection since I got here."

He rested his head in his hands and sighed. "I don't know. It's several things."

"Like what?" I demanded. When he didn't respond, I nudged him with my foot. "Hey. Come on. Spill it."

"I'm new to all of this," he replied. "I've never shared someone before. I don't know how it works. And I didn't want to seem presumptive about how *you* feel. I was worried you might be weirded out by the age difference, too."

"You're not *that* old," I said.

"No," he said with a wry smirk, "but I'm old enough for it to be weird. Not to me or you, but to others."

"I don't care what other people think," I said automatically. After a moment, I realized I meant it.

"There's also *him*." Derek gestured at the sleeping bundle of joy in the bassinet. "I've been totally focused on him. He's occupied almost all of my attention and thoughts for the past two weeks."

"I get that," I said. "But it seems pointless to worry about things you can't control."

"You're not wrong. But that doesn't mean I don't do it. Being in charge is a burden." He shook his head and twisted to face me on the couch, dark eyes glistening in the soft lamp light. "I like you, Clara. I really do. Especially now that I've gotten to know you."

"You have a strange way of showing it," I muttered.

Annoyance flashed in his eyes, and then something like a challenge. Before I could react, he slid down the couch, grabbed my head with both strong hands, and crushed his lips against mine

I tensed with surprise, but then I felt the desire inside of him. He was telling the truth: he had wanted to do this for a long time, and had been holding himself back.

I breathed in his scent, full of smoke and cedar wood and his deeper, musky fragrance. My body came alive as his lips churned against mine with need, and soon I was kissing him back just as passionately.

Where has this man been hiding for the last two weeks?

Derek pulled away and gave me a satisfied glare. "How's that for showing it?"

I bit my lip and nodded. "Mmm hmm. That's better."

One of his eyebrows climbed up his forehead. "Just better?"

He dove into me again, kissing me harder than before and pushing me back against the cushions with his body. My hips surged upward with need as he laid me flat, finally proving to me how he *really* felt.

I glanced at the hallway leading to the front door of the station. "What if someone else wanders into the station in the middle of the night?"

"I don't care," Derek said.

He means it. The only thing he cared about right now was what he was going to do to me.

We clung and clutched to each other as the kiss deepened. His fingers danced their way down my navel, sending shivers up my spine. I spread my legs for him eagerly, and he took the hint and shoved his hand underneath the elastic of my pajamas, beyond the panties and into the warm depths of my pussy.

I craned my head back and sighed loudly.

"You're drenched," he whispered, breath hot and tickling against my neck.

"For you," I replied.

A smiling snarl touched his lips, and then Derek went to work undressing me. I don't know how he yanked off my pajamas and panties without tearing them. The air was cool on my wet lips while I watched him pull off his own blue fireman's pants, and the briefs underneath.

I caught a glimpse of him for a brief second—he was already as hard as could be—before he smothered me with his body. Our motions were desperate and eager as he guided his crown into my lips, breath quickening.

I gasped as he plunged into my wet folds, throwing the weight of his entire body behind the erotic joining. Both of us groaned together, muscles tensing together and fingers clawing while we savored the moment.

And that makes three, I thought faintly.

But Derek wasn't here to take his time. He was a man who knew what he wanted, who was going to *prove* it to me, and nothing was going to make him delay any longer.

I cradled his head in my hands and kissed him, as the two of us lost ourselves in the pent-up, unleashed desire.

26

Derek

For the past two weeks, I couldn't even begin to think about a romantic relationship. Hell, it was downright selfish while we had Baby Anthony to take care of. To say nothing of our actual job at the firehouse.

But Clara was here, and I wanted her desperately. I had wanted her ever since she first set foot in the station, making her first pizza delivery a year ago. She was so many things: she was cute, she was gorgeous, she was devastatingly *beautiful,* in a natural, curvy way.

She was a real woman. She was everything I never knew I wanted.

And no matter what else was going on, I couldn't delay what I wanted anymore.

There was electricity to our frenzied lovemaking on the couch. It was more than just physical attraction: we shared a passion for taking care of another living soul. We were two people united by our desire to do the right thing, no matter the consequences.

Being on the same team like that made everything different. The way I felt when I kissed her was out of this world.

And now that I was *inside* of her?

Clara's pussy was the kind of thing men wrote epic poems about. It was the Helen of Troy of lady-parts. The moment I sank into her, all the way to my base, I could have died happy. And I'm only exaggerating a *little bit*.

Being inside of her felt like comfort. Like safety. Like it was the home I never really knew I had.

I drove into her on the couch without holding back. Clara wrapped her legs around me and surged upward with need, taking every stroke with her entire voluptuous body. I could feel her hard nipples through her pajama top, brushing against my own shirt, so I slipped my hand inside to cup one of them. She was full and warm beneath my fingertips, even better than I had imagined.

And I had been doing a *lot* of imagining these past two weeks.

There were no words as we lost ourselves in the motion of our hungry bodies. Knowing that anyone could walk into the station at that moment somehow heightened the pleasure, and added urgency to our act.

Clara's entire body went tight like a wire and she opened her mouth in a silent cry of pleasure. She clamped her pussy lips around me while she climaxed, which made me absolutely fall apart in her arms. I pushed myself as deep as I could go, even deeper thanks to the way she was arching her back to take all of me, and then I was destroyed by an overpowering orgasm. My cock erupted inside of her and I had to clench my teeth to keep from screaming with ecstasy.

Clara gazed up at me with desire, and continued squeezing her lower lips tightly, like she was trying to milk every ounce of my seed. I throbbed and gasped and pulsed inside of her, unleashing two weeks of sexual tension while she squeezed her hand into my hair and held me close.

For the first time since I could remember, I lost myself in a woman.

*

We clung to each other, bodies sweaty and still hot from the act.

"Glad no cyclists walked in," Clara purred up at me.

Her neck was exposed, so I bent down and gave her a soft kiss. "We should probably get dressed. Just in case."

"You say that," she replied softly, "but you haven't moved."

"My body won't let me. It wants to stay right here, inside of you."

She giggled, which caused her inner muscles to clamp down even tighter on my shaft. "I don't mind."

Eventually, we pulled apart and started to get dressed. Clara reached over and tried to smack my bare ass when I bent over, so I grabbed her arm and pushed her down on the couch, giving *her* firm backside a satisfying smack. She giggled and pushed me away playfully, and then we grinned while collecting our clothes.

This woman has me acting like I'm twenty again. But it wasn't an act. She made me *feel* like I was twenty. Like we were a couple of kids fooling around. Young, frisky, and fun.

I certainly didn't mind it.

I sat back on the couch. Clara gave me a long kiss, then rested across me with her head in my lap. I gently stroked her hair. It was silky and smooth, much more than I had expected.

I've waited a year to run my hands through this hair. The thought made me happy. And peaceful.

"You should have done that a week ago," Clara said. "Instead of being a grump."

"I have an excuse. I've had a lot on my mind, in case you didn't notice."

"That doesn't mean you can't be a nice guy," she said.

"I'm a nice guy. I baked Taylor a birthday cake."

"You could have been nicer to *me*," she clarified.

I ran my thumb along the side of her eyebrow. "Is that what you want? Someone who's *nice* in bed? Because I can be gentle next time, if you want."

She twisted and giggled up at me. "Don't you *dare* change a thing."

I bent down and kissed her. "Wasn't planning on it."

We relaxed together for a while, and then eventually she got up to use the bathroom. When she was done, I did the same thing to clean myself off.

As I looked at myself in the mirror, I realized I was smiling. A *genuine* smile. I couldn't remember the last time I had looked this way.

She's right, I thought. *I should have made a move on her a week ago.*

Suddenly a siren pierced the air. It wasn't very loud since I had dimmed the volume, and sounded more like someone's nearby phone alarm going off than a station-wide siren, but it was enough to get my attention. And enough to wake the baby.

Anthony was crying in Clara's arms as I rushed back out to the living room. For a brief second, I was distracted by how *beautiful* she looked. Cradling the baby protectively, she looked motherly and powerful. The caveman part of my brain was immediately attracted to the sight.

"A call at one in the morning?" she said while comforting the baby. "Hope it's not serious."

"We'll see." I gave her a kiss on the cheek in passing, patted Baby Anthony on the cheek, then ran toward the garage. Jordan and Taylor were only seconds behind me.

Adrenaline was a hell of a drug. Even with the heart-pounding excitement that I had just shared with Clara, it paled in comparison to throwing on my gear and preparing to head out on a call.

"Dispatch, this is Riverville station," Jordan said into the radio as I drove the fire engine out of the garage. "What do we have?"

"*Kitchen fire at one-three-niner Alston Street,*" she replied. "*They put it out with their kitchen fire extinguisher, but the neighbors still called it in.*"

Taylor scoffed in the back cab. "Pete's making midnight quesadillas again."

I grimaced. This wasn't the first call we'd gotten to that address, and it was always because Pete Delgado got hungry in the middle of the night, started cooking food, and then fell asleep again.

As I drove to the scene, I thought about Clara, and what we had done together. I hadn't realized how much I *needed* that. I felt clear-headed for the first time since I could remember.

"You okay, Chief?" Jordan asked me.

I realized he was staring at me. "Why?"

"You look... happy."

"Me being happy worries you?"

"A little, yeah," he replied.

I tried to act casual, but I couldn't keep that same smile from sliding onto my face. And of course, trying to suppress it only made it more obvious.

"Wait a minute. Did what I think happen finally happen?" he asked.

I pulled up in front of the Delgado residence, which was trailing faint smoke from the left side. "Maybe."

"What happened? What'd I miss?" Taylor demanded.

"Chief finally *buried the hatchet* with Clara."

"Oh shit!" Taylor looked as excited as a puppy. "Is this a metaphor? Is the hatchet his penis?"

"Shut up and move out," I said while climbing out of the fire engine.

The two of them continued laughing and congratulating each other while we approached the house.

And me? Well, I couldn't stop smiling.

27

Clara

"I need your honest opinion," I said with grave seriousness. "If I'm being dumb, then don't be afraid to tell me. Okay? Here goes. I'm dating three men at the same time."

Baby Anthony stared up at me from his bassinet.

"It was their idea!" I said defensively. "They *want* to share me. They don't even seem weird about it, aside from some joking comments to each other. Is that so wrong? Is it totally scandalous and crazy?"

Baby Anthony scrunched his face up like he was trying to fill his diaper.

"Yeah, well, nobody asked you," I muttered to him.

I kept replaying the night in my head. It felt like Derek and I had gone from polite acquaintances to lovers in the blink of an eye. I guess all that awkward sexual tension really was real all along.

And boy was it worth the wait!

All three men were good in bed. *Better* than good. But Derek had a confidence unlike the other two. A deliberateness that was incredibly sexy. If that's what came from an extra ten years of age, then sign me up.

I glanced at my watch. It was one-thirty. When I had woken up an hour ago, I was anxious and filled with stress. Now everything seemed like it would work out.

I guess a girl just needs to get laid sometimes.

Derek came home and joined me in bed some time later. "Everything okay?" I asked.

"Kitchen fire," he said while slipping under the covers with me. "Already put out before we got there."

I sniffed. "You smell like smoke."

He froze in the process of pulling the blankets over him. "I already showered, but I can take another one..."

"Shut up and cuddle with me," I said. "I don't mind."

The scent was a little distracting, but it was worth it to have his warm, powerful body spooning mine. As long as I was cuddled up into his frame, I felt safe.

And happy.

When I woke up the next morning, I wondered how I was going to bring up the subject to the other two. It seemed uncouth to blurt out, "Hey, I slept with the Chief," while eating bacon and eggs.

But when I went into the kitchen, the three men were already awake and talking about it.

"Heard you had a busier evening than us last night!" Jordan said with a knowing smile.

Taylor was bouncing the baby against his chest. "He finally opened up, huh? Well, I think it's great!"

"We don't need to discuss it," Derek grumbled while sipping coffee. "This isn't a town hall meeting."

Jordan clapped him on the shoulder. "Aw, come on, Chief. We're *really* teammates now."

"I believe the term is *eskimo brothers*," Taylor chimed in. He took one of Baby Anthony's little hands and waved it for him. "Say good morning to my eskimo brothers!"

"I regret everything about this situation," Derek said.

"Everything?" I asked.

He got up and strode toward me with a loving smile. "Everything except for one thing. This." Derek took me in his arms and gave me a long kiss.

"Good morning," he rumbled.

"I haven't even brushed my teeth yet," I said, but I was grinning like an idiot at the same time.

"I never understood people who do that," Taylor said. "Brushing your teeth as soon as you wake up makes *no* sense. You should wait until you've had breakfast, *then* brush your teeth."

"Speaking of breakfast, would any of you boys like to fix me a plate?"

"Right away, dear," Jordan said. He began scooping sausage links off a skillet. "How many do you want?"

"Three, please," I replied.

Jordan sniggered.

I glared at him.

"What?" he asked. "It's a funny metaphor."

"If you're *eleven*," Derek said. "I would expect that from Taylor, but not you."

Taylor frowned. "Aw, come on."

Jordan put the plate in front of me at the table. I realized I was starving, so I quickly began wolfing down eggs and sausage.

"What do you think?" Jordan asked.

"The eggs are a little runny, but I don't mind," I said.

"I meant about... the *situation*. And I don't mean that idiot from *Jersey Shore.*"

"Oh." I put down my fork. "Why are you asking me now? I agreed to it, didn't I?"

"But you hadn't actually gone through with the whole thing," Taylor pointed out. "It's different now that you've slept with all three of us. So what do you think?"

"I think discussing it over breakfast is kind of weird." I looked at him, then Jordan, then Derek. "But aside from that? I don't mind being shared by you three."

"Don't mind?" Jordan asked incredulously. "I thought you would be more enthusiastic about the whole thing. I know I would be if I had three gorgeous women sharing me."

I gave him a look. Jordan turned two shades of red.

"Not that I want three other women," he quickly said. "You're plenty for me."

"That's what I thought." I speared a sausage and gestured with it. "It hasn't been going on very long, though. Let's give it some more time before passing judgment. Being with all three of you may get tough when we sit down and, say, try to watch a movie together."

Derek barked a laugh. "Jordan likes watching rom-coms, and Taylor hasn't even seen *Silence of the Lambs.* If a fight about movies is all it takes to scare you away, Clara, then I don't think we'll last beyond next Saturday."

"It's a dumb movie!" Taylor insisted. He turned Baby Anthony around in his arms and began speaking to him in a soothing voice. "His name is Hannibal, and he's a *cannibal.* If that movie came out tomorrow, social media would rip it apart."

Derek rolled his eyes and flipped to a different page of his newspaper.

Jordan leaned against the kitchen counter and crossed his arms over his chest. He watched me eat for at least two straight minutes.

"What?" I finally asked. "You're making me feel like a zoo

animal."

"Oh, nothing," he replied. "I was just wondering which of us you like the best. In bed."

I almost spit out my bite of eggs. "Seriously? I would expect you guys to be more mature than that."

"What a childish question," Derek agreed. Then he slowly lowered his newspaper. "Especially since the answer is clearly me."

Taylor scoffed. "Fat chance, old man. Err, I mean, Chief."

"You think it's *you?*" Jordan asked Taylor. "She wants a real man. Put on another thirty pounds of muscle and maybe then you can throw her around in the bedroom."

"I'm *lean*, unlike you gorillas," Taylor shot back.

Baby Anthony happily flailed his arms as if he were part of the argument.

"You all have your strengths," I said diplomatically. "That's what I like about being with all three of you. Your different styles compliment each other well."

All three of them were silent for a moment.

"That's not an answer," Derek pointed out.

"Ugh!" I carried my plate to the sink, rinsed it off, and put it in the dishwasher. "My attraction to you three is dwindling by the minute."

Jordan came up and hugged me from behind. "We'll stop. We're just having some competitive fun."

I sighed happily in his arms. "It's eight in the morning. Let's save this kind of discussion for later in the day, after I've had coffee, okay?"

"Deal."

He kissed me on the crown of my head, and then we heard a noise deeper in the station. Seconds later, a familiar face appeared in the doorway to the kitchen.

I gawked. "*Mom?*"

My little Sicilian mother barely even acknowledged me. She hurried over to Taylor and took the baby out of his arms. She immediately began cooing to him in Italian, rocking him back and forth and smiling like she had gone to heaven.

"Uh," Derek said. "Mrs. Ricci? What are you doing here?"

"Shush," she said to him. "Baby time." She twisted him around and opened her mouth wide for him. Thus prompted, Anthony opened his own mouth in a toothless smile.

Derek gave me a look. I nodded.

"Mom, you can't be here," I said. "It's too risky. Nobody is supposed to know the baby is here."

"I do not care!" she announced stubbornly. "I have been patient. I have waited. I have even lied for you! I want to see baby, now."

I gave a start. "You lied for me? When?"

She sat down and bounced the baby in her lap. She had the magic touch, because everything she did made Anthony squeal happily. "That man came to the restaurant. Awful man. Yuck. Romancing Angelina even though she is married woman."

"Did he say anything to you?" Derek asked.

"He asked about the baby. I pretended to be angry with you about it, and said I would not discuss my daughter. He believed me, I think. And so, I deserve my reward!" She began smothering the baby with kisses.

Derek's jaw clenched. "I knew Billy would snoop around. Checking our story."

"He asked about the baby's father," Mom went on, "but I said nothing. I only acted angry. It was good acting, because I would not be angry! I would be very happy to have grandbabies."

"You have a grandson already," I reminded her. "Jason and

Maurice's son..."

"I love LeBron, but he lives down in Los Angeles, and you are *here*," she said. "Then she stood up and walked over to Jordan. "I want *many* babies. Do you know who can give them to her, hmm?"

Jordan looked like a deer caught in the headlights as Mom cackled and patted him on the cheek. She even gave one of his arms a squeeze and said, "Strong babies! Very strong!" before resuming focusing on Anthony.

I cringed through the whole thing. "That's enough, Mom."

"What?" She gestured at him. "He is big and strong. Very good. I approve." She turned toward him. "I approve, fire man! Take my daughter!"

I let out a long, embarrassed groan.

Derek allowed Mom to stay for half an hour. We went into the living room and she played with him on the floor. When Jordan tried to turn the TV to a replay of last night's Giants game, Mom snapped at him and insisted that we play the Dodgers instead. Jordan changed the channel without a fuss.

"Mom may only be a hundred pounds, but she gets what she wants," I whispered to him. "It's best not to fight her."

"I can see that."

Eventually Derek cleared his throat and made some comments about needing to clean up the firehouse. Mom took the hint and finally got up off the floor.

"I bring you food later," she said. "No charge. A thank you for playing with the baby."

"That's real nice of you," Derek said. "But we'll insist on paying."

She ignored him and patted Jordan's cheek. "My daughter loves bringing you the Friday order. When you call, she makes the giggle face!"

"Ugh, *Mom*. Stop it!"

Taylor grinned. "I want to hear all about the giggle face, Mrs. Ricci."

"Mom has to open the restaurant," I said, ushering her out the front door. "Lots of prep-work to do before lunch."

She made an annoyed sound. "Restaurant does not need me so much. Nobody comes for lunch."

Derek cleared his throat. "Is business not so great, Mrs. Ricci?"

"It had a few people in it the last time I was there!" Taylor said hopefully. "I mean, I guess it was just two, but still..."

Before Mom could tell them all about the restaurant's money problems, I continued pushing her toward the door. "Thanks Mom, love you, bye."

The guys were all smiles when I returned to the kitchen. "Grandbabies, huh?" Jordan asked.

"Don't start," I warned.

Taylor playfully squeezed Jordan's bicep. "So strong!"

"You're just jealous she likes me," Jordan said.

"It seems to me she doesn't want a son-in-law," Derek said. "She wants a sperm donor for her daughter. You just happen to be her best chance."

"Or so she thinks," Taylor said with a smile. "Wonder what she would think of this whole arrangement."

"We're going to *keep* wondering," I cut in forcefully, "because she's never going to find out. We're lucky it was Jordan hugging me by the sink when she walked in. If it was one of you two, I don't know how I would have explained it."

"I like her!" Taylor said. "For such a small woman, she's got a whole bucketload of attitude. I bet she was even feistier when she was young."

"Contrary to what you might think, she's gotten more feisty

with age." I took Anthony out of his bassinet and checked his diaper. "And she won't be satisfied until she has an entire Italian soccer team worth of grandchildren."

"I bet she'd like all three of us, then!" Taylor insisted. "More guys dating you means more chances for..."

He trailed off at a glare from me.

"It's been a week," I said dryly. "Let's not get ahead of ourselves."

But as I went to put the baby down for his nap, I couldn't help but smile at the fact that the guys had met my mom, and everyone had gotten along.

It was a weird step in this weird four-person relationship, but it still felt like a step forward.

28

Clara

Like last weekend, we transferred our whole baby-taking-care-of troupe to Derek's house in phases. I left the fire station around seven, to avoid seeing any of the second-shift guys.

I wasn't sure how much it mattered. Billy already knew I was staying there sporadically, even if he didn't know the true reason. And word had probably spread among the other guys. But the less I saw of them, the less Billy could interrogate me. I didn't exactly consider myself to be a master liar, so I was happy to avoid any chance at getting caught in a gotcha-moment.

I settled into the living room with Baby Anthony. The Dodgers had already won today (yay!) but that meant the only game on TV was the Giants (boo). But the baby seemed to enjoy having some background noise on, and I enjoyed rooting *against* the Giants.

The guys got home ten minutes after nine. They tip-toed into the house like teenagers who were afraid of waking their parents, but they relaxed when they saw me feeding Baby Anthony.

"He's been up a while," I said. "He's having a cranky night."

Derek smiled and gently put his hand on the baby's back. "I'll never get tired of seeing you with him."

I raised an eyebrow. "Why? Because all a woman's good for is taking care of babies?"

I was only teasing him, but he gave me a serious response. "No. Because you always smile when you're holding him. Like you're happy, in a different way than normal."

I frowned, unable to think of anything good to respond with.

"Your favorite fireman asked about you," Jordan said.

It took me a moment to realize who he meant. "Ugh. Don't even say that."

"He was awfully suspicious that you weren't there," Taylor chimed in. He gave me a quick peck on the cheek, then looked abashed about it, and began to blush. "The other second-shifters didn't seem to care. But Billy was awfully curious about your life."

"They probably understood that you didn't want to be around Billy," Jordan said. "Everyone knows how creepy he is."

"How about we don't discuss him?" I suggested. "What's the plan for this weekend? Relax and watch the Giants lose to the Padres? Oh wait—we're already doing that. They're down six runs in the ninth inning." I gestured at the TV and smirked.

Derek rolled his eyes. "I have a plan. About Baby Anthony."

I blinked. "Oh?"

"My sister and I are driving up to Sacramento to talk to an administrator with Social Services," he explained. "We might be able to speed things along, or get some emergency funding, without tipping our hand too much. My sister thinks it's worth it. At the very least, we'll get a feel for how much longer we should wait before putting him in the system. Then we'll know the best way to proceed."

"That's great," I said. "How long will it take?"

"We're leaving first thing in the morning. It's only three hours away, so hopefully we'll be back by tomorrow evening. Regardless, I'm not coming back until I have some idea of what to do." He gently caressed the baby's tufts of black hair.

"Hopefully we'll have a better understanding of what happens next," I said. "Regardless, I'll keep helping with the baby for as long as we need." I kissed Anthony on the forehead for emphasis.

Derek smiled at me, then turned to his fireman teammates. "I've got a job for you two."

"A job? Anything, Chief," Taylor said.

"I need you to watch the baby for a little while."

Jordan frowned. "Why?"

Derek gave me a wolfish grin. "Because I'm late to the Clara-sharing party, and I have some ground to make up."

The moment Jordan took the baby out of my arms, Derek bent down like a football player making a tackle, wrapping his arms around my waist and then *hefting* me over his shoulder. I let out a yelp as he carried me to the stairs.

"I probably smell like baby powder!" I protested.

"You could smell like skunk," Derek growled, "and it wouldn't stop me from what I'm about to do to you."

I giggled as he carried me up the stairs. The last thing I heard was Jordan muttering, "Show off."

Derek's bed was big and comfortable, and after our erotic activities, I slept like a log. That probably had more to do with how much the fire captain wore me out, rather than the comfort of the bed itself, but either way I slept happily until my alarm went off.

But I woke up alone, with a note on my pillow:

Let's do more of that when I get back.

I grinned and went downstairs to get some breakfast. Then I grinned even harder when I was greeted by the other two firemen, sitting and eating breakfast. Taylor looked totally normal with a spoon in his hand, but Jordan had a new accessory.

A chest baby-carrier. Which Anthony was sleeping soundly in, his limbs all hanging limply while the huge fireman ate his Corn Flakes.

"Now *there's* a gorgeous sight," I said.

"I was about to say the same to you," he replied. "I like those pajamas."

I went to the fridge and made sure to bend over like I was reaching for something, even though the orange juice was on the top shelf. The guys were staring so hard I could practically feel their gazes.

Jordan swiveled on his breakfast stool until he was looking away from me. "What's the matter?" I asked. "Don't want to get too much of an eyeful?"

"Definitely not worried about that," he replied. "I'm just turning this way so Baby Anthony could get a look." He bent down and lowered his voice. "Trust me, little dude. You're going to appreciate this some day."

"Gross," Taylor said. "She's been, like, caring for him like a mom."

"Eh, she's more like a nanny," Jordan replied. "Or a babysitter. I had a *huge* crush on my babysitter when I was a kid."

"I think it's different when the baby's so young that I'm feeding him with a bottle," I said dryly. "To him, my breasts are like a salad bar rather than something sexy."

Jordan groaned and swiveled back around. "Fine. Go bend over again so I can enjoy it all myself."

"Nope," I replied while pouring orange juice. "You missed your chance."

"Thanks a lot," Jordan muttered to the baby, who continued sleeping peacefully against his chest.

After a breakfast filled with more playful teasing, Taylor drove up to visit his family so they could celebrate his birthday. Jordan and I spent the day binging romantic comedies on Netflix, and then discussing how realistic the plots were.

Jordan made us grilled cheeses for lunch while I fed the baby. After more romantic comedies, I cooked chicken marsala with roasted veggies.

It was fun. It was like the two of us were playing house—even though it wasn't *our* house. There was no pressure, aside from keeping the baby happy and his diaper clean.

I liked it. The whole thing was deeply satisfying, like I was getting a glimpse into the future. Of a future I *could* have with someone.

Or three someones, I thought.

Derek called and told us that he wouldn't be home until tomorrow. He and his sister hadn't been able to get a meeting with the administrator they were looking for, but she was making time for them on Sunday after church.

Taylor got back from his family birthday celebration a little after that. "I need a drink," he said the moment he came through the door.

"You had that much fun, huh?" I asked.

He dropped his backpack into a chair. "Don't get me wrong. I love them. But they're best in small doses. And six hours with them was about five too many."

Jordan opened the cabinet to the liquor bar. "Derek did tell us to make ourselves at home. Looks like he has all the ingredients to make margaritas."

"I'll take seven," Taylor said.

I raised an eyebrow at him. "Are you old enough to drink?"

"Ha ha," he said dryly. "Just for that, you're not getting a *nice to see you again* kiss."

I carried the baby over to him and then kissed Taylor on the lips. He returned the kiss eagerly, without trying to stop me.

"That's what I thought," I said with a wink.

Jordan made his margaritas *very* strong, with lots of salt around the rim. I was good and tipsy after one of them, and it looked like the guys weren't too far behind me.

Taylor fiddled with his phone, then suddenly frowned at the TV. "What the hell are we watching? Tom Hanks and Meg Ryan?"

"*You've Got Mail* is a classic!" Jordan argued.

"Classic is just another word for *old*."

"You're not allowed to give your opinion on movies anymore," I teased. "You can watch cartoons in the morning."

He gave me a playful glare. "You know, your mom arrived at the perfect time yesterday."

I reached down and placed Baby Anthony in his bassinet on the floor. "Perfect, how?"

"She helped you dodge the question we had asked. About which of us was best in bed."

I laughed it off. "I forgot all about that. Thanks, Mom."

Taylor slid closer to me on the couch until our thighs were touching. He was wearing jeans, but I could still feel his warmth against my skin. "Well? Are you going to answer the question now?"

"Like I said: you all have your strengths."

"That's a cop-out," Taylor complained.

"It's true," I replied while sipping on my second drink.

On the other side of me, Jordan snorted. "She's trying not to hurt your feelings, buddy. I'm pretty sure you wouldn't like the answer."

"Pfft. Yeah, right." Taylor ran his fingers through his blond hair. "That's not true, is it, Clara?"

I shrugged casually. "If you guys keep pestering me, I'll tell you that you're *all* bad in bed."

Jordan's arm slid around my shoulder. "Now I know you're lying."

"Definitely lying," Taylor agreed.

"If you say so," I said innocently.

Jordan's fingers began caressing the back of my neck. "You sound like you need some convincing. Taylor, do you mind watching the baby tonight?"

Taylor made a face. "You hung out with Clara all day. I was hoping to spend some alone time with her tonight."

"Neither of you called *dibs* on me," I said.

Both of them stared at each for a moment, then shouted, "DIBS!" at the same time.

"Shh, you'll wake the baby," I whispered.

"I called dibs first," Jordan said.

Taylor shook his head. "Did not!"

"This bickering is *very* sexy," I said.

Jordan ignored me and began caressing my leg. "I'm taking Clara upstairs."

Taylor jumped to his feet. "Then I'm coming too."

"Are you suggesting we share her?" Jordan asked mockingly.

"Why not?" Taylor shot back. He put his hand on my other leg. "We're sharing her in every other way!"

"Fine by me!" Jordan replied stubbornly. "As long as Clara doesn't mind!"

I froze. "Wait a minute. Are you suggesting what I think you're suggesting?"

29

Clara

The guys seemed confused, like they didn't really understand what they had agreed to in their possessive bickering. Then Taylor's mouth curled into an O shape of surprise.

"Yeah," Jordan said. "I think we are suggesting that."

Slowly, Taylor nodded.

It took me several heartbeats to find the words I wanted to say. "You want to have a *sex threesome?*"

"I think you can just say threesome," Jordan replied. Taylor nodded in agreement.

"How am I supposed to know that!" I hissed, trying to keep my voice low for the sleeping baby's sake. "I've never done this before!"

Taylor awkwardly rubbed the back of his neck. "Neither have I."

"I haven't," Jordan said quietly. "Not precisely."

I whirled toward him. "Not precisely?"

"Okay, not at all," he admitted. "I've never had a threesome. But I'm willing to try it."

I looked at each of them in turn. I was kind of bewildered that they would be interested in this. It was one thing to share me on different nights, by themselves. But together like this...

I want to do it, I realized. I had never really fantasized about having a threesome before, but maybe that was because I had never known the right two guys. But now that I was flanked by them on the couch, the target of their possessive desire? I wanted it badly.

"What about you?" I asked Taylor. "Are you comfortable with this?"

Taylor gulped down the rest of his second margarita. "Okay, yeah," he said while wiping his mouth. "I'm comfortable with it. Especially if it puts us ahead of the Chief."

I gave him a look. "Is that the only reason you want to do it? To one-up Derek?"

Taylor grinned. "Not the main reason, no."

Slowly, we all got up from the couch and went upstairs. Jordan carried the baby in his bassinet. The steps seemed extra creaky tonight, like the house knew what we were doing and was judging us for it.

Judge me all you want, I thought. *This is really happening.*

We went into my room, the one with all the typewriters. Taylor closed the door behind us, even though there wasn't really a need. Jordan carefully put down the baby bassinet, then paused to make sure Anthony was still sleeping quietly.

Then he turned to me, threw me up against the wall, and kissed me like he was trying to win a contest.

I melted under the churning of Jordan's lips, and the unexpected force of his passion. The whole thing took me by surprise—in a good way. A *really* good way.

Jordan hadn't acted like this before.

I liked this side of him.

Then Taylor was there, pulling me away from his friend and

taking his turn with me, holding me against his body while nuzzling at my neck. I craned my head and panted, catching my breath while I could. Jordan leaned against the wall and watched, eyes hungry and waiting.

I can't believe I'm doing this.

I had been with each of them privately. Everyone knew what was going on. But kissing Taylor in front of Jordan, and Jordan in front of Taylor, gave me a happy tingle of naughtiness that I didn't expect.

It cranked the entire thing up to ten. And we hadn't even gotten started yet.

Jordan yanked me away from Taylor, hugging me from behind and kissing the back of my neck while grinding against my ass. I felt the hard length of him through our clothes. He was as turned on as I was. Maybe even more.

Taylor removed his shirt and sat on the edge of the bed. His eyes raked over me, drinking in the sight of Jordan manhandling, fondling, and kissing me. This time he didn't need to pull me away—Jordan gave me a little shove toward the bed, and I fell into Taylor's waiting lap.

I could feel Jordan's gaze on me while Taylor and I made out. It was like a caress moving up and down my back, creating goosebumps in the cool room. Taylor's hands moved up and down my back, then took hold of my shirt and pulled it off. I closed my eyes and exhaled softly as he leaned forward and took my nipples in his mouth—first the left, then the right, lips nibbling with just a *little bit* of pressure.

"You okay?" he paused to ask, eyes wide and waiting.

I nodded without thinking. "I've never been more okay in my life."

Jordan answered behind me in a barely formed word—it was more like a grunt: "Good." And then he pulled me away from Taylor, one hand on my thigh and the other curled around my waist, lifting me to my feet.

And then bending me over the bed next to Taylor.

I gasped as Jordan pulled my pants down, taking my panties with them. His fingers danced up the bare skin of my thighs while Taylor leaned back on the bed and watched. I felt my body tense, every muscle from my toes to my neck, waiting to see what Jordan would do. His breath was hot on my skin; on the back of my knee, up my thigh, then against my ass. Taylor's eyes tracked his movement as he waited to see what would happen next.

Every muscle in my body relaxed as Jordan buried his face in my pussy from behind. I moaned in surprise, arching my spine and pushing my hips back into him. His tongue felt like it was an animal all on its own, wriggling and licking in every direction, hitting every inch of my inner walls.

I tried to open my mouth to tell him to keep going, but all that came out was another long moan.

"She's going to wake the baby," Jordan rumbled into my wet heat. "Shove something in her mouth to muffle her, will you?"

Taylor was already slipping out of his pants, the hard ridge of his cock coming into view. In the soft light I saw the glisten of pre-come on his tip, more proof of just how much these two were enjoying this.

And then Taylor caressed his fingers into my hair, made a fist, and pulled my face down onto him.

I scarcely had time to think before his cock was shoving into my mouth. But rather than being alarmed or surprised, the way he took control turned me on more than I expected. He wasn't too forceful—it wasn't like he was choking me or anything. Just using me, and my mouth, the way he desired.

I groaned around his shaft as he used the grip on my hair to move me up and down.

"That's more like it," Jordan gritted out before returning his tongue to my clit, swirling around the nub before plunging deep into my depths again.

They took me like that for a while—one eating me out from behind while the other held my head down on his cock. *This is it*, I thought while allowing myself to appreciate the moment. *I'm doing it. I'm having a threesome with two of the firemen.*

I never expected this to happen when I delivered pizza to their station.

And then the thought was gone, overwhelmed and overwritten by the waves of erotic pleasure buffeting me from both ends as they had their way with me.

30

Taylor

It was awkward with Jordan at first. How could it not be? I had my dick out in front of him, getting sucked-off by Clara, the girl we were both seeing. Meanwhile, he was back there treating her lady-parts like an all-you-can-eat buffet—something he was *very* good at, judging by the noises Clara was humming into my dick.

A week ago, I was a virgin. Now I was having a freaking *threesome*.

I'll be totally honest here: I never thought I'd have a threesome. It just wasn't the kind of thing I expected to happen to me. Like winning the lottery, or getting struck by lightning. But in the times I fantasized about it, I pictured the threesome math a little differently. Two girls and me, not me, a girl, and another guy.

But screw all that nonsense. Sharing Clara between us was freaking *hot*. Jordan making out with her, then pushing her onto me so I could have a turn. And now him eating her out while she sucked the life out of my cock. It was great. It was better than great. It was goddamn amazing in a way I never expected.

Maybe it helped that Jordan and I were already as close as brothers. Working together at a fire department did that. Jordan had *literally* dragged my half-conscious body out of a burning building when my respirator valve malfunctioned. I'd saved his ass countless times too.

Compared to that, sharing a woman was *easy*.

Clara took hold of my shaft with a hand and began stroking to go along with the suction of her lips, and all thoughts of teammates and firefighting immediately disappeared from my head.

I squeezed Clara's silky-blonde hair in my hand and pulled her off me, raising her up until I could jam my tongue into her mouth. We shared a long, deep kiss like that, humming vibrations of pleasure moving from her tongue to mine, until finally I couldn't take it anymore.

"Move," I said to Jordan.

He barely had time to get out of the way before I took his place behind Clara. I put my hand on her lower back to get her at just the right height. Her ass was a masterpiece from this angle, two full orbs tapering to her waist. Her little rosebud in the crevasse of her flesh, with the dripping-wet lips just below.

It was even more beautiful when I slid my cock into its depths, finding her pussy to be every bit as soaked as it looked, and then filling it in one long stroke.

She gasped and leaned forward on the bed, face on the covers and ass still up in the air. I squeezed her right cheek, feeling the heft of it in my palm while keeping myself as deep inside her as I could.

I'm afraid to start moving, I thought with a grin, *because I already feel like I might explode.*

Jordan had undressed while all this was going on, and knelt over on the bed. As I had done before him, he grabbed a handful of her hair and pulled her lips to his cock. She took his crown eagerly into her mouth, allowing it to muffle another long moan.

Clara was absolutely drenched for us. Even though her pussy was clamped around my cock like it was trying to squeeze the life out of me, when I finally moved, it was effortlessly smooth. I barely pulled back, only an inch or two, before I couldn't take it—I *had* to push back into her, to feel the entirety of her. Half measures simply would not do.

I grabbed hold of her ass with both hands and fucked her steadily, marveling at just how *incredible* she felt. I watched my shaft slide in and out of her while her perfectly-round cheeks bounced softly against my thighs.

I think I just became an ass man.

I don't know how long we took her from both ends like that. Ten seconds, or maybe ten minutes. Time stopped making sense whenever I was inside of Clara. Like some kind of sex black hole. But eventually, Jordan pulled Clara forward onto him. He rolled her sideways so that she was on her back, legs spread wide. Jordan wasted no time sinking in between those legs, and I knew the moment he was inside of her from the way her whole body went tight like a wire.

Clara reached in my direction, fingers grasping and beckoning me.

Who was I to withhold what the lady wanted?

I knelt on the bed next to Clara, leaning down to cup a breast and suck on her nipple. But she had other things in mind—she grabbed me by the shaft and pulled me to her face, wrapping her lips around me and resuming the earlier blowjob like she was making up for lost time.

Jordan and I had avoided eye contact up to this point. Seems like a logical rule of a devil's threesome, right? But now, accidentally or on purpose, our gazes happened to connect.

Can you believe this is happening? Jordan seemed to say with his eyes.

No, I can't, I gazed back at him. *But I'm glad it is.*

Jordan began pounding Clara's pussy then, long, hard strokes that made her entire body shake. New moans rumbled up from Clara's throat, and she sucked me off faster.

I'm not going to last very long if she keeps this up, I thought.

Fortunately, the other two were on the same wavelength as me. Clara squirmed and arched her back while Jordan jackhammered into her, thrusts that were so hard it was like he was trying to prove something. But it was doing something special to Clara, who bucked and thrashed on the bed underneath him. One of her hands raked across his chest, and the other cupped my balls, squeezing them urgently while her tongue swirled around my crown.

Finally she arched her back almost violently, and let out the beginning of a climactic cry. She bit her lip to stop her screams, and her hand slid up to my shaft and stroked me with more fervor than I could handle.

A tingle ran up my balls and through my manhood, the trembling beginnings of an earthquake of an orgasm. I tried to warn her, to tell her what I was about to do, but she seemed to know—despite her eyes being clenched and her mouth open in a silent scream of ecstasy. She yanked my cock toward her chest, aiming me at her cleavage and gripping my shaft with tight, desperate fingers.

I came so hard that I'm surprised I didn't roar loud enough to shake the walls. Somehow I managed to contain the majority of my animal-like grunts as Clara tugged the load from me, splashing it all over her chest, covering her tits with my cloudy white strands.

And then Jordan was pulling out of her and climbing up onto the bed too, kneeling over her with his dick gripped tightly in his hand, and he added his come to Clara's chest too. Her fingers found his cock and took over for him, stroking us both at the same time, milking us for every ounce we had until none of us could move.

31

Clara

"I can't believe we just did that," I breathed.

The three of us were lying on our backs in bed, one guy on either side of me. We had already cleaned up but we weren't really cuddling yet—we were just splayed out on the bed, limbs overlapping here and there, trying to catch our breath and process what had just happened.

I just got double-teamed by two guys.

"That did just happen, didn't it?" Taylor asked. He reached over and pinched his arm. "Yep. This isn't a dream."

"I will admit that I was skeptical at first," Jordan rumbled next to me. "But that wasn't awkward at all."

"Not once we got going," Taylor said. "It was like we were working together."

"Which we do every day," Jordan said. "Like teammates."

"Except instead of putting *out* a fire," I said with a giggle, "you were *igniting* one between my legs."

Both of them turned their heads toward me.

"That was really cheesy," Taylor said.

Jordan nodded. "It's a good thing you're cute, because from anyone else, that might ruin the entire night."

I arched my back on the bed in a long stretch. "Nothing could ruin the night I just had."

Taylor caressed my cheek. "That good, huh?"

I nodded vigorously. "Mmm hmm."

"Enough to do it again?" Jordan asked.

I let out an offended noise. "If we *don't* do that again, then I'm breaking up with you guys."

Their laughter must have been too loud, because suddenly Baby Anthony began to stir and cry. Our sounds of merriment turned to groans.

"I've got this one," Taylor said, giving me one final kiss before hopping out of bed. He walked over to the bassinet, totally nude. "Thanks for waiting until we were done, little buddy. You're already learning not to cock-block your friends."

"It wasn't weird earlier," Jordan said. "But—ugh, dude! Maybe put some pants on before you *bend over* to pick the baby up?"

Taylor spun around, dick swinging freely. "We've used the communal shower together plenty of times. You've never been weirded out before."

"This is different." Jordan threw a bicep over his eyes. "Get dressed, man."

"When I'm done changing this diaper." Taylor began humming to himself while placing the baby on the table and removing his diaper.

I giggled at the sight of his lean body, while Jordan continued complaining.

*

The next morning, my brother Jason called to ask how things were going with the baby, and to see if I needed any other pointers or advice.

"Nope, I'm great," I replied. "The spreadsheet has been a lifesaver. I feel like I actually know what I'm doing!"

"*Wait until he turns one,*" Jason replied. "*It only gets harder from there, but in different ways.*"

I frowned down at the baby in the bassinet in front of the couch. A strange realization came over me. One that had been obvious from the start, but had become more muted as I focused on the day-to-day tasks of caring for the little baby.

"I won't get to see him when he's a year old."

"*Oh. Right. Clara...*"

"It's fine," I quickly said. My voice was strangely wooden, like I was hearing it through a door. "I knew this was how it would go. It was always just temporary."

There was a long pause on the line. "*It's normal to get attached. Whatever emotions you're feeling right now are fine, and—*"

"I said I'm fine," I repeated, more forcefully this time. The lump in my throat began to recede. But the damage was done. It felt like I had been stabbed, and all the happiness I had accumulated was slowly leaking out.

Maybe Baby Anthony wasn't a sign, I thought. *Maybe him sharing a name with my late father was just a coincidence.*

"Anyways, thanks for the spreadsheet," I said to my brother. "If there's nothing else...?"

"*Wait, Maurice wants to talk to you.*" There was a scraping noise as he handed the phone over to his husband. Maurice's higher-pitched voice came through. "*Clara. Hows your situation? And I do not mean the baby. You can't tell, but I'm winking at you right now.*"

"If you're referring to everything with the firemen, things are good," I replied. "*Really* good."

"*I don't want broad strokes. I want details!*"

I cocked my head to listen. The guys had run out to get breakfast, and everything in the house was silent. Even still, I gave Maurice a measured response. "I'm getting along very well with all three of them."

"*I said details! Have you had a threesome yet? Two of them at the same time?*"

I sucked in my breath in surprise. "I can't tell you that! You're, like, my brother!"

"*Jason is your brother,*" Maurice said dryly. "*I'm the cool brother-in-law who you can tell every juicy detail to. In fact, you're obligated to. I'm pretty sure it's written on my marriage license.*"

"I don't think that's how marriage licenses work."

"*Well, tell me anyway, because it's Sunday and I'm bored.*"

I glanced down at Baby Anthony in his bassinet, and he gazed up at me with curiosity. It felt wrong to discuss these kinds of things in front of him. Then again, last night we had *done* it while he was in the same room. So I guess talking about it wasn't weird.

"I had a threesome last night with Jordan and Taylor," I whispered. But Maurice missed most of what I said, because as soon as he heard the word *threesome* he started squealing with excitement.

"*I knew it! I knew you were having way more fun than you were letting on! Keep talking. Tell me more things about this.*"

Behind him on the line, I heard my brother asking something. Maurice shooed him away.

"I'm not telling you anything while my brother is in the room with you!" I protested.

"*It's fine. I'm walking outside. The mosquitoes are bad, but this is worth hearing about this. Okay, I'm alone now. Tell me all about it!"*

"I'm not giving you any more details than that," I said with a laugh. Just discussing last night's activities gave me an excited tingle in my gut. "But I will tell you that it was enjoyable by all parties involved."

"*Oh em gee. You're the luckiest slut in the world!*"

"Maurice!"

"*Don't get your newly-desirable panties in a bunch. I mean it in an endearing way. I would kill to be in your position.*"

I heard my brother in the background: "*What position?*"

"*Oh nothing, dear. I'm just kidding around with your sister.*" Maurice lowered his voice to talk to me again. "*I'm not kidding. I'm so jealous. Get it, girl!*"

I spent the rest of the morning thinking about the conversation with Maurice, and how it affected my own reaction to last night's event. Threesomes weren't something that happened *normally*. They were the kind of sizzling affair that only happened in college, or with weird couples who wanted to liven things up in the bedroom after exhausting all other options. Under such an assumption, I had felt vaguely embarrassed about last night, even though I had thoroughly enjoyed it.

But talking to Maurice, and speaking about the event out loud, was strangely liberating. He was excited for me. He was *jealous*. That kind of reaction took away the stigma from the event and made it acceptable in a normal kind of way.

Jordan, Taylor, and I had a threesome. It was great. And there was nothing wrong with that, no matter what anyone else thought.

The three of us relaxed all day. Taylor did some studying in his room, while Jordan and I snuggled on the couch and watched reruns of *Mork and Mindy*. The show was well before my time, but it had Robin Williams in it, and had aged pretty well.

Derek got home later that night, the headlights from his car sweeping across the house as he pulled up the driveway. Excited for his return, I met him at the front door with Baby Anthony in my arms. Derek smiled at me like a husband returning home after work, gave me a kiss on the cheek, and then swept the baby away from me.

"How was our little guy?" he said, cradling the baby against his chest and kissing him on the crown of his head. "Did you behave while I was gone, like I told you to?"

"Anthony was good, but he, uh, drank a bunch of your tequila," Taylor said. "The really expensive stuff."

"Did he now?" Derek asked dryly.

Taylor nodded gravely. "Yep. We've got a lush on our hands."

As I watched Derek, I couldn't help but admire how *happy* he was to see the baby again. He was treating Anthony like he was his son, and not just a burden that they were trying to be rid of.

It's a shame his ex didn't want kids, I thought. *He's going to make a wonderful father someday.*

"How'd it go, Chief?" Jordan asked. "Did you get any clarification about how we should proceed?"

Derek handed the baby back to me—reluctantly, it seemed—and pulled his phone out. "I took some notes. The administrator I talked to at Social Services gave us a lot of information. A lot of it isn't really relevant to us, which is my fault, since I was asking a lot of questions without coming right out and telling her what our situation was. But the key takeaway is this: they'll have a new budget in two weeks, along with a dozen newly-approved foster families. The situation will greatly improve then."

"Two weeks?" Jordan asked hopefully. "You're certain?"

Derek nodded once. "Two more weeks, and then we'll be able to turn Baby Anthony over to the system and know that he'll be going to a good infant-specific foster home."

Jordan and Taylor clapped each other on the back. Derek smiled along with them, but the happiness never touched his eyes. He looked like he was having the same revelation I had earlier: that our time with Baby Anthony had an end-date, and one that was now just around the corner.

I moved the baby to my other arm and gave Derek a hug. Wordlessly, he squeezed me back, then let out a long sigh that might have been relief and might have been disappointment.

I know the feeling, I thought.

We celebrated that night by grilling steaks on Derek's back porch. It was a cool, peaceful night, and the sun turned deep orange as it dipped below the treeline.

"These margaritas would be better with the other tequila," Derek grumbled while flipping a steak on the grill. He gave the other guys—but not me—a sideways glance of judgment.

"You said to make ourselves at home," Jordan replied. "We took your offer at face value."

Derek grunted in disapproval.

Taylor was playing with the baby in his bassinet, so I got up and went to Derek. I wrapped my arms around him from behind, pressing my face against his firm body. The shirt he was wearing smelled like smoke and spicy deodorant.

"Are you practicing good fire safety with the grill?" I asked.

His torso shuddered as he chuckled. "The open flame is ten feet away from any awning or overhanging wood, and I have a fire extinguisher underneath the grill. Not to mention a backup in the kitchen."

"I was just teasing you."

"You can never be too safe," he said. "Can you imagine if a fire broke out and the guys on second-shift had to come put it out?" He let out a hiss of pain. "Billy Manning would never let me hear the end of it."

I smiled, then came around the side to sit next to the grill, facing Derek. "It's okay to be sad about it."

His face darkened in a way that told me he knew what I was referring to. He glanced over his shoulder to make sure the others weren't in earshot and then said, "Why would I be sad?"

My dad used to tell me that a silent response was often better than a vocal one. Now, I stared at Derek and said nothing.

He focused on the steaks for several moments. I didn't think he was going to say anything. Finally, he sighed. "Putting him in a good foster home, and then finding someone to adopt him, has been the goal from the beginning. I shouldn't feel this way, and that frustrates me."

Taylor let out a loud laugh that was echoed by the baby. Jordan said something that prompted Taylor to flip him off. Jordan grinned and sipped his margarita.

"Emotions don't always have to make sense," I said quietly. "As a woman, trust me: sometimes they make *zero* sense. But that's okay. It just means you're human."

"I don't have to like it," he grumbled.

I got up and hugged him again, this time from the front. "Then let's enjoy it while it lasts."

We kissed, and there was a deep understanding in the way our lips touched. Both of us were emotionally in sync, going through the same thing at the same time.

The moment ended as Taylor carried the baby over to us and began explaining to him in a lecturing tone. "This is *fire*. It's really bad. Our job is to fight it. But it's also good sometimes, like when it's turning raw meat into yummy steak." He paused to reflect on that. "Huh. I guess a lot of things in life are like that. Good or bad, depending on the context."

"I think he's a little young for philosophy," Derek said.

We laughed and joked and then sat down to dinner. More than ever, it felt like the four of us—plus Anthony—were playing house. Like one big, happy family. What we had wasn't normal. In fact, it was very much *abnormal*. But for some reason, it felt right.

And that was good enough for now, I decided.

The next day, we packed our things and prepared to return to the fire station. It was starting to feel like a normal routine, as commonplace as a daily commute to work. There was comfort in that as I packed my little suitcase and put a fresh diaper on the baby. And if that comfort was overshadowed by the knowledge that it would only last another two weeks? Well, I could ignore that for now. Because for now, I was happy.

That happiness ended when we got to the station.

32

Derek

I had an interesting conversation with my sister on the drive up to Sacramento yesterday.

"I'll tell you straight: it's kind of messed up," she had said bluntly.

I glanced over at her in the passenger seat. "Tell me how you really feel, why don't you?"

She held out her hands. "Don't bite my head off. I'm just giving you my honest opinion. That's what you asked for."

"Sorry," I made myself say, because she was right.

"It's kind of messed up," she continued, "but that's not necessarily a bad thing."

"How do you figure?"

She shrugged. "I work in Social Services. I've seen every kind of family unit on the planet. Traditional couples, gay and lesbian couples, single parents of all types. And you know what I've learned? Everyone is messed up. Those so-called *normal* families are often the most dysfunctional, once you get beneath the outer layer where everyone pretends like they're doing great."

"Okay," I said, not really understanding her point.

"So for you to mention a polyamorous situation, where you're sharing a woman with your two colleagues?" She shrugged again. It was something she did a lot. "It's kind of messed up, but *all* relationships are kind of messed up. If you can make it work, then hey, more power to you."

I frowned while driving along. "Wait a minute. So you're giving your blessing?"

She laughed. "I may be your older sister, but there's no blessing to give. If you're happy, then great! That's the lesson I've learned in all this: do whatever makes you happy. Within reason, of course. I'm not telling you to start shooting up heroin."

I had always come to my sister for advice, ever since we were little kids. Usually, I didn't like what she had to say. She was blunt, and rarely told me what I wanted to hear. I had expected her to say that my weird relationship with Clara and Jordan and Taylor was insane, and that I should end it before things went too far.

"Does she want the same things you do?" she asked me.

"You mean kids?"

"Of course I mean kids. That seems like an important thing to figure out up front." Her laugh held all the bitterness that I felt about my first marriage, and the contentious way it had ended.

"I don't know what she wants," I admitted.

Now she gave me a sharp look. "Then you sure as hell need to find out."

"She's great with the baby."

My sister rolled her eyes. "Stop it. There's a world of difference between *babysitting* and wanting to be a mother. Stop screwing around and ask her, Derek."

I knew she was right. The question about children was one that I knew I needed to ask Clara, but it still felt too soon. That our relationship, as messed up as it might be, was still too fragile to handle the stresses of such a deep, loaded question.

As we drove toward Sacramento, I realized that I was afraid of asking the question because I liked Clara a lot. Since we slept together, I couldn't stop thinking about her. I ached to be away from her right now, and if I imagined really hard, I could still taste her strawberry-flavored chapstick from the last time we kissed.

I'm happy, I realized. *And that scares me. I don't want to know if she wants children some day because I'm terrified of what the answer may be.*

That realization had come yesterday on the way to Sacramento, and by the time I got home to Riverville, it had burrowed under my skin like a thorn from a particularly nasty plant. An itch that couldn't be scratched.

I drowned it with margaritas made from cheap tequila and told myself that I would worry about it in the future. Once Baby Anthony was taken care of.

We returned to the station on Monday evening. Once again, we left Clara and the baby behind with instructions to wait for our text message to meet us. I wasn't sure if we needed to continue doing it that way since Billy knew about things, but I still didn't want him around her and the baby. Only trouble could come from that.

Unfortunately, trouble was waiting for us at the station regardless.

"Where's the pizza girl and her smelly little baby?" Billy asked when we walked into the firehouse.

Taylor and Jordan tensed, but I had spent all day mentally preparing for Billy's attitude. "Brought her home for the weekend. Figured you wouldn't want a smelly baby lingering around the station."

Billy's face contorted in a sneer. "She coming back?"

"Might be," I said. "Up to her. We'll help however we need to."

Billy stared at me a long time, then wandered back into his

bunk.

I shot the shit with the rest of second-shift. They were a good group of guys, and several of them asked about Clara—not in the grating way that Billy had, but with genuine concern. When nine o'clock rolled around, everyone gathered their things and left.

Billy was the last to go, and lingered in the kitchen. His wormy lips moved together like he was mumbling to himself, or like he was trying to work up the courage to say something.

"Need something?" I asked.

He glanced at me with his beady eyes. I could see him stand up a little straighter, as if height could add strength to what he was about to say.

"I've been thinking," he said with a smile that held no warmth. "That baby doesn't look anything like her."

I stared at him. "It's a baby."

He shrugged one shoulder. "Yeah, but still. He had dark hair, and hers is blonde. Unless she's dyed it, but I don't think she did."

"Whoever the father is probably had dark hair," I replied evenly.

"And who might that be?" he wondered out loud.

I didn't like his line of questioning. He was implying that one of *us* was the father, and although that was incorrect, I was beginning to worry about *why* he was pursuing this.

"If you have a point, why don't you skip all this subterfuge and get right to it," I said bluntly.

He puffed himself up again. "I don't think it's her baby."

I forced myself to sound bored. "And what makes you think that?"

"Just a hunch."

I was about to tell him off, to insist that I didn't have time for this and that if he wanted to indulge in conspiracy theories, he was welcome to do that at home.

But then he reached into his pocket and pulled out a folded piece of paper.

"Oh, I also have this," he said while unfolding it. My stomach sank as he pulled the ends taut to show me.

The birth certificate.

"That was in my room," I growled.

"Maybe someone left the door open. And maybe I checked inside to make sure everything was safe and secure."

He was obviously lying; I had locked my door before leaving, and Anthony's birth certificate was inside my locked desk drawer. It would have taken some thorough snooping to find it.

I took a step forward without knowing what I was doing. "Listen here, you little shit—"

"No," he interrupted. He took a step back, then steeled himself once more. "*You* listen to *me*, Captain Dahlkemper. The game is over. I know everything. That baby was *surrendered* here. And you've been keeping him for yourself."

"That's not true!"

"It *is* true." He tapped the birth certificate. "Because this girl? The real mom? I looked her up and called her. She confirmed everything. And oh boy, she was really surprised to learn that her precious baby wasn't put in the California system."

A coppery taste flooded my mouth. It felt like someone had just shone a spotlight on me, and there was nowhere I could run. The feeling was worse coming from Billy.

"Listen to me," I said slowly. "You shouldn't have called her. In Texas, they have sixty days to surrender a child, but in California it's only three. She could face legal consequences."

"Oh, I'm well aware of that," Billy replied. "*She* wasn't, though. Not until I explained it to her. She got real scared then. Started crying.

Ugly crying on the phone." Billy let out a laugh like it was all a big joke.

My legs felt numb, so I pulled out one of the kitchen chairs and sat. "Okay. Let's come to an arrangement about all of this."

Billy scoffed. "What, you want to offer me another *commendation* on my performance review? Fuck that." He pointed. "I want to wear your shoes. I want to be Fire Captain of this station. Resign and recommend me to be your replacement, and I won't tell anyone about the baby you stole."

My stomach turned. "Stole? You have no idea what's going on. My sister works for Social Services. They're overloaded and have no funding. Foster families are stretched thin. We're holding the baby for a few weeks until things get better. *That's* why we've been keeping it a secret."

Billy's laugh was high pitched and manic, like a child who had just won a board game. "Don't care! Only thing I care about is your position. Give it to me and I won't tell anyone about your secret."

The despair in my gut slowly transformed into anger, white and hot. I wasn't a violent man. I spent my life *saving* people, not hurting them. But right then, I had the overwhelming urge to haul off and punch Billy. The fingers of my right hand ached to curl into a fist.

The desire was so strong that it scared me.

Billy leaned forward and patted me on the shoulder, a meaningless gesture after what he had just said. "Relax, Dahlkemper. If you really do care about that little blob, step down and give me your position. Should be an easy decision, right?"

He hopped up with a spring in his step. "Take a week to think about it." He folded the birth certificate and placed it in his shirt pocket, then patted it through the fabric. "I'll hold onto this until then. For safe keeping."

Billy strode from the station, whistling a tune to himself.

"You okay, Chief?" Jordan asked a few moments later. He and

Taylor were standing in the doorway.

I sighed and held my head in my hands. "Things just got complicated. Billy knows everything."

33

Clara

I enjoyed the little routine we had gotten into. My three fireman boyfriends—that's what they were, right?—left early. I hung out at Derek's house a little longer with Baby Anthony, playing peek-a-boo with him on the floor of the living room. He wriggled and giggled and smiled as if it was the most fun game in the world.

"You and me both, little dude," I said.

I was growing attached to him, I knew. He was starting to feel like *my* baby. It was impossible to take care of a child for several weeks in a row and not feel that way, I guess. But I knew it was destined to end.

Until then, though, I would enjoy every second of it.

Around nine-thirty, I loaded up the car and drove Baby Anthony over to the station. As soon as we walked inside, I could tell something was wrong. A sour mood hung in the air like smoke.

"What's going on?" I asked when I found them sitting in the kitchen.

And then they told me.

"He can't do that!" I said bitterly. I was holding the baby to my chest protectively, as if I could shield him from it all.

"He can, and he is," Derek replied in a hollow voice. "The question is: what do we do about it?"

"What about handing him—the baby—over to Social Services as soon as possible?" Jordan suggested. "If the baby isn't here, then Billy's accusation won't hold any weight."

"Like flushing a bag of weed down the toilet before the cops barge in?" Taylor said. "Dude."

Jordan grimaced. "Aw, man. I didn't mean it like that." He took a step toward me and put his hand on the baby's back.

Derek shook his head. "Handing him over to Social Services now won't accomplish anything. Billy has the birth certificate. He would still report me, and I'd lose my job anyway. *And* the baby would be placed in a piss-poor foster family, and his mother would be prosecuted for abandonment. It's the worst of all possible scenarios."

I could see the determination in his eyes, and the pain from his own childhood. No matter what happened, he wouldn't let Anthony grow up the same way he did.

"It's blackmail," I said weakly. "That's illegal. You should turn Billy in to the police."

"As tempting as that sounds, it would reveal what we've been doing with the baby," Derek said. His handsome face was more grim than ever. "There's a reason blackmail *works*."

He stood and looked at each of us. "No matter what I do, I lose my job. If that's going to happen, then the least I can do is ensure the baby goes to a good home. I'm going to give Billy what he wants. I'm going to resign."

Jordan hunched over the kitchen table, fingers gripping the wood so tight it looked like it might snap. "Billy Manning isn't a leader. He would make a terrible captain."

"I don't disagree," Derek said, patting him on the shoulder. He waited until Jordan looked him in the eye before continuing. "But we're out of good options. Which means we have to choose the least-shitty one."

Jordan hung his head in defeat, eyes clenched shut. Finally he nodded in acceptance. The two of them hugged, clapping hands on backs, and then Derek embraced Taylor.

"I'm so sorry," I said to Derek. To my surprise, he gave me a smile.

"I knew this was a risk when we took this little guy in." He pinched Baby Anthony's cheek. "Maybe we should've kept him at my house the entire time, and taken the risk of future legal trouble."

"Could've, should've, would've," Jordan said, putting a hand on Derek's back. "We did the best we could with the information we had at the time."

The mood was funereal. It felt like someone had died, and we were all just starting to come to grips with it. When I spoke, my throat was tight with emotion.

"What happens next?"

Derek grabbed a bottle of water out of the fridge. "Billy gave me a week to decide, but I'm assuming he'll want an answer when second-shift takes over on Friday. I intend to keep working until then. It'll give me time to figure out the paperwork involved, and back-filling Billy's position once he's promoted..."

He trailed off at a noise by the front door of the station. Not quite a knock, but more than just the wind blowing.

"If that's Billy..." Derek growled.

We all paused, listening for more noise. A car door closed, and then a car engine rumbled. It grew quieter as it disappeared.

We all went to the door to check it out. Derek opened it wide and looked outside in both directions. The street was deserted.

"Chief!" Taylor said. "There's a note on the door."

Underneath the door knocker was a crisp white envelope. There was no writing on the exterior. Taylor snatched it away and ripped open the letter inside.

"It says *we need to talk*," Taylor read out loud. "There's a phone number underneath. That's it. Signed by someone named Melanie."

Derek gave a start. "Did you say Melanie?"

"Who's Melanie?" I asked.

The color was draining from Derek's hard face. "Melanie is the name on Baby Anthony's birth certificate. It's his *mother*."

*

We sat around the living room at the station. Taylor brought a bag of tortilla chips with him, but none of us had touched them. We were all too tense to eat.

"What would the mother want now?" I wondered out loud.

"Billy said he called her," Derek explained. "She's probably upset that after surrendering Anthony, he wasn't put into the Social Services system. I'd be upset if I was in her shoes."

"Maybe it's something else," Jordan suggested.

"Maybe she wants to keep the baby after all," Taylor said. He was pacing back and forth with Anthony in his arms. "She surrenders the baby. Two weeks go by. Now she feels guilty and wants a do-over."

"She's not getting a do-over," Derek growled. "I can accept someone surrendering a baby because they can't take care of them. But waffling back and forth? Absolutely not. She made her choice."

"Uh, guys?" I said. "She left her phone number. Why don't we just ask?"

The three of them looked at me like the idea had never occurred to them.

Derek pulled out his phone and thumbed in the number from

the note. But before hitting *dial*, he paused. "What should I say?"

"Just ask her what she wants to discuss," Taylor said. "Keep it vague. Let her do the talking."

Derek nodded, then hit dial. He put it on speakerphone, so we all heard the rings. The silence between them was so absolute that you could hear a pin drop.

There was a click, and then the voicemail message played. "*Hiya! This is Mels. You know what to do.*"

The beep sounded, and Derek ended the call. Then he dialed the number again. This time, it went to voicemail after one ring. He didn't leave a message.

"She's ignoring us," he grumbled. "It's probably a stalling tactic. To make us sweat."

I rolled my eyes. "She sounds young. She probably just prefers texting. Give me that."

I snatched the phone and composed a message, reading it out loud as I typed. "This is Captain Derek Dahlkemper of the Riverville Fire Station. I received a note on my door. I understand you want to talk? I've tried to call you twice." I nodded. "There. Sent."

Derek took the phone back. "I don't know. If she wouldn't answer a phone call, I don't expect her to answer a text, no matter how young she—oh! She's replying!"

We all huddled around Derek's phone. The three little dots appeared to indicate that the other person was typing a response. The dots disappeared, reappeared, then disappeared again.

"What's taking so long?" Derek wondered out loud.

Finally the message appeared.

Melanie: Meet me at Tony's Pizza tomorrow at 5:00.

Taylor gasped. "He wants to meet at your family's restaurant? That's a crazy coincidence!"

Derek clenched his jaw. "It's not a coincidence. That means she knows Clara is involved. Billy must have told her."

I winced. I had been involved in the whole thing, but up to this point I wasn't directly implicated. Having the baby's mother mention my family restaurant by name suddenly made the entire ordeal a lot more real.

I wonder if she could sue, I thought. Then I shook off the notion. Right now, the only thing that mattered was Baby Anthony. Once he was taken care of, everything else could come later.

Derek started typing a response.

Derek: Can we meet at the station? We're on-call for the next four days.

Melanie: It has to be at Tony's. 5:00.

"Well, it looks like we don't have a choice," Derek said. He rose and nodded once. "We're meeting Anthony's mother tomorrow."

34

Clara

The next day leading up to the meeting was the most nerve-wracking day of my life.

I went through my tasks taking care of Anthony, but my mind was full of questions without answers. What if she wanted to take Anthony back? That would solve some of our problems. We could pretend that she never actually surrendered the baby, which would absolve us—and her—of any legal ramifications. The only problem was that Billy still had the birth certificate, but we could figure out a way to explain that later.

Derek didn't like the idea of giving Anthony back, not to someone who had surrendered him in the first place. But if that's what the mother wanted, what could we do about it?

There was a worse scenario than that, though: what if the mother was mad we didn't properly hand over Baby Anthony to Social Services? We could explain *why* we didn't—since we had an honest, legitimate reason—but what if she didn't care? What if she was furious about the whole thing? I wasn't sure if we could be sued for that, but people sued other people for all sorts of reasons. If the roles were reversed, I might feel the same way as her.

The guys received two calls: a kitchen fire in the morning, and a faulty smoke detector in the early afternoon. That helped distract them. But it left me home alone with the baby, which only seemed to heighten my own emotional response.

During the second call, after changing Anthony's diaper, I clutched him to my chest and started to cry. An ache had formed in the pit of my stomach and wouldn't go away, and once I started crying, I couldn't stop. It was beginning to feel like the meeting with Melanie might be the end of everything. That I would never see Baby Anthony again.

"I'm not ready to say goodbye," I whispered to the baby between sobs. "I've only just started to get to know you."

In retrospect, I should have expected this. It was naive of me to agree to help watch the baby and expect to *not* grow attached to him. But I didn't realize it would be this hard. It was like being told that my arm was going to be cut off tonight.

"I love you so much," I told him. "I know I'm not your mom, and I've only been taking care of you a few weeks. But I still love you. I want you to know that."

I wished I knew more about the woman. If I knew her full name, I could stalk her social media and see what kind of person she was like. That would help me mentally prepare for the meeting tonight.

But only Derek knew her full name, and Billy had the birth certificate. So there was no way for me to know.

Since the guys were technically on-call, we loaded up the fire engine and drove it to my family restaurant. That way, if a call came in during the meeting, they could quickly leave. They parked the engine on the street behind Tony's Pizza. Derek got out.

"You two stay in the truck with the baby," Derek told the others. "I don't want to bring him inside unless Melanie asks. I'll call if we need you." He nodded at me. "You ready?"

I gave a start. "You want *me* to go inside with you?"

"She mentioned your restaurant specifically, so that means you're involved. Besides, it might put her at ease to know a woman has been helping take care of the baby."

Numbly, I followed Derek off the fire engine and around to the front of my restaurant. We couldn't have been more different: him in his baggy fire trousers and tight white shirt, and me in a summer dress and sandals. It accentuated the feeling that I shouldn't be here.

We walked into the restaurant. We were half an hour early, because Derek insisted on seeing the woman approach: he wanted to know what kind of car she drove, or if she was arriving with other people. At this time of day, there was only one booth occupied by a grey-haired couple splitting a small pizza.

Mom was standing behind the counter, counting bills in the register. Doing the evening count before the dinner rush, a job which had been mine when I was working here. She glanced up, looked back down at the register, then realized what she had seen.

"Clara!" she came around the counter and hugged me tightly. "Why do you come and not bring the baby?"

I glanced over my shoulder at the elder couple eating in the booth. "Mom, shh. We're here to meet with the baby's mother. I need you to *not* get involved. Okay? Just stay behind the counter and pretend like everything is fine."

"The woman who abandoned the baby?" She sniffed, then glanced at Derek. "She tells me not to get involved. Her own mother. I remember when she was *this big*, and I was the one giving orders."

Derek chuckled. "I bet she was a handful."

"I have photos!" Mom put her hand lightly on his arm. "I show you! Wait here!"

"*Mom*," I insisted. "We just need some privacy until the meeting is over. Then you can show him all the photos you want. Okay?"

She rolled her eyes and went back behind the counter,

muttering to herself in Italian.

"Please do not let my mom show photos of me as a child," I said.

Derek smirked over at me. "Why? Would that be embarrassing for you? Maybe you should have thought about that before making fun of my typewriter collection."

We chose the window booth in the corner, both of us sitting on the same side so we could see the restaurant and parking lot. Derek glanced at his watch. "We still have twenty minutes."

I started to reply, then froze. "Look."

On the other side of the restaurant, a young woman came out of the bathroom. She slipped into the closest table, where a cup of soda pop was sitting. She took an anxious sip, then glanced outside nervously.

"You don't think that's—" I began.

The woman swept her gaze across the restaurant, and her eyes locked onto ours. They were wide and frozen for three long seconds.

Then she began to cry.

It's her, I realized. *That's Anthony's mom.*

35

Clara

After letting out a choking sob, the woman shouldered her bag and rose from the table. She walked across the restaurant like someone approaching the gallows, pausing in front of our booth.

"Melanie?" Derek asked gently.

She nodded, then sat in the booth across from us. Now that I got a really good look at her, I realized she was younger than I expected. She had holes in her jeans, out of a punkish style rather than normal wear and tear. She was wearing a black Billie Eilish T-shirt. Her dark hair had purple highlights above the ears, and her eyebrows were sharp above young, inexperienced eyes.

She's a teenager, I realized.

Derek cleared his throat. "I'm Captain Dahlkemper, but you can call me Derek. I just want to say up front that Billy Manning—"

Melanie held up a hand to stop him. "Can I just, like, explain myself first? Before you say anything?"

Her hand was trembling. My heart went out to her. She was terrified.

"Okay," Derek said.

The girl—it was impossible to think of her as a grown woman—reached into her bag and pulled out a three-ring notebook, the kind I used to take notes in back in high school. She flipped to an earmarked page and then began to read.

"It started at the homecoming dance my senior year," she said in a shaky voice. "My boyfriend and I, we, um..." She stopped and put the notebook down. "Can I just, like, talk to you guys?"

Derek reached across and put a hand on hers. "You can do whatever makes you comfortable." His voice was gentle, and it seemed to reassure Melanie.

She nodded. "So, yeah. Homecoming. I know, we were stupid teenagers. We made a mistake. Anyway, a month later I was late. Like, *late* late. I didn't know what to do, so I told my parents. My parents flipped out, which I can't blame them for. Once everything cooled off, they convinced me to keep it. I didn't know *what* I wanted, but they made some good points, so I did that. I kept the baby."

Melanie cleared her throat and glanced between Derek and me, then went on. "The pregnancy wasn't bad at first. Everyone at school was *super* supportive. But the third trimester really sucked. I started panicking about what to do. My mom said it was just the hormones making me freak out, but it was more than that. I didn't *want* a baby. I wasn't ready to be a mom yet, and I definitely didn't want my life derailed." She looked down at the table and shook her head. "I know that sounds shitty. I hate to think of a baby as a burden like that, but... Yeah. I knew I wasn't ready to be a mom."

"We're not going to judge you," I said softly. "That must have been really hard."

She glanced at me, then back down at the table. "We were on vacation when I had the baby. Down in Texas, visiting my cousins. So of course, the baby decided to come three weeks early. But he was healthy and beautiful."

That explains why he has a Texas birth certificate, I thought.

Her dark eyes lit up, and for a brief moment I could see Baby

Anthony's features in her. "He was so beautiful! I held him and held him and didn't want to let go. I've never loved anything so much in my life. Oh, and we even shared a birthday! I turned eighteen on the day he was born."

Eighteen, I thought. So young.

Melanie's smile wavered and she slumped her shoulders a little more. "Everything got hard once we left the hospital and came back to California. I didn't get any sleep. He cried *so much,* which I know is normal for a baby, but it was tough. My parents didn't help as much as they said they would." Her eyes shimmered. "I tried to take care of him. But I was such a bad mom. Nothing I did calmed him. My cousin Suzanne has a baby boy, and he *always* stops crying when she holds him. Anthony didn't do that for me. And I knew it would only get harder when school started back up. My mom works, so we would have to pay for daycare, and that's expensive. Like, *so expensive*, you have no idea. We didn't have any way to pay for it. So..."

She closed her eyes, sending tears rolling down her cheeks.

"When I was in the hospital in Texas, I did research on what to do. And I learned how there are laws where you can surrender a baby up to sixty days after he's born."

Derek and I glanced at each other, but said nothing.

"You have to understand, I *tried*," she pleaded. "I tried so hard to be a good mom. But when the sixty-day deadline got close, I knew I couldn't give him the life he deserves. That's all I want, you know? What's best for the baby. Even if it's with some other family."

Melanie pulled out a tissue and blew her nose. "We live on the north side of Fresno, so I drove down to this side to surrender him to a fire station where nobody would know me. Just in case. After dropping him off at the door, I cried the whole way home." She let out another sniffle. "But I knew I was doing the right thing. That's what I've kept telling myself these last few weeks: that he's probably with a good family by now. In a nice home, with a white picket fence and maybe a golden retriever who sleeps next to his crib, to protect him. That's what I told myself."

She blinked a few times. "Then I got a phone call from a fireman at the station, and he told me..." She looked at me, then at Derek. "You still have the baby? I don't understand. Why isn't he with a loving family now?"

The last part had a hint of accusation in it. I felt Derek tense next to me. It was time to tell her the truth, and hope she understood our reasons.

"When we found the baby on the door of the station," Derek began to explain, "I wasn't sure what to do. I knew about Safe Haven laws in theory, but had never had it actually *happen* to me before. I have a sister who works for the California Department of Social Services, so I called her. She gave me all the information on what paperwork to file and how to turn him over to the system.

"And then," he said with dramatic emphasis, "she made a casual comment. She said it was a shame he wasn't surrendered a few weeks later, because *then* they would have a bigger budget and a broader foster parent pool to use. It turns out, the system was overloaded and under-budget. There were only a few foster families in the Fresno area with availability, and all of them had complaints on their record."

Melanie sat very still. "Oh."

"I grew up in a foster family like that," Derek said. "I didn't want Anthony to experience the same thing. So I made the decision to hold him for a few weeks until the new budget and foster family pool came in, and *then* turn him over."

Melanie had tears in her eyes again. "I didn't... I didn't know that my baby..."

"No," Derek said emphatically. "You had no way to know. This isn't your fault. This is something *I* decided to do for the baby's well-being. That's the reason I didn't turn him over immediately: because I was waiting for my sister to tell me when the situation was better. So that the baby would go to a good family, like you wanted."

"You did that for him?" Melanie asked. "You took care of a

baby you didn't even know, while doing your own job as a fireman?"

"I did."

Melanie relaxed visibly. "That's so selfless of you. Thank you." A smile touched her lips. "Thank you for doing what was best for my baby."

He glanced at me, and then told Melanie, "I was also trying to do what was best for you, too."

"What do you mean?" she asked.

Derek hesitated before answering. "Safe Haven laws require that the baby be surrendered within seventy-two hours of birth."

Melanie blinked in confusion. "The other fireman on the phone said something like that, but he's wrong. I looked it up when I was in the hospital with Anthony. It's sixty *days*..."

"In Texas, yes," I said gently. "In California, it's seventy-two hours. And since you surrendered him in California, that's the law that matters."

The blood drained out of Melanie's face as the ramifications of that sank in. Then she started crying again.

I slid out of the booth and joined her on the other side, putting an arm around her shoulder. "You didn't know. It's okay. You did what you thought was best."

"If we turned him over to Social Services," Derek explained, "you could have been legally prosecuted. Maybe a judge would go easy on you, but..." He shrugged as if there was no way to know. "My sister was working on a way to slip the baby into the system and back-date it. So it would appear like you surrendered him earlier than you actually did."

I held her while her sobs petered out. My mom stuck her head out from around the counter to look at us, but I waved her away.

"Thank you," Melanie finally said after blowing her nose. "Thank you for doing what was best for the baby, and for trying to help me. I'm glad everything worked out in the end."

Derek cringed. "Well, it hasn't totally worked out. That man who called you, Billy Manning, found out that we were keeping the baby off the books. He's blackmailing me over it."

Melanie's eyes widened again. "Oh no..."

"Everything is going to be fine with you and the baby," Derek quickly added. "I'm going to give Billy what he wants and make sure nobody finds out about you and the baby."

"Oh. Okay." Melanie blinked. "What does he want?"

Derek smiled sadly. "It's not important. It's worth making sure Anthony goes to a good home. But I wanted to make you aware, in case Billy contacts you again."

"I won't talk to him again. I'll ignore his calls, I promise."

"Thank you," I said.

Melanie smiled hopefully. "I'm just sorry it's a big hassle for you guys. When I surrendered the baby, I didn't think it would cause a problem for anyone. The last thing I want is for someone to get in trouble over it."

"I'll be all right," Derek said. "As long as I know it's for the baby."

"I didn't *want* to surrender him." Melanie smirked ruefully. "I originally wanted to try to find a family to adopt him directly. Without an agency or anything in the way. That way I could know he's going to a good family. But then the surrender date was here, and I didn't have the time... It's a shame I didn't know anyone who wanted to adopt. That would have been the easiest solution without getting all of you in trouble, right?"

I was about to tell her not to worry about it, that we would figure out what to do thanks to Derek's contacts in Social Services, but the older fireman had a curious look in his eyes. He was staring at the cushion between Melanie and me as if he was a chess master who had just found a really good move, but was still trying to make sure it was fool-proof.

"Are you okay?" I asked.

Derek blinked, then smiled at me. "I think I just figured out what to do."

36

Derek

It was all so simple, now.

I had always wanted a family. Not just a wife, but *children*. A house full of love and laughter, and little ones running around who I could take care of. I had so much love to give. Deep down in my bones, I knew I was meant to be a father.

It was the reason I got divorced. I loved my ex-wife fiercely, but she would never be enough on her own. I needed a full family. That was on me, not her.

After that, I always thought of things sequentially.

I needed to find the right woman.

We needed to get married.

Then we would start a family together.

But now that I sat here in the booth with Clara and Melanie, I knew I had been going about it all wrong. I didn't need to do things in any particular order. I could skip a few steps if I needed to.

And in this case? Skipping a few steps was the solution to *all* of our problems.

It was a wonder I didn't think of it sooner.

"I'll adopt Baby Anthony," I said.

The two women across from me acted like I had told a joke with a confusing punchline. "You'll what?" Clara asked.

"A private adoption," I explained. "You sign over Anthony to me. I'll adopt him. No agencies, no red tape, except for a few forms to fill out and a lawyer."

Clara was dumbstruck. Melanie said, "Do you even *want* to adopt a baby? I want him to go to a good home, not just someone who is trying to stop a guy from blackmailing him..."

"I've always wanted children," I explained. "It ruined my first marriage, because I wanted children and she did not. These past few weeks taking care of Anthony..."

I didn't have to fake the huge smile that spread on my face.

"These past few weeks have been the happiest of my life. Taking care of Anthony, changing diapers and feeding him. Hell, even waking up in the middle of the night and rocking him back to sleep. I've loved every minute of it. The experience has reinforced that I was made to be a father."

"Derek would make an amazing father." Clara was talking to Melanie, but her eyes were locked onto mine. "I've never seen a man so focused on doing what's best for a baby. He's already been treating Anthony like his own son. If you want someone to adopt your baby, I can't think of anyone better than him."

I blinked, and realized my eyes were watering. That was impossible. I hadn't cried since I was six years old and my dog died.

Clara's mom must be cutting onions in the kitchen, I thought while discreetly wiping my eyes with my sleeve. *That's the only thing that makes sense.*

"A fireman," Melanie said slowly. "I can't think of a better father for Anthony."

"We can pretend like you never surrendered the baby," I

explained. "There's no official record of it. The paperwork will show that you were the mother of the child up until the date of adoption, and nobody will know about the last few weeks when things were in limbo."

"What about Billy?" Clara asked.

I shrugged. "What evidence does he have?"

"The birth certificate, for one thing."

"Don't worry about that," I said. "I have a way to get that back without a problem."

Clara reached across the table and took my hand in hers. "Derek. Are you *sure* you want to do this?"

I smiled. "More certain than I've ever been about anything, Clara." I felt my smile waver. "As long as you would want to keep dating someone who has an infant."

Now it was Clara's turn to have tears in her eyes. "Of course I would! And I want to help you take care of him!"

"Good," I said, "because I'm going to need the help."

I wanted to lean across the table and kiss her, but her mom was watching us from the counter. And out of all the drama happening today, I'm sure Clara did *not* want to have to explain to her mother about how she was being shared by me, Jordan, and Taylor.

Instead of hugging, we all leaned across the booth and shared an awkward three-person hug. The women were crying, and the onions in the kitchen were bothering my eyes again.

"So, you've been helping take care of the baby?" Melanie asked Clara.

She nodded. "For the last two weeks."

"It's a funny story, but Anthony is kind of the reason we started dating," I explained. "He brought us together."

"That's amazing!" Melanie let out an exhausted laugh. "I was kind of wondering who you were, and what your affiliation with the fire station was."

I frowned. "Wait a minute. You didn't know who Clara was?"

Melanie blinked. "No. Should I?"

"Well, you insisted we meet here at Tony's Pizza, so I assumed that was because of Clara's involvement with the baby."

Melanie looked at her, then at me. "What does this pizza place have to do with you?"

Clara and I shared a worried glance. Something wasn't right here.

"Why *did* you insist on meeting here?" Clara asked carefully.

"It's a silly story," Melanie said awkwardly.

"Tell us anyway," I insisted. "We promise not to judge you."

"Well..." Melanie blushed. "It started when I found out I was pregnant. This was before I told my parents, so I made Jake—that's my ex-boyfriend, the biological father of Anthony—I made him drive me to a pregnancy center far away from Fresno, to make sure nobody would recognize us."

"Oh, you went to the one two blocks north of here?" Clara asked.

Melanie nodded. "That's where we took the first sonogram or ultrasound or whatever. The procedure where you see the baby on the blurry screen. We were both kind of freaked out afterward, so we came here to get pizza and talk about it. Jake wanted me to *take care* of the baby, if you know what I mean, but I wasn't sure what I wanted to do. We had a big fight over it. It kind of caused a commotion in this place. Jake said he had to get his wallet out of the car so he could pay for the pizza, but then... He drove off and left me here."

"He left you?" Clara asked. "What an asshole!"

Melanie smiled. "He *was* an asshole. I'm glad he made it obvious then, because it was easy to break up with him after that. So I was here, alone and scared. That's when the owner of this place came up to me. At least, I *think* he was the owner of this place. His name was Tony, like the restaurant, so I assumed."

Next to her, Clara suddenly froze. But Melanie kept going like she didn't notice.

"He was a frail little man. I think he was Italian, but he spoke really good English. I thought he was going to demand that I pay, but he was *so nice*. He sat down and asked if I was okay. My hormones were already going crazy, because I broke down and told him everything. Every single detail, like he was my own personal therapist. I must have rambled for at least ten minutes, but he didn't leave or interrupt me. He just *listened*."

Clara's mouth was hanging open, now.

"He told me the pizza was on the house. And then, instead of calling me an Uber, he offered to drive me home. Normally I would never accept a ride from a stranger I had just met, but Tony seemed different, you know? Really genuine. He drove me back to Fresno, which was over an hour in traffic, but he didn't complain. He listened to more of my story and told me everything was going to be okay. That's kind of why I came back here to Riverville to surrender the baby. I figured if this little town was full of people like him, then it would be a good place for my baby."

She chuckled and looked over her shoulder toward the counter. "That's why I insisted on meeting here today. Because this place feels *safe* to me, you know? I was hoping to see Tony today, but I don't think he's working. I kind of have to tell him..." She trailed off.

"What?" Clara asked, voice barely above a whisper. "What did you want to tell him?"

Melanie shrugged her shoulders. "Throughout my pregnancy, he was the kindest person I met. The one person who made me feel like everything was going to be okay, and he wasn't just *saying* that. I kind of named my baby after him. I know that sounds silly, to name a baby after a guy who gave me free pizza and a ride home, but..."

Tears were streaming down Clara's face by this point. Finally

Melanie realized something was wrong. She looked at me in confusion, like she had accidentally kicked a puppy.

I can't imagine what Clara must be feeling right now, I thought. *To learn about this a year after her father died...*

"This place," I said, gesturing. "It's Clara's family restaurant. The man you met was her father."

"He was sick," Clara choked out between the tears. "You must have seen him right before he went on hospice care. He wanted to keep working right until the end, so he was frail in his final days..."

"Oh no!" Melanie said. "I'm so sorry! I didn't mean to mention—"

"No! Don't apologize!" Clara said with a happy laugh. It was a strange sound at odds with the tears still streaming down her face. "When I started helping them take care of the baby, I thought it was a sign that he had the same name as my father. It turns out it really *was* a sign. You have no idea how good it feels to hear your story about my father. If he were here right now he would be so happy..."

I pulled Clara from the other side of the booth into my side, and held her as she wept.

37

Clara

I was right. The baby *was* a sign. Just not in the way I expected.

For the past year, I had struggled to accept my father's death. Sure, I logically knew he was gone. I had been to the funeral, and had been helping my mom handle all of the details that came *after*. But I hadn't accepted it in my heart. Emotionally, it kind of felt like knowing I had failed an exam but was too afraid to look at the actual score.

His death, and his absence from my life, stayed in the back of my head. A pulsing pain that could be dealt with later.

Hearing Melanie's story brought that pain straight to the forefront of my mind. My father was gone. Forever. But he had left a legacy behind without knowing it. A funny twist of fate that had changed the course of my own life.

As I cried in Derek's arms, a calm realization came over me. My father was gone, sure, but he *had* left a sign for me. A sign in the form of a baby who was named after him, because he had been kind enough to help a stranger in need.

I was meant to take care of him, I thought as the tears began to subside. *Baby Anthony really was the sign I thought he was.*

I still didn't know what I wanted to do with my life. Long-term, at least. But for now, I had a clear path forward. Especially if Derek was going to be adopting the little guy.

The other guys were sick of waiting in the fire engine, so we told them they could come in. I was afraid that Melanie might change her mind about the adoption once she saw her baby again, but she was loving and friendly and couldn't stop talking about how happy she was that a fireman was adopting him.

We ordered three pizzas and spent the next hour discussing how to proceed.

We had a few days until second-shift began. Normally, that wouldn't be enough time to complete all of the paperwork, but Derek called in all the favors he had. His lawyer friend—the one who had recommended keeping the baby at the station as much as possible—drew up the private adoption papers. The first was a consent form to transfer permanent legal custody to Derek. Melanie signed it immediately, but we still had to get the biological father to sign. Derek was worried that might be a problem.

It turned out to be a non-issue. Melanie's ex signed the document the next day. Melanie told us he practically fell all over himself trying to sign it, because he was afraid of being on the hook for child support.

Derek's sister then expedited the paperwork through the Social Services department. "Don't you need the birth certificate for that?" I asked as he folded the documents into an envelope to give to her.

Derek smiled. "I already got it back and made a photocopy for processing."

"How'd you manage that?" Jordan asked.

Derek leaned against the wall and crossed his arms. "I made a call to Billy's wife. I suspected they don't have the best marriage, and sure enough, I was right. She said she would do anything to get back at that cheating, lying asshole. Her words, not mine. So she rummaged through his office, found the birth certificate, and gave it back to me.

250

And the letter Melanie left when she surrendered the baby."

Logistically, we pretended like the baby had never been surrendered at all. This saved the three firemen from legal trouble for not turning the baby over to Social Services immediately, and it protected Melanie from prosecution for child abandonment. If anyone asked why the firemen had been taking care of a baby for the last couple of weeks, we would tell them that we were in talks to adopt the baby and were doing a trial run of taking care of him.

By Friday morning, everything was done. Well, *almost* everything. California had a thirty-day period of revocation. That was the period where the birth mother—or father—could change their mind about the adoption and veto the entire thing. But we knew the father wouldn't do anything, and Melanie insisted she wouldn't change her mind.

"I know my baby is going to a better home than I could ever give him," she told us at the station on Friday afternoon. She wasn't sad or overly emotional—she spoke matter-of-factly. "It makes me *so happy* knowing you're adopting him."

I put my arm around Derek and hugged him. "You're going to make a great father."

He raised an eyebrow. "What makes you say that?"

Taylor snorted. "You kidding, Chief? The last two weeks prove you're made for this. It's a shame you haven't had a bunch of kids already."

"I don't know about that. But I promise to do the best I can." He nodded once at Melanie. "I owe you a lot of thanks, too. And not just for letting me adopt Anthony."

She frowned. "Why's that?"

Derek hesitated. I got the impression he wasn't sure he wanted to say a lot in front of Jordan and Taylor. But then he charged forward anyway.

"I grew up in a foster home," he explained. "My mother put

me up for adoption when I was young. I never met her, but I hated her for it. For abandoning me."

Melanie's eyes went wide. "Um, is this supposed to make me feel better? Because it's kind of doing the opposite..."

I nudged Derek in the ribs. "Get to the point before she starts crying."

"I hated my mom because I couldn't wrap my head around why she would do that," Derek said. "But after talking to you, and hearing your story about the pregnancy and why you're giving up your baby? I understand, now. I can't know for sure the circumstances of my own mother, but I'm choosing to believe she was a lot like you, Melanie. A young woman who was just trying to find the best life for her baby."

Melanie crossed the room and hugged him. "I've never had anyone thank me for being such a big screw up."

"I'll try to be more empathetic with other people's situations," he replied.

"That'll come in handy now that you're a dad!" Taylor chimed in.

"Especially if the baby grows up and does something *really* bad," I said. "Like leaving an oven on *warm* for an hour to keep some Italian food from getting cold."

Derek glared at me, but it was playful rather than bitter.

We said our goodbyes with Melanie and got back to work for the afternoon. Derek and the guys had chores to complete in the firehouse, like re-folding the fire engine hoses and cleaning the spare equipment. I spent the time watching Baby Anthony sleep in his bassinet in front of the TV.

Before we knew it, it was evening and nearly time for the switch-over with the other shift. Jordan was practically hopping from one foot to the other with excitement.

"I can't wait to see the look on Billy's face when you don't step down."

Derek let out a long breath. "Actually... Well, now's as good a time as any to tell you guys. I'm still stepping down as Captain."

All of us gasped. "What? Why!" Jordan demanded. "You found a way around Billy's blackmailing."

Derek smiled sadly. "I've loved working here in Riverville. But the unorthodox hours aren't going to work now that I have a baby."

"We can keep the baby here!" Taylor said. "Just like we've *been* doing."

Derek gave him a patient look. "We all know that's not ideal. Besides, it's too late. I already put in for a transfer. There are already three stations vying for me to take over."

Jordan and Taylor looked at each other quietly. "You're just going to leave us here?" Jordan asked.

"Jordan," Derek said gently. "This will be good for your professional development. Both of you. A new Captain with a different leadership style..."

"Fuck that," Taylor said. "Take us with you!"

Jordan whipped his head around to him. "Us?"

"Why not?" Taylor ran his fingers through his yellow hair. "A Fresno station would be closer to my college classes. And Jordan, you don't have any roots here in Riverville. Why *not* transfer to Fresno?"

"I doubt the station Derek applies to would have positions for both of us," Jordan replied.

Derek's eyes brightened. "Actually, I could throw my weight around. Insist that whichever station takes me also approves your transfers as well. I don't think it would be a problem."

"What about your house?" Taylor asked.

"I'll keep it. It's only a twenty-minute commute to Fresno."

Jordan glanced at me, then at the others. "I'm going to need to think about it. I know Fresno isn't far away, but... What about you,

Clara?"

"What about me?"

"Are you staying here in Riverville long-term?" Jordan asked. "I know we've only been together a couple of weeks, but your plans might have a bearing on what I decide to do." Suddenly he blushed. "Shit. That probably sounds *really* clingy. I'm not trying to plan out our futures together or anything. I'm just, I guess, trying to figure out..."

I walked over and shut him up with a long kiss. "You're not being too clingy. I like that you're factoring me into your plans."

He sighed with relief. "So, then what are you going to do?"

"Honestly? I don't know," I replied. "I still feel obligated to help with the family restaurant, but I know it hasn't been doing well financially. But whatever I do, I know I want to keep *this* going. The four of us. And I definitely want to keep helping with Baby Anthony."

As if he understood his name, Anthony let out a flurry of baby-babbling from his bassinet.

"Good," Jordan said. "Then whatever happens, we'll all try to stay together. Whether that's here in Riverville, or in Fresno."

The second-shift guys arrived shortly after that. Greetings and fist-bumps were shared, and then the newcomers gathered around the bassinet to play with the baby.

Except for Billy Manning. He casually sauntered over to Derek and lowered his voice, but I was still close enough to hear.

"Have you made a decision, *Captain?*" he asked.

"I have. Do you have the child's birth certificate?"

Billy let out an awkward cough. "I, uh, do still have it. It's at home somewhere. For safe keeping. I'll bring it to you later."

A faint smile touched Derek's lips for an instant, and then was gone.

"Well then?" Billy insisted with hunger in his eyes. "Do you have an announcement to make while everyone is here?"

"I do." Derek raised his voice. "Everyone. I have something to tell you. I will be resigning as Captain of the station. I'm transferring to a Fresno station within the next few weeks."

There was a murmur of surprise from the other three guys on second-shift. Billy beamed smugly, like an olympian on the podium right before receiving his medal.

"I've been here over ten years, and it's time for me to move on," Derek explained. "You're a good group, and I know you'll thrive under new leadership."

"Who will be replacing you?" Billy asked casually.

Derek nodded at him. "I'm not in charge of choosing my replacement. I can only make a recommendation to the municipal fire chief for the greater Fresno area. But recommendations hold a lot of weight with the decision, and I'm proud to announce that I will be recommending..."

Billy took a step forward and began to open his mouth.

"...Brandon McDonald."

Billy tripped over his own foot and almost fell. The other second-shift guys broke into cheers and began clapping Brandon McDonald on the back.

"What are you doing!" Billy got right up in Derek's face, and snarled with rage. "We had a *deal*."

Derek frowned. "A deal? I don't know what you're talking about."

"The baby." Billy pointed at the bassinet from across the room. "I'll tell *everyone*."

"Tell them what? That I'm legally adopting the baby? That's hardly a secret, and everyone will know about it soon enough. It's the reason I'm transferring to a Fresno station. To get on a traditional twenty-four slash forty-eight schedule."

"You *stole* that baby!" Billy said, louder this time. A few of the other guys glanced over. "That baby was surrendered to this station, and you kept him for yourself!"

Derek's face became a mask of confusion as he looked around the room. "I've been discussing adoption with that baby's biological mother for several weeks. We were taking care of him on a trial basis. He was never *surrendered* here. What would even give you that idea?"

Billy's bloodshot eyes widened in surprise. "I... But you... I have proof! I have the birth certificate! And the letter from the mother when she dropped the baby off!"

"That's impossible," Derek replied. "I have the birth certificate. And there's certainly no letter of surrender. Are you feeling well, Manning? Perhaps you're too sick to work this weekend's shift?"

Billy panted with rage, then stormed down the hall into one of the bunks. The door slammed closed behind him.

We said our goodbyes to the second-shift and collected our things. On the way out to the cars, Taylor suddenly started chuckling. Jordan took it up next, and then all of us were laughing. It was a laugh of relief and victory.

"So," Derek said to me. "How would you like to become the baby's full-time nanny?"

I let my hand drift down to cup Derek's ass cheek. I gave it a squeeze and said, "I want to be a lot more than just that!"

We laughed even harder as we walked to the car.

38

Clara

It took two weeks for Derek to finalize the transfer to Fresno Fire Station Number Sixteen. It was on the east side of the Fresno city limits, which meant an easy commute from his house in Riverville without ever needing to cross any major city highways.

Jordan came along with the transfer along with Taylor and Derek. In the end, it was an extremely easy decision. "The four of us have something special," he said after making the decision. "It feels like I'm adopting the baby, too. Or like I'm one of the cool uncles."

"Cool uncle," Taylor said, tasting the words for the first time. "I like that. I'll be the one to buy Anthony his first case of beer."

Derek gave him a look.

"Um, I'm only joking," Taylor said. But the look he gave me, and a secret little smile, told me he wasn't joking at all.

It took *another* two weeks to backfill the Riverville fire station. Then the guys had their first shift at work at the new station. Unlike the crazy Riverville shift, this station was larger and adhered to the standard firefighter shift: twenty-four hours on, then forty-eight hours off. That still seemed kind of nuts to me, but all three guys were *very* excited to move to it.

It also made it easy for me to help take care of the baby. Rather than taking care of him for several days in a row, I only watched him every third day.

Which was a good thing, because I had a new schedule of my own to work around.

Tony's Pizza wasn't doing well in Riverville. The town was just too small, and *just* far enough away from Fresno proper to get any of that business. It had been scraping by since before my dad passed away, and things had only gotten worse in the year since then. Within another year, it would be out of business entirely.

It took a lot of convincing, but eventually I talked my mom into closing down the restaurant.

Well, I guess *technically* we weren't closing down. We were moving. Because Derek's lawyer buddy was married to a commercial real estate agent, who happened to know of a corner location in downtown Fresno. It was just a few blocks from the stadium where the Fresno Grizzlies baseball team played, and at eleven hundred square feet, it was just big enough for a small pizza place.

Mom grumbled and complained about it: the location was too small, they only had six tables instead of twenty, the prep table in the kitchen was half a foot shorter than the old location. But her complaints disappeared after opening night, when we had a line of patrons out the door waiting for pizza.

I hadn't seen Mom smile so much since before Dad died. I was working in the kitchen on opening night, and I heard her happily greet the patrons.

"Tony was my husband!" she said to every single customer. "Anthony Allessandro Ricci. The sauce recipe was my family's, but he perfected it over the years..."

I was surprised about the huge crowd until I told my three fireman boyfriends the next day.

"Taylor told all of his college friends," Jordan explained.

"You have that many friends?" I asked.

Taylor shrugged. "I just walked around telling everyone in my dorm about it. And the girl's dorm next door."

"What a surprise," Derek said dryly. "All the college girls were eager to help the hunky fireman."

"It's not like that!" Taylor replied. He glanced nervously at me. "I didn't flirt at all."

"What were you wearing?" Jordan asked.

"Same thing I always wear," Taylor replied. "My blue work trousers, boots, and the Fresno Fire Department T-shirt."

"The tight white one?" I asked with a laugh. "Yeah, now I'm beginning to understand why we had such a huge crowd! It was sweet of you."

I gave him a soft kiss, and he grinned the rest of the night.

The commute from Riverville to Fresno wasn't bad. It was twenty minutes to the new fire station, and thirty-five to Tony's Pizza downtown. So we all kept our homes in Riverville.

I babysat Anthony every third day, when the guys were on their twenty-four-hour shift. It was remarkably easy now that we weren't trying to hide it from anyone. I watched him at home, then brought him to the restaurant with me. He was such a good baby—I could put him in his bassinet in the back room of the restaurant, within sight of me at the food prep station. He rarely cried, and happily focused on the spinning toys of his mobile.

Mom gave him lots of attention. She even hired an extra person to help run the cash register and take phone orders. She insisted it was because they were busy, but I knew it was because she liked to sneak away to the back room and play with Anthony. Soon she was doing more of that than *actual* work.

I didn't mind. She had stopped bugging me about grandchildren. That's what we call a win-win scenario.

She continued believing that I was only dating Jordan, and that

I was nannying for Anthony as a favor rather than because of my relationship with Derek. Sometimes I wondered how she would react if she knew I was dating all three firemen. Maybe I would tell her in the future. But for now, she was just happy to have a new baby to play with several times a week.

Speaking of dating all three of them, that part of things was going *very* well. The new shift schedule made it so much easier to spend time with each of the guys individually. Sometimes I crashed at Derek's house, and other times I was at Jordan's apartment.

I had the most fun with Taylor. He was in his final year of college at Cal State Fresno, but continued to live in the undergraduate dorms.

"I'm only here a few nights a week," he told me. "The dorms are cheaper than getting my own place. I'm saving *so* much money."

He had a dorm room all to himself, so I didn't mind. And it was kind of fun fooling around in his small dorm bed while shouting and partying went on down the hall. It kind of made me feel like I was in college again.

And of course, Taylor was totally worth it. As our relationship progressed, he was the most loving, affectionate of the three. After sex, he would roll me over onto my belly and gently run his fingertips over my skin, caressing my back until I fell into a deep sleep. He liked to give foot massages, especially after I had been standing up during my shift at the restaurant all night. And he *loved* to cuddle. In the morning before we got out of bed, at a restaurant while we shared a booth, and at Derek's place when we all hung out together on the couch. If Taylor and I were sitting next to each other, his arm was around me.

Everything was just as great with Jordan and Derek, too. Jordan and I had a traditional dating life, going out to dinner and watching whatever rom com was in theaters. Meanwhile, Derek and I had a *deep* connection through our mutual caring of Baby Anthony. It felt like the two of us were always playing house. Eventually, it stopped feeling like *playing* house and started to feel real.

Anthony may have been his baby on paper, but I couldn't help but feel like the mother. It was such a satisfying feeling.

That feeling intensified once the thirty-day revocation period ended, and Derek received the paperwork officially making him Anthony's father.

"I can't believe it's been a month already," Jordan said. We were all sitting around the living room, with Anthony in the bassinet on the floor. "It feels like just yesterday we were scrambling to fill out the paperwork before Billy Manning found out."

"Maybe it flew by for you," Derek said, "but for me? It was the longest month of my life."

"You didn't *really* think Melanie would change her mind, did you?" I asked.

"No, I didn't think so. But I'm still a lot more relaxed today, now that it's official." He leaned down and pinched the baby's little foot. "You're mine now, little guy. And I'm always going to love you."

I smiled at the fatherly look in Derek's eye. For the first time in his life, he was *exactly* where he wanted to be. And it made me feel all tingly inside. Especially knowing that I was a part of it all.

We spent the next two days formally preparing a nursery. We moved all of Derek's typewriters to the attic—which was no small feat, considering how heavy they were to carry up the steep attic ladder. Then we painted the room a soothing shade of robin's egg blue. Taylor used his artistic flair to add little clouds and tiny flapping birds to one corner of the room.

Once we added a crib, and a diaper-changing station, the room was complete.

We celebrated that night with margaritas (made with *good* tequila.) Taylor cooked chicken tacos with spicy guacamole and a smooth crema fresca.

By the time we put Baby Anthony to bed, the four of us were nice and sloshed.

"The Dodgers are going to come back," I said, gesturing at the TV with my fourth margarita. Or maybe it was my fifth. "They're only down one run."

"Not a chance. The Giants closer is going to shut this rally *down*," Jordan argued.

"Bet you he blows the save," I said.

Jordan shook my hand. "You have a bet."

Not two minutes later, the Dodgers hit a three-run home run to take the lead. I jumped up and did a little dance in the living room.

"You're not a very gracious winner," Derek pointed out.

"Screw being gracious! The Giants suck! Hah!"

Taylor stretched out on the couch with one arm propped up behind his head. "You made a bet, but you never mentioned what the winner would get."

"A back massage?" Jordan suggested.

I smirked at him. The margarita was going to my head, and made me braver than I normally was. And after being with the guys for close to two months, I was a lot less shy around them.

Which meant I wasn't afraid to ask for what I wanted. Something I'd been considering for a while.

"How about some *group* activities?" I said.

"What, like a board game?" Taylor asked.

Derek snorted. "Not sure that's what she means, champ."

Taylor blinked, then suddenly sat upright. "Oh?"

I raised an eyebrow at them.

A lusty smile spread across Jordan's face. "I'm all for that. Not sure about the Chief, though."

Derek frowned. "What's that supposed to mean?"

"There's no way you would have a threesome, or foursome," Jordan said.

"Why do you think that?"

"You're kind of high-strung," Taylor piped up. "And possessive."

"You like things a very specific way," Jordan added.

Derek gave us a confused grimace. "When did this become the *shit all over Derek variety hour?*"

I went over to the chair and sat in his lap. "You wouldn't want to share me?"

"I already share you," he replied, his voice a deep rumble.

I stroked his cheek. "I mean in the bedroom. Together. All of us."

A glimmer of interest sparkled in his eyes. "I could do it."

I leaned in close so that my lips were close to his, and whispered, "Prove it."

39

Clara

Derek hesitated only a moment, then stood up from the couch. He took me by the hand and led me upstairs, with Jordan and Taylor following close behind.

Once we were in the master bedroom, he didn't wait for the others. He threw me up against the wall, smothering me in a passionate kiss that I felt with my entire body. I didn't even notice the bedroom door closing.

As quickly as he had kissed me, Derek ripped his lips away and shoved me to the left. I tumbled into Jordan's waiting arms, and he picked up the kiss where Derek had left off, tongue forcing its way into my mouth possessively.

Next to him, Derek made a hungry noise deep in his throat. I felt his eyes raking over my body while Jordan had his way with me, drinking in the sight of it.

Then there were hands on me—two sets of hands, and neither of them were Jordan's. Hands that removed my top, unbuttoned my jeans, and forcefully pulled them down to my ankles. All of their movements—Derek, and Jordan, and Taylor—were possessive and hungry tonight, like a pack of wolves fighting over dinner.

It's finally happening, I thought as goosebumps ran up my arms. *They're all taking me at once.*

Jordan didn't want to stop kissing me, but Taylor ripped me from his arms to take his turn. I surged upward with need as he kissed me, holding the back of my head with one hand and digging the other into the front of my panties. I moaned as the fabric pushed inward, and longed to feel more of him inside me.

Derek fell to his knees behind me and gave me my wish. He pulled my cotton panties down with so much force I was surprised they didn't tear—although I wouldn't have cared if they did. The only thing I cared about was the way my three men were fighting over me.

As soon as my panties hit the ground, Derek put a hand on my lower back and pushed me forward so he could bury his face in my pussy from behind. I groaned while two tongues pleasured me from both ends—Taylor's in my mouth, and Derek's in my wet heat.

While they worshipped me, I caught a glimpse of Jordan to the side. His muscular frame was silhouetted by the window as he slowly undressed. First his shirt went over his head, then he unbuckled his belt and let his pants slip to the floor. The stiff rod of his cock hung in the air, proof of just how much he wanted me.

"I love tasting you," Derek murmured into me. "Even if I'm sharing you with them."

Before I could respond, he plunged his tongue deeper inside my pussy. I broke away from Taylor's kiss to crane my neck and moan loudly in the room.

Jordan approached and gently pulled me away from the other two. He gave me a quick, rough kiss, then stared deep into my eyes.

"I can't wait. I have to have you."

I gasped as he bent me over the bed. I was putty beneath his powerful arms as he pushed me lower to get just the right angle. I surrendered to his whims, and there was a beautiful, erotic trust that came with surrendering.

I would take whatever these three men gave me. I loved them, and they loved me.

Jordan's crown pressed against my entrance, and then both of us moaned a duet of pleasure together as he gripped my ass with his palm and buried himself inside of me in one long, forceful stroke. The force of it sent shockwaves of tingling ecstasy through my body, and I lost my balance and fell forward. Jordan came with me, ensuring that he didn't slip out, until he was on top of me on the bed.

I was as wet as could be, and Jordan couldn't hold himself back. He covered me with his body, wrapping his arms around my chest and cupping one breast, as he began gyrating into me. I was vaguely aware of Derek and Taylor undressing while Jordan slammed his hard length into me, intense and wonderful from this prone angle, our skin slapping together loudly with every thrust.

His breath was hot against my ear as he said, "It's time to show Derek what sharing *really* means."

He grabbed a handful of my hair and tugged, forcing my head up. Derek was kneeling on the bed in front of me, his own massive cock already as hard as it could be. I opened my mouth wide and accepted him eagerly, wrapping my lips around the crown. I couldn't move my head—Jordan held a vice-like grip on my entire body as he continued to fuck me—so Derek had to move his hips back and forth.

He was tentative at first, like he wasn't sure how rough he could be. But soon my moans were so loud, even muffled by his hard length, that he knew I was loving every sweaty second of it. He pushed Jordan's hand away and took hold of my hair in his fist, holding my head in place so he could relentlessly fuck my mouth.

I closed my eyes and savored the sensation. Being filled from both ends by these huge, hulking firemen. I was their sex toy, to be used however they saw fit.

And I didn't want it any other way.

Jordan pumped me from behind, let out a sigh, then slid out of me. Taylor took his place immediately, sitting back on his haunches and then pulling my hips back so that I was in a kneeling position on his cock. I began riding him like this, guided by his hands on my hips.

The position was awkward while still leaning forward, so Derek rose to a standing position at the edge of the bed, pulling my head up with him until I was riding Taylor properly in the reverse-cowgirl position. Derek lessened the grip on my hair so I took the opportunity to grab hold of his hard length, stroking him while sucking on his tip.

He craned his head back and let out the deepest, most satisfying moan I've ever heard in my life.

I sped up, jacking him off into my mouth while bouncing on Taylor's cock.

Jordan was next to me on the bed then, pulling my head away from Derek and toward him. His cock jumped the moment I wrapped my lips around it. I gave him a long suck, taking as much of him in my mouth as I could, then moved back to Derek and did the same thing. Back and forth I went, sucking one and then the other, all while stroking them with each hand.

Even though I was on top of Taylor, he was fucking me just as much as I was fucking him—he was thrusting his hips upward, meeting me stroke for stroke. The slapping of our skin grew louder the faster he went. We were all a sweaty mess, temples and chests glistening with moisture from our combined efforts.

Finally Taylor wrapped his arms around my chest and pulled me away from the other two. He held me in a bear hug from behind, kissing the side of my neck, before throwing me sideways on the bed.

As if it were a choreographed dance, Derek slid over and fell between my legs, burying into me from base to tip with slippery, lubricated ease.

I lost myself in the hungry arms of my men, grabbing and grasping and *pushing* into me from all sides. When Jordan was fucking my mouth, Taylor pawed at my breasts and wrapped his lips around my nipple, squeezing with *just* the right amount of pressure. Then Jordan pushed my head to the side and made me take more of Taylor's cock for a few seconds. I accepted it all with eager enthusiasm, surrendering to the mindless drive of our bodies on the bed.

My orgasm was sudden and powerful, a trembling sensation that surged through my entire body. I clamped myself around Derek's cock, milking him while I came, and he sped up to match my cries of pleasure.

With three men around me, knowing that I was having a foursome, my climax went on and on. Wave after wave of it slamming into my body as roughly as Derek's hard length. I arched my back and moaned around Taylor's cock, then around Jordan's, then Taylor's again as they passed my head between them.

Finally I felt Taylor shuddering inside my mouth. His fingers clawed at my neck, then my cheek, grabbing onto whatever he could as he rumbled with his own orgasm. I kept my lips wrapped tightly around him as he exploded in my mouth, hot ropes of his seed that pulsed again and again. I swallowed him down, gripping his cock between my fingers like I could squeeze every drop from his rigid length.

"Oh my God," Derek said while bottoming out inside of my pussy. His hand pawed at my breast, squeezing with a desire so powerful it bordered on pain. "Clara! *Clara!*"

A jolt of new pleasure shot through my spine like electricity as Derek came inside me. His roar of pleasure was so loud I almost didn't notice Jordan climbing up over me, straddling my chest while gripping his own cock in a meaty fisty.

Jordan's eyes locked onto mine, dark and lustful and loving, and then they clenched shut as he blew his load all over my chest. I felt the strands of his come hit my breasts, my neck, my shoulder. Taylor finally pulled his cock out of my mouth and pushed me forward, allowing Jordan to shove his crown into my lips, giving me the last couple of spurts of his love.

Then all four of us trembled, and our cries died down, and then we were still.

*

"Told you I could share."

Derek was sitting upright in bed, with his back against the headboard. I was stretched out between his legs, my head on his chest while he stroked my hair gently. Jordan and Taylor were to either side of me, resting their heads against my knees and caressing my legs with their fingertips.

A girl could get used to this, I thought.

"I'm very happy you proved them wrong," I said.

Taylor sighed happily. "I never doubted you, Chief. I was just egging you on."

"I had my doubts," Jordan admitted. "Consider me corrected."

"I'm always happy to put one of my firemen in his place," Derek said smugly. "It's one of the perks of leadership."

"That wasn't too... *intense* for you, was it?" Taylor asked. It took me several seconds to realize he was talking to me.

"Too intense?" I giggled. "That was *exactly* the right amount of intensity. I like being with all of you at the same time."

"Makes sense," Derek murmured. "More dicks, more hands, more lips."

I tilted my head back to kiss him gently. "It's more than just math. The three of you are *different* when you're all together. Like you're trying to compete with each other."

"Sorry," Jordan said. "I was just going based on instinct, and sometimes I—"

"No!" I interrupted. "Don't apologize. It was amazing. Keep doing more of that, please."

The four of us chuckled together.

"I'm just surprised the baby slept through all of that," I said. "Thin walls, you know."

I felt Derek nod behind me. "He's gotten better in the past few weeks. Pretty soon he'll be sleeping through the night."

"A full night of sleep? *Every* night?" I snorted. "What a novel concept."

"Parenting certainly isn't easy," Derek said. "But I wouldn't trade that little guy for anything in the world."

"Cheers to that," I said. "Hey, while I'm thinking about it. You guys have tomorrow off. Want to see that new movie, the one with James Maslow in it?"

"The rom com?" Taylor asked. "I saw the trailer for it the other day."

"Say no more. I'm in," Jordan said.

Taylor grunted. "You don't even know what it's about."

"It's a romantic comedy, and I get to go with my favorite girl. What more do I need to know?"

I leaned over and kissed him on the crown of his head. "Then it's a date."

"Mind if I tag along?" Taylor asked. "I haven't been to the movies in a while, and I don't have class tomorrow."

"Who says I want you to come along?" Jordan asked.

Taylor twisted and gave him a look. "Dude. We just spent the last hour tag-teaming Clara. If you can do that, you can share a movie experience."

"Watch out. Jordan is a movie-talker," I warned. "He likes to whisper during the entire thing."

"No problem. I'm used to tuning Jordan out."

Jordan reached over to playfully smack at Taylor.

Behind me, Derek shifted. "Can, uh, I come too?"

All three of us twisted to look at him. "Really, Chief?" Taylor asked.

Derek shrugged. "Sure. Why wouldn't I want to go?"

"What about the baby?" I asked.

"I'll find a babysitter. How much would your mother charge?"

I scoffed. "Are you kidding? She would pay *you* for the privilege of watching him for an evening. She already treats Anthony like he's my child."

"He kind of is," Derek pointed out. "Maybe not on paper, but in reality? You've spent just as much time with him as I have. Maybe even more."

I grinned. It *did* feel like he was my baby. A voice in the back of my head told me that was a bad idea, that I couldn't get too attached to Anthony in case Derek and I broke up.

But I quickly shushed that voice. I was too happy to worry about such things right now. Sometimes, a girl had to live in the *present*.

Taylor looked up the movie on his phone. "There's a showing at eight."

"Eight's kind of late," Derek said. "Can we do something earlier?"

"Jesus, *grandpa*," Taylor teased. "Want to make dinner reservations for three-thirty while we're at it?"

"I am not above kicking you out of my house," Derek replied.

"Sorry, sorry," Taylor said. "I'll behave. I like being here way more than my dorm."

"There's a six o'clock showing," Jordan said. "It's a dine-in theater, so we can get food delivered to our seats."

"The food is never good at those places," Derek said.

"I'm cool with anything!" I said. "I'll eat anything."

Jordan snickered. "Phrased another way: you'll put anything in your mouth?"

I gave him a playful shove. "Just for that, you're not putting anything in *this* mouth for a week."

He twisted around and grinned at me. "What if I offer to put *your* things in *my* mouth?"

"I'm listening."

Baby Anthony picked that moment to start crying. I quickly hopped out of bed and grabbed Derek's bathrobe from the bathroom. It was *way* too big for me, but I didn't care because it was warm and soft.

"You guys decide on a show time while I take care of the baby."

They continued arguing about that while I went across the hall to the nursery. I picked Baby Anthony up and checked his diaper. It was wet. I moved him to the changing table and set to work.

"Did you know you were named after my dad?" I said softly.

Anthony wriggled his legs and frowned up at me.

"His name was Anthony. Anthony Allessandro Ricci. He was such a kind, loving man. He was friendly to everyone who ever walked into his restaurant. Including your mom! Your biological mom, I mean. That was before Derek adopted you. And now here you are!"

Deep down, I knew that coincidences happened in life. Not everything had to be a *sign*. Maybe that's all Anthony was. A series of weird coincidences in a small town outside of Fresno. Crazier things had happened in this world.

But regardless of how our lives had crossed, I was so happy that Anthony had come into my life. Because as long as I had him, I felt like I had a deeper *purpose* to everything. A reason for getting up in the morning beyond knowing that I would be working at the family restaurant.

And my three fireman boyfriends, I thought while taping down the new diaper and lifting the baby into my arms. *I have them to look forward to each day.*

    Whether it was all a coincidence, or an actual supernatural sign, I didn't really care. All that mattered was that my life had changed for the better.

Epilogue

Taylor
One Year Later

"Trick or treat!" the kids on the porch squealed.

I grinned at them. I loved kids. Always had. That was one of the cool things about being a firefighter: kids looked up to you. Working at the Riverville fire station, and then the one in Fresno, we had entertained countless field trips and school assemblies. Dressing up in our gear and explaining the importance of fire safety. Stop, drop, and roll. Driving kids around in the fire engine and honking the horn. They ate that shit up.

So, yeah. I had always loved kids. But I especially loved them now that we were taking care of Anthony. It gave me a new appreciation for the entire *idea* of a child, you know?

"Look at all these costumes!" I said with an enthusiasm I didn't have to exaggerate. "Let's see. We have a spider, a spooky ghost, and Spiderman." I gave the Spiderman, who was actually a girl with long blonde hair, a fist-bump. "You're one of my teammates, you know that?"

She looked up at me in awe. "I am?"

I flexed my own costume and held out my paper mache hammer. "I'm Thor! Specifically, the short-haired Thor from *Ragnarok*. Thor and Spiderman are on the Avengers together."

"Thor?" she asked.

"Oh man. You need to watch all the Marvel movies," I said. "But you have to watch them in chronological order, not the release order. It's better that way." I paused. "Wait. How old are you?"

The little girl Spiderman held up eight fingers, four on each hand.

"Okay. Maybe you're too young to watch those movies. But in, like, six more years? You'll love them. Trust me. Okay, who wants some candy?"

Riverville wasn't a huge city, but it still had its fair share of trick-or-treaters on Halloween. And even though Derek's house was a few blocks off the beaten path, we had gotten a steady stream of knocks on our door.

It probably helped that we spread the word that we were handing out king-sized candy bars. That drew the kids to us like moths to a flame.

After handing out the candy, I waved goodbye and closed the door. Derek was standing just inside, giving me an impatient look.

"What?"

"An eight-year-old doesn't need to be watching Marvel movies," he said.

"Hey. She's the one dressed as Spiderman. I was just making conversation." I gestured. "Besides, you're one to talk, *Captain*."

Derek was adorned in the blue spandex and circular shield of Captain America. He had never seen any of the movies, and in fact turned his nose up at all superhero movies, but since the rest of us were dressed in the theme he eventually relented.

Clara appeared at his side. She was wearing the tight black outfit of Black Widow. An outfit which clung to her curvy frame so wonderfully that I continuously had to look away from her. Here's a secret: it's impossible to hide an erection when you're wearing spandex shorts.

"Leave Captain America alone," she said, threading her arm through Derek's. "He's eighty years old. Respect your elders."

Derek grunted. "Captain America isn't that old. He's played by that guy. The young one."

"Chris Evans," I said. "And he *is* that old. He was frozen in ice. Haven't you seen Captain America fighting nazis?"

"I haven't seen Captain America do anything, except for the commercials on TV," Derek grumbled. "I wouldn't have let you dress me up as him if I had known he was so old."

"We chose that costume for you because you're a *Captain,* not because you're old." Clara kissed him on the cheek. "Don't be so sensitive."

Suddenly, Clara's brother-in-law Maurice came around the corner. He had his son, LeBron, in his arms. "I like a sensitive man. I think it's good to be balanced. A rough, muscular exterior, but emotional and sensitive on the inside..." He gave a happy little shiver.

Jason, Clara's brother—and Maurice's husband—put an arm around him. "Okay, I think you've had enough of Clara's rum punch for one evening."

"What's wrong with telling the hunky firemen that they're hunky and muscular and yummy?" Maurice demanded. "It's not a secret." He turned to me. "Do you have a fireman uniform my lovely husband can borrow? We need it. For a thing."

Jason groaned and rolled his eyes. "I think it's past LeBron's bedtime."

"Which LeBron?" Maurice gestured at his jersey. "I'm LeBron from the Cavaliers." He bounced the infant in his arms. "This is LeBron from the Lakers. And *you* are LeBron from the Miami Heat."

"It's past *both* of your bedtimes," Jason replied. "It was good to see you guys. Clara, walk us out?"

I shook hands with Jason—and accepted a *very* long hug from Maurice—before they went through the door.

"You don't need me to wear a fireman uniform," Jason told his husband. "If you're good, I'll pull out my Navy whites tonight."

The last thing I heard was Clara groaning and telling her brother not to talk about their sex life in front of her.

The last year had flown by. First was the new fire station in Fresno and getting used to different schedules and different customs. Before we knew it, it was May and I was graduating from Cal State Fresno. My whole family came down for the graduation, and I finally got to introduce them to Clara.

I'd had serious girlfriends before, but nobody like her. She was the first one who I liked enough to meet my family. And she handled it with grace and charm, winning over everyone—including my mom.

Of course, we didn't tell them about the whole arrangement with Derek and Jordan. But they didn't need to know about that.

After graduating, I was promoted from *Probationary Firefighter* to a full-time firefighter. It was mostly a meaningless distinction, but it felt like a huge honor. It meant I was doing this *for real*, and wasn't just a rookie anymore.

Derek let me crash at his place until I found one of my own. That was five months ago, and I was still staying at Derek's big house. Everything just sort of *worked* when we were all here together: Derek, me, Jordan, and Clara. We went from playing house to actually living it day-to-day. The closet in the master bedroom was slowly being taken over by Clara's dresses and blouses.

That's how we all liked it, though. We were happiest when we were together, as crazy as that seems.

I finished handing out candy and then went back inside to help put Baby Anthony to bed. He was really more like *toddler* Anthony at this point: he was twenty-five pounds and growing every day. He had a full head of dark hair now, and had just learned how to walk last month. Now he was a walking machine, marching around the house whenever we turned our back for a second.

The four of us went through the nightly routine of putting him in his jammies, then individually kissing him goodnight in his crib. But I had my own routine. After the others went back downstairs, I slipped into the nursery again and bent over the crib. Anthony smiled up at me happily.

"Taylor," I whispered to him, enunciating it carefully. "Tay-lor. Tay-lor. Taylor. Can you say Taylor?"

Anthony had been speaking in gibberish for months now, but he still hadn't said his first *real* word. And I was determined to make his first word Taylor. Sure, that was a more complex word than *mama* or *dada*. But I was determined, damnit.

"Maybe tomorrow." I gave him a final kiss on his head. "Stay cool, little dude."

I gave him a fist bump—that was one of the first things I had taught him when he started walking!—and then left him alone to sleep.

"How much candy do we have leftover?" I asked as I went downstairs. The others were on the couch, but the TV was off. "Is the Giants game still on?" I asked.

"Actually, we have a different surprise," Jordan said. As the Hulk, he was still covered in green body paint, although he had washed most of it off his face.

"A surprise?" I asked.

Jordan aimed the remote at the TV. A movie began to play, with a lion roaring when the MGM logo appeared. The scene opened on a misty forest, with violin music.

"What are we..." I trailed off when I saw the name on the screen: JODIE FOSTER. Then another name: ANTHONY HOPKINS.

"No..."

Clara erupted into a fit of giggles. "Yes!"

"We're not watching *Silence of the Lambs!*"

Derek took me by the shoulders and pushed me down onto the couch. "It's time to become a man, Taylor."

Clara reached over and laced her fingers into mine. "I'll hold your hand the whole time."

Jordan fell into the recliner to my right with a bowl of popcorn. "Is everyone ready?"

Derek was rummaging around in the kitchen. "Start the movie, I'm just checking my mail. Hey. Clara. You got a letter. From the..." He paused. "California Department of Social Services?"

Clara jumped up from the couch. "Oh! Gimme gimme gimme!" She grabbed the letter out of Derek's hands. "I have something to tell you. All of you."

I snatched the remote off the coffee table and paused the movie. "Yes! A distraction!"

"Clara?" Derek asked. "What is it?"

She took Derek's hand and pulled him down onto the couch with her. "The last year has been amazing. Raising Anthony with you. With *all* of you." She nodded at me, then Jordan. "It's like we're one big, happy family. We work really well together."

"We do," I agreed.

"I never knew I could be this happy," Jordan said.

"What's the letter, Clara?" Derek asked.

She held it up, still unopened. "I applied for us to become foster parents."

Derek gasped. "What?"

"I've thought about it a lot," she explained in a rush. "You all know that I want to eventually have my own family. I haven't kept that a secret."

A feeling of warmth spread in my chest, like a flower blossoming and reaching for the sun. I felt that way whenever Clara talked about having kids, because I wanted the same thing. Over the past year, I was absolutely *certain* that I wanted her to have my children. And I suspected that Jordan and Derek felt the same way.

"But there are so many children out there who need good homes," Clara went on. "I called your sister last week. There are currently *eight hundred* children in California waiting for new foster families. We can't help all of them, but we can help some. That way nobody has to be stuck in a bad, or overcrowded, foster home. The way we were afraid Anthony might be."

She cupped Derek's cheek. "And the way you were, growing up."

I had never seen Derek Dahlkemper cry before. The mere *idea* of that was insane, like being told the ground was made of chocolate cake. But now tears shimmered in his eyes, and he sat very still while looking at Clara.

"You would do that?" he asked. "Be a foster mother for kids in need?"

"Of course I would," she replied gently. "As long as you'll be a foster father with me." She glanced at me. "And Taylor and Jordan, too."

Jordan and I shared a look. We both knew we were on the same page. "Of course we will," Jordan said.

I let out a more enthusiastic, "Hell yeah!"

The four of us crowded together on the couch in a big hug. Derek never *actively* sobbed, but tears ran down his cheeks, and he didn't trust his voice to speak. He just smiled and hugged Clara.

That was the measure of a good woman. The ability to bring out the best in a man, and the more sensitive, vulnerable parts too. I clapped Derek on the back and hugged Clara tightly.

"Don't you have to be married to be foster parents?" Jordan asked.

"Woah, hey, let's not get ahead of ourselves," Clara replied with a laugh.

Jordan smirked. "We can raise foster kids together, but discussing marriage is a bridge too far?"

It was a running joke between all of us. How does a polyamorous group like ours take things to the next level? The legal system wouldn't acknowledge one woman being married to four men.

"To answer your question: nope!" Clara said happily. "Unmarried couples can be foster parents, as long as they meet all the other requirements, and pass the home inspection process. It's actually pretty common, especially in couples who have been together longer than a year. If we're approved, we can raise foster children."

"Well?" Derek finally said in a choked-up voice. "Open the damn letter already!"

You could hear a pin drop as Clara tore open the letter and then read it. Tears welled in her eyes. For a brief moment, I was terrified that they were tears of disappointment.

But then she smiled, and nodded, and then the four of us were hugging all over again.

I still wanted babies of my own with Clara. She was *the one*, a fact which I knew with a certainty deep inside my gut. But we were still young, and we were in no rush. For now, I couldn't wait to raise foster children with her. Kids who were in desperate need of a warm and loving family.

Clara was wiping away tears when she said, "How are we supposed to watch a scary movie now!"

I seized on the comment. "Good point! Let's switch to the Giants game."

Derek grabbed the remote and hit play. "You're not getting off that easy."

We settled in to watch the movie. "Hannibal the cannibal," I muttered. "What a stupid name for a character."

"Shut up," Clara said, squeezing my hand. But she said it with a smile, and her eyes said, *I love you.*

I love you too, I said with my eyes as we snuggled together and watched the movie.

Bonus Scene

Excited to see what the future has in store for Clara and her fire-proof men? Want to know how bit their family is? Click the link below (or type it into a browser) to receive a special fast-forward bonus chapter that was cut from the original book. It's extra sappy and extra sweet!

https://bit.ly/39kFPHk

Cassie Cole
Romance Author

Cassie Cole is a Reverse Harem Romance writer living in Norfolk, Virginia. A sappy lover at heart, she thinks romance is best with a kick-butt plot!

Books by Cassie Cole

Broken In

Drilled

Five Alarm Christmas

All In

Triple Team

Shared by her Bodyguards

Saved by the SEALs

The Proposition

Full Contact

Sealed With A Kiss

Smolder

The Naughty List

Christmas Package

Trained At The Gym

Undercover Action
The Study Group
Tiger Queen
Triple Play
Nanny With Benefits
Extra Credit
Hail Mary
Snowbound
Frostbitten
Unwrapped
Naughty Resolution
Her Lucky Charm
Nanny for the Billionaire
Shared by the Cowboys
Nanny for the SEALs

Printed in Great Britain
by Amazon